Praise for the

DAUGHTER

 series

A beautifully written dystopian that has you chasing resolution and begging for the happy ending Daughter4254 desperately deserves.

—Jennifer Jenkins, *Nameless* author/ Teen Author Boot Camp co-founder

The Best Dystopian YA Novel Since Ender's Game

—Amazon Review

Daughter 4254 reminds me a lot of *Under the Never Sky* and the Divergent trilogy. It's like a mixture of the BEST ELEMENTS from both series, plus some extra bookalicious dressing on top.

—Reading with Jax

GIRLS OF WAR

Leigh Statham

OWL HOLLOW PRESS

Owl Hollow Press, LLC, Springville, UT 84663

Girls of War
Copyright © 2021 by Leigh Statham

Library of Congress Cataloging-in-Publication Data
Girls of War / L. Statham. — First edition.

Summary:
After a narrow escape from wipers, Imani faces an uncertain future where the key to peace rests in her artificial memory—if only she can figure out how to access the information.

ISBN 978-1-945654-73-2 (paperback)
ISBN 978-1-945654-72-5 (e-book)
LCCN 2021932601

The view outside my tent is grim as I step out in the morning light and walk to the edge of the canyon. On the opposite edge people in dirty, torn uniforms mill around the remains of the bridge that used to span the void. One reaches toward me, then slips and falls, sliding down the steep, rocky slope into the river below. I can't tell if it's a man or a woman, but it screams until it submerges. I don't see it again. Another one plummets into the swift rush of water, but he bobs back to the surface and scrabbles onto a boulder. His faint moans drift up to me.

I don't want to look at them, but I can't help it. They used to be normal people like Thomas and me. Now they are mindless wanderers, stripped of their personalities and any other sign of humanity thanks to the Mind Wipe and whatever else Haman did to mess with their brains. Several small fires still burn on the wipers' side, leftover from when the mountain people blew up the bridge the day before. It worked to keep Haman's men away from us, and once they realized they couldn't get across and were trapped with the wipers, they retreated. Now it's time to plan our next move.

"Come away from there, love." I hadn't noticed Thomas's approach. He takes me by the arm and pulls me gently back to camp.

The small outpost of mountain people is no longer hiding. The tent city sits in an open clearing by the bridge cabin. A fire burns in the center of the circled dwellings, and smoke plumes from some of the stove pipes puncturing the tent roofs. Haman and his Blue Spider Alliance know we are here. The Leaders know we are here. The tension is thick as we make our way into an unsure day.

The mountain people are suspicious of Thomas and me, as are the Leaders and the rebels. We have defied each of them but have returned to the mountain people, out of necessity but also out of choice. Now we face their judgment. Considering we disobeyed their laws and snuck away to save my mother from Haman, they might not welcome us back.

"I don't understand how Haman can justify all of this," I say as I follow Thomas to the center of camp, holding his large, calloused hand in mine.

"What do you mean?" he asks.

"He ruined all of those people," I point across the river, "and left them in the mountains to die. They don't have any way of protecting themselves or feeding—"

"Actually, they do quite nicely feeding themselves," he cuts in.

"That's gross. Stop it."

The wipers had attacked as we rescued my mother from Haman's compound the day before. They bit and clawed and scratched anyone who came within grasp, including the guards of the compound. Haman's experiments tried to replace memories and personalities by implanting secret information—forbidden information. I too was the subject of one of his experiments, and now that my mother is with me, the fear that I will turn into a wiper—become yet another failed experiment—grows stronger. But I can't let myself wallow in doubt and worry. There is still too much to be done.

As if sensing my stress, Thomas squeezes my hand. "There's going to be a meeting soon. We need to decide if we're heading back to the mines or not," he says.

A few of his people give us and our joined hands strange looks. They must have known of Thomas's assigned partner, a quiet girl I've only seen a handful of times, or maybe there is some rule against hand holding. I am too tired to worry about things like that. I guess he feels the same way.

"Do you think they will let me come back to the mountain with you?" I ask.

"I'm sure you don't need to worry your head about that." Thomas always has a positive attitude and a plan. Even in the depths of a prison with no hope of survival, he found a way to smile and look ahead to better times. I trust him, but I can't guess how anyone else will react.

"I dunno," I say. "I haven't exactly made friends with the people who matter."

"How about you go check on your ma and meet me at the main campfire in a few minutes?" He smiles and squeezes my hand again before letting it go as we reach my tent.

My mother.

It feels so strange to say the words. I'd given her up for dead long ago only to learn that Haman had her in the same facility where he experimented on me and put all knowledge, both censored by the Leaders and not, into my head. When the mountain people made it clear they weren't going to help save Mother, Thomas and I rescued her and managed to avoid letting Haman capture me. Now I have my mother and Thomas. It's almost too good to be true.

A reference pops into my mind—something that happens less frequently as I learn to control and access the information crammed in my brain. A translucent person. It is called a ghost, a spirit come back from the dead to haunt the living. They float around making scary noises and throwing things. But as I lift the flap to the tent, my mother stands there—real, solid, smiling.

"Good morning," she says.

There is no one to stop us from showing love here like the awful auto-eyes that recorded our every move in our community back home. Ignoring the wiper bite on my shoulder from the day before, I embrace her and hold on like a young one. She still has the smell of antiseptic and steel from Haman's facility, but there is also the underlying smell I know so well. It only belongs to her— berries and fresh cotton, warm summer nights and crisp winter mornings. I let it fill my mind and mingle with the cool air of the pines and wood smoke and feel truly, deeply happy for the first time in years. I don't want to let her go. She doesn't want to release me either, her thin arms tight and unrelenting around my body. When we separate, she takes my hand, and we sit down on my cot.

"They are having a camp-wide meeting in a few minutes," I say.

She nods calmly. "I hear food is scarce. Though that might not be a concern for me if they don't let me stay." A weak smile crosses her lined features.

Nothing has changed. Mother was always worried about feeding everyone in our community back at home, and now she is starting up with complete strangers in the middle of a dire situation.

I squeeze her hand. "They'll be deciding what to do with me as well. Not many of the mountain people are happy about me wandering into their lives and bringing one regime and one rebellion down on them."

Instead of the regret or fear or uncertainty that I expect, her eyes fill with pride as she cups my cheek. As she opens her mouth to speak, a man outside calls for everyone to gather for the meeting.

She stands and wraps a blanket around the white sleeping clothes she was issued at Haman's compound. Our escape didn't leave any time for dressing appropriately for the weather, and her soft cotton booties are torn and dirty.

"Mother, let me try to find something warmer…" I look lamely around the small tent for something else she can wear, already knowing there is nothing of use.

"I'll be all right. I don't need anything more than what I have now." She smiles and pulls the blanket more tightly around her shoulders with one hand and squeezes my arm with the other.

"You'll feel differently if we end up hiking back to the mines," I say. "Let's head to the firepit and see what they have to say." I pull back the flap and let my mother walk into the cold, sunny air. I follow, glancing only quickly behind me at the distant shore where wiper movement still catches my eye. Thomas meets up with us as we approach the clearing, and I take his hand. Mother smiles at him.

The fire is stoked and feels warm and welcoming. Several men and women, holding shock rifles and dressed to blend in with the brush and trees, sit on stumps and rocks at the edge of the small clearing. The refugee scientist, Dr. Bowman, who followed us out of the compound, stands off to one side looking awkward in his white institute clothing and an oversized bark-brown jacket. He holds a mug of something steaming, and my mouth waters.

A man approaches us carrying a moss-green coat and smiling at mother. "We found this in our supplies. Here." He offers it to Mother, who takes it gladly.

"Thank you," she says. Thomas takes her blanket as she slips the coat on and zips it up.

The man lingers, as if debating saying more. He's about her age, and his black hair is flecked with white and gray strands over his ears—salt and pepper, my artificial memory tells me. Something we didn't see often in the towns. Older people are not *of use* there. Mother smiles back at him. It is a strange exchange—quick, but I catch it.

"I'm Grimley. We have venison soup cooking and a lot to talk about," he says, offering her his arm. She takes it and steps ahead of us.

"I am Imani's mother," she says, and I wonder at her phrasing. Why didn't she just say her name is Imani too?

Thomas looks back at me, eyebrows raised. We follow them into the gathering. I lean in and whisper, "Do you know what the plan is? For us?"

"I don't," he whispers back. "But don't fret your head. It's not going to be anything bad. I'll make sure of it."

I frown. Surely Thomas hasn't already forgotten about how the council lied to us about finding my mother.

Thomas seems to read my mind. "They can be as shady as they like. I still have friends, and I know things just as well as they do." He smiles at me, his eyes searching my face—for what, I don't know.

"But Joe is officially in charge," I remind him. I don't want to remember, let alone talk about, the night with Joe in the kitchens.

"He's only head of the council. Plenty of levelheaded people still have sway down here and up there. They're not all nutters."

"Just don't hold anything back. I need to know everything too. We need to do this together."

"Says the girl who sneaks off in the night," he says with a smile.

"That was different."

"I know. But I love to tease you." He squeezes my arm and rubs his fingers down to my elbow, lingering.

Mother and I are settled on stumps close to the fire, sipping stew offered to her in a clay mug and to me in a tin can that once held some other type of food. The men and women around us begin to talk. The salt-and-pepper man, Grimley, stands to one side of a taller, dark skinned man with a stern face. He holds his gun like he means to use it at any moment. His feet are spread shoulder width apart and he looks from face to face as he speaks.

"This is what remains of our outpost team." He motions to the group of thirty or so people gathered around the fire now. The spaces between every two or three people seem to mark the ones who were lost. I didn't know them, but some faces are grief stricken, others hard. "As far as we can tell without people on the ground there, the Blue Spider rebels have fled their side of the canyon and are likely holed up in the Institute. Dr. Bowman," he pointed at the scientist, "has offered to fill us in on any intelligence he is privy to in exchange for asylum. We have agreed to this arrangement with certain restrictions. He will not possess a weapon, he will be accompanied at all times, and he will speak to the council at the mines when we return. Those responsible for his guard rotation have already been informed."

Heads nod around the circle and he turns from the scientist toward me and Mother. "Now, there is the matter of our new flatlander companions. Do you have anything to add?"

I look at my mother. Before either of us can speak, Thomas answers for us.

"They also have information on Haman and the Leaders we can use. I propose we take them to the mines and let them speak to the council."

"That one's already reported and a fat lot of good it did us," a woman to my right says, sneering as she points at me. I don't recognize her.

"Silence," the serious man says. "I'm aware of the history. Thomas, they will speak for themselves."

I don't hesitate. "My mother and I would like to request asylum."

"I'm not sure that will be possible given the fact that you violated your original agreement," the man says, folding his arms.

"There were extenuating circumstances." I can be just as serious.

"Would you like to report these *circumstances* to us now?"

"I was threatened by Haman and lied to by those inside your organization. I felt it best to take matters into my own hands, without endangering any of the mountain people by asking them to accompany me and get my mother out of the Institute."

"What manner of threats did you receive?"

I look at Thomas, who clearly doesn't know what I am talking about. I'm not sure I want him to know.

"Haman was going to kill my mother if I didn't return to the Institute. The council wasn't going to let me leave and lied to me about their plan to free her."

"And do you have proof of these lies?" He is defensive, like he doesn't believe me.

"I do. The guards who were sent to retrieve her never left the mines. You can talk to them, or anyone who knows them, when we get back."

A murmur filters through the group.

"Enough," the man says. "We will deal with this in front of the council. We have no quarrel, that I've been informed of, with your mother. She may accompany the group heading back to the mines until her asylum has been approved. Unlike some"—he nods his head in the direction Haman's institute—"we do not leave our brothers and sisters to wander the wilderness helpless and alone."

I look at my mother, relief filling my chest. One problem solved—for now.

"Commander, what do we do about them?" Grimley gestures to the few bodies still stumbling along the other edge of the river.

Sorrow softens the man's hard expression, but only for an instant. "There is nothing we can do. We man the guard house and keep our eyes on them. I'm not sure what the next few days will bring. Dr. Bowman, would you care to fill us in on the status of your mindless army over there?"

"They aren't mine," he says, wringing his hands. "I spoke against the choices the Leaders were making regarding Mind Wipe science, specifically how much it changed people. I thought there was a way to improve the wipe. I was transferred to Haman's lab, and he recruited me to work on his plan to improve the wipe and prepare patients to receive the old knowledge. What I learned from those ancient medical records was amazing." His eyes got distant, but when the commander cleared his throat, he quickly resumed speaking and hand wringing. "It was a year into the project that we started seeing issues. The subjects we retained to observe were beginning to regress mentally. I felt we should issue alerts for communities where other subjects were serving in case they experienced the same regressions, but Haman said no."

"Haman knew about these effects and didn't stop the program?" I ask in disbelief.

"We were only starting to understand when—" He is cut off by the commander.

"What I want to know is where did all of these sodding wipers come from? All of a sudden, your side of the shore is crawling with them when this entire region was deserted before. Are the flat lands having that many disciplinary issues?"

Dr. Bowman's hands are writhing like snakes, and he's unable to keep eye contact with the commander as he speaks. "Haman kept a facility underground for test subjects that would not be released back into communities. I'm not sure how he managed that, as it was strictly against the Leaders' Mind Wipe policy of wipe and return, but he had hundreds housed beneath the Institute and many more at two other facilities. Last night the Institute's security systems were disabled and they escaped."

Thomas coughs and digs his toe in the dirt. I look up at him from my stump. He avoids my gaze and instead puts a hand on my shoulder.

"What did you do?" I whisper.

He shakes his head and nods to the conversation in front of us.

"I know where they came from." Mother speaks, her lilting voice a welcome change from the deep timbre of the men.

"They are like me, people who were assigned to final rest that Haman smuggled out for experimentation."

There is a moment of silence while everyone digests this information.

"He healed them and then destroyed their minds?" The man shakes his head and doesn't wait for an answer as a murmur rolls through the group. "Hundreds of those buggers roaming around over there. All right, Bowman, I only want to know one more thing before we haul you up to the council. Why defect now?"

This question seems easy for Bowman, and he straightens and meets the commander's eyes. "Haman is a madman. He's done far more experimenting than I or any one person in his organization could know. There's more than just the Mind Wipe at play here. I should have stopped him when I first saw the effects, but he always assured me that they were temporary, and I chose to believe him in order to continue my research. After seeing the numbers of subjects in the forest last night, I'm now certain he was lying. You are my last hope. My community thinks I'm dead, and without an identity, the Leaders will find me and label me a traitor. I'd probably get the wipe, and I'd rather take my chances with you than risk that."

My mother leans forward, putting her head in her hands. I feel sick to my stomach as all of this information shifts into place. There is only one piece of the puzzle I don't have yet.

"How long?" I ask quietly in the silence that follows.

"How long what?" Bowman says.

"How long after Haman messes with them before their brains begin to rot?"

"The subjects sent back to their communities early on seem to be functioning well. But something in the last year changed for the subjects we retained, and the results were not favorable. Anyone we added information to began to display symptoms of aggression after about six months."

"Six months?" My throat feels tight and my stomach turns over. I suddenly regret the soup I ate.

"Give or take," he says.

Thomas squeezes my shoulder and says to Bowman, "We don't know what he did to them for sure, right? Not everyone has turned bonkers."

"Without my notes and cell numbers, I'm not sure what he did to the people wandering the woods now. And I wasn't a part of the addition experiments—just the team who wiped subject prior to information addition."

"Enough," the man in charge says. "Imani, you can talk with Dr. Bowman in greater length later. We need to move on to coordinating who is going back to the mines."

Shock at my short timeline—*six months*—overshadows the faint surprise that the commander knows my name. I manage a nod. "Hey, lass." Thomas leans over and whispers, "There's nothing to be afraid of."

I know he means well. I want to believe him. But there are so many things he doesn't know, so many things we can't control. The commander makes assignments and the meeting winds down. We are to pack up and start back to the mountain.

"Mother?" I say as the group around us disperses.

She looks at me and smiles. "It's so good to hear that name again."

"Did he implant anything in your mind?" I ask. "Were you ever hooked up to his machine? There would have been music and bright colors, a lot of information coming very quickly. Do you remember anything like that?"

Mother just shakes her head. "I was very sick when I arrived at the Institute. My early memories of that time are hazy at best. I remember different treatments and medicines, but nothing like what you're describing."

"Do you have any strange memories you don't recognize? Any visions or flashing images?"

"No. I have had strange dreams since living there, but not consistently. Nothing during the day."

I fold my arms and think for a minute, looking at the ground. Then I ask, "What are your dreams about?"

She frowns in thought. "There is one where I'm recording a list of numbers on a writer for your brother and father, and one where I'm walking in the orchard with you back in our community. The rest are hazy."

"Brother joined the auto-eye program," I say, realizing she wouldn't know this.

"Well," Mother says, "that suits him, I suppose."

She doesn't sound pleased, and I don't have the heart to tell her that he's the reason I went to prison, that he spied on me in hopes of catching me at something bad enough to warrant a Mind Wipe. I definitely gave him something to report.

I try to relax the worry from my forehead, but Mother sees my concern for her. She takes my hands. "Listen, I know you're worried that I'm going to turn into a wiper, but Haman didn't ever do anything like that to me. I didn't even see him that often. We spoke a few times. He told me a bit of his life now and how his goals had panned out. We talked about our school days and the foolishness of youth. I begged him to let me go to you or at least know what you and your brother were doing. He refused, and the more I insisted the less he came to see me. He hadn't been to my room for more than a week before you showed up."

I'm still uneasy, but I want to relax and trust her story. She's telling me her truth, but that doesn't mean Haman didn't secretly do something to her.

"I'm sure your mum is right," Thomas adds.

"Let's help pack up," she says, standing from her stump. "I'm looking forward to meeting the mountain people." She rubs my back and I nod, turning to the camp. Her affectionate touch feels strange in public, but her warmth and easiness soothe my nerves and I let it flow through me.

"You'll love them," Thomas says as he looks at me, his eyes full of concern. We don't have to speak to know what the other one is thinking.

"I'm sure I will." She smiles at him and takes my half-finished can of soup from me. "Are you sure you don't want this?"

"I'm fine," I lie. My stomach feels like a pit of acid. I can't eat another bite. How much time do I have left?

TWO
Marian

23 was brushing her long dark hair in slow, deliberate strokes. She smiled at her reflection and nodded when her roommate came in to see what was taking her so long.

"You're going to be late, 23," she said as she reached for a rubber band and twisted her carrot-colored hair into double braids down her shoulders. She was tall and thin and her skin was the color of a peach blossom.

"I've told you not to call me that when we're alone. Someday no one will have a number, and I feel much more like a Marian every day. Plus, no one cares if I'm a little late for breakfast." She'd been spending extra time getting ready and braiding her hair in the mornings. Secondary School never regained complete order after 4254 left over a year ago. Her actions were like a never-ending wake from a passing boat. Schedules had relaxed a bit and punishments weren't as severe, but there was still an air of imminent threat.

"You just like it because 4254 gave it to you," her roommate said as she closed a drawer and checked her teeth in the mirror.

Marian braided her hair and pursed her lips. There was a boy in her nutrition class she was hoping to get closer to today.

"You're not wrong. I could have picked one for myself—I thought about that, you know. But I think it's pretty cool that the rebel of the century gave me a name as a parting gift."

Her roommate rolled her eyes.

"And in turn, I gave one to you, Ashley," Marian said and slapped her on the back.

"Be quiet! Mother has been lurking in the halls lately," Ashley gathered her bag off the floor and turned to leave.

"Relax." Marian gathered her own things and sauntered after. "It's been over a year since our fearless hero wreaked havoc here. She's probably long dead and the Leaders are convinced we are under control. Life is good and we are safe."

Before she left her room, she slipped an apple and some bread from her dresser drawer into her satchel. *Old habits die slowly*, she thought. *Especially useful ones.*

"I wish I could be as confident as you," Ashley said, jealousy tinging her voice. "I have to grab something from the study room. I'll see you and the others at lunch."

Marian walked through the bustling hall like a queen surveying her kingdom. It helped that she was taller than many of the students. They literally had to look up to her. Hushed chatter filled the corridor, one of the biggest differences since 4254 left.

She pulled her apple out of her bag and tried not to think about the times when the Leaders had restricted food and an apple could buy you a huge favor. Food could again become a currency in a heartbeat, so she kept hoarding it, just in case. She never wanted to see another friend starve to death.

She took slow thoughtful bites out of the yellow fruit as she made her way to her first class. Students in the halls nodded and smiled at her. Some greeted her with a wave or a "Hello!" but she kept walking.

A short boy wearing the standard gray tunic was waiting for her at the door to her first class. He had nondescript brown hair, bright hazel eyes, and a chubby build, the result of undesirable genes and many failed attempts by his community Leaders to control his metabolism through diet. Marian had dubbed the kid Charlie because he reminded her of the bald boy in the ancient comic strips she'd found in the archives before they were moved to a secure location off campus.

"You ready?" she asked, her smile loaded with mischief.

"No, not really," he said.

"Oh, come on. You've got this," Marian said.

"I dunno. It seems like a really stupid thing to do."

They walked into class side by side and took seats next to each other in the back.

"But you need to prove you can be trusted, that you're brave and worthy of my pack." She made her face serious, but the smirk beneath revealed her true feelings and kept her from being too frightening.

Marian had collected a small group of like-minded students in the months following 4254's exit. She never opened up to anyone she didn't already trust. She vetted everyone who attempted to broach her inner circle before they even came close to speaking to her about it.

Charlie was as good a recruit as she could find. He was fourteen years old, intelligent and cautious, just the right amount of classroom knowledge and street smarts. Plus, he looked innocent. His doughy features and ability to paste on a blank stare made it seem like he wasn't thinking about much beyond his next meal. And yet, he never stopped thinking. Charlie was the only person in Marian's gang that she thought might possibly be smarter than she was. Best of all, he hated the Leaders. He just had to pass one final test of loyalty.

"Charlie, it's going to be easy. And I'll have your back. They'll never know what hit them," Marian said.

Charlie looked thoughtfully into his bag as they pulled out their supplies for the class. "I still think it's an archaic tradition and completely ridiculous."

"Yeah, well, I'm in charge and that's what I say you have to do. Like it or not, I make the rules around here."

"I'm not sure about trading one filthy group of Leaders for a crazy matriarch." Charlie shook his head. He was smiling. Marian loved spouting off at him because she knew he could take it. Some of the other kids couldn't. They would crumble under her intense gaze. But not Charlie. He smirked and shrugged his shoulders.

"Fine." He was going to do it.

The rest of the class went by quickly. More of the same nonsense—hoops they had to jump through to graduate and be "decently educated citizens." Nutrition was the next class, right before lunch, and Marian gathered her friends as she walked the halls to their designated classroom. She noticed a boy talking loudly to a younger boy in the hall. A house mother from another wing was coming toward them as well. Marian caught up to the boys first.

"No talking in the halls," she said loud enough for the Mother to hear. She furrowed her brows and stared the boys down for good measure.

"Everyone talks in the halls—" one boy started.

"Not while I'm around. No talking. Get to class." She wore her authority like a custom-made jacket, leaving no room for argument. The boys looked at her, then at the Mother, and nodded without protest, walking to their class silently.

"Thank you, 23," she said. Her identifying tag said Mother 2A. She was from dorm A, second in charge.

"Of course," Marian said and continued on her way.

A few steps later, Charlie ventured to whisper, "You're such a hard-nosed fake."

"Yeah, but it gets me what I want." Marian smiled and elbowed him as they approached the door to Nutrition.

Marian checked her reflection in a window before stepping into class. She bit both of her lips in turn, giving them a rosy red bruise. Love was not *of use*. Coupling was only to be administered by government assignment, and physical intimacy was relegated to family units looking to reproduce offspring. But what Marian had discovered a few years ago, and what she was slowly teaching the other students, was the fact that even if it wasn't *of use*, physical contact in certain ways was an excellent pastime and stress reliever.

776 sat in his usual seat. His dirty blond hair was cut very close to his scalp. She bet it would feel amazing if she could rub her hand over it. It looked like the pictures she'd seen of the ancient fabric called velvet. His eyes were blue and large, like a young one's, and they questioned everything and nothing at the same time. She'd already named him Ethan in her mind. She'd seen the name in a book a few weeks ago, and it stuck in her head.

He looks like an Ethan, she thought.

He had soft full lips, the kind she'd love to kiss. She was certain he'd never kissed anyone before. She hadn't met a boy yet, older or younger than her, who had. Or a girl either. During her school tenure, she'd dabbled in both sexes, always making sure to carefully choose the people she spent time with, rotating frequently, and occasionally offering her expertise to those she wasn't attracted to in exchange for favors.

Her favorite trade was homework for a little French kissing in the bathroom. She never figured out why it was called French kissing. But she liked the ancient nickname—she liked the names of all banned things—so she used it.

"Hey," she said as she sat next to him.

"Hello," he said.

"How was your break?" she asked, referring to the day they had the week before to visit home.

"It was satisfactory. Yours?"

He was so formal, so stiff. His muscles twitched as he looked at her then looked away. She knew boys looked at her. Even instructors occasionally looked at her. In ancient times she would have been considered very desirable with curving hips, a full chest. and big brown eyes. Her dark hair was braided back but she knew just how to pull it out and toss it around a partner to make them drown in her scent.

She wanted to make Ethan drown now. She wanted to see him breathe deeply, see those first feelings of longing cross his face as his eyes closed and his hands held onto her body like the edge of a cliff.

"My break was also satisfactory," she said. This was the first step. Make him feel comfortable. "Have you been able to work on this assignment yet?"

"Yes, I completed it," he said.

"Would you mind helping me with it later tonight? I'm struggling with the isometric calculations."

"I should be free after dinner."

"Perfect." Marian smiled and licked her lips. His left eye twitched before he looked to the front of the classroom where the instructor was beginning her lecture on lipids and fatty acids.

The rest of the class went by like that; Marian stretching every few minutes to distract Ethan, smiling and answering questions to appear as engaged and interested as he was. After the time was up and they were packing their things, Ashley came up beside Marian and waited so they could walk to lunch together.

Marian nodded and they made their way out of the classroom. But when Marian glanced back, Ethan was still in his seat, so she made an excuse to Ashley, telling her to go ahead, and went back to search for a "lost" reader.

"I know you have a lot of acquaintances," Ethan said, surprising her. She expected she would have to be the one to speak first. "You know almost everyone in the school. Why would you ask for my help in this class?"

She checked to make sure the rest of the students had already filed out. "Because you're the one I want to spend time with." This sort of blunt approach usually caught her target off guard and made a hole in their unassuming armor big enough for her to weasel in and get what she wanted. But 776 just tipped his head and looked at her as if he couldn't understand why anyone would want to spend time with someone else.

"I find that odd," he said.

"You have a lot of odd things to find out. Trust me," she said.

"What do you mean?"

"You help me with this assignment, and I'll explain later."

Marian was used to people playing into her hands. This guy was harder to navigate. He still seemed perplexed. The typical hint of wonder and curiosity hadn't crossed his face yet. Maybe he wasn't a good target.

Then again, she liked a challenge.

"Where should we meet?" he asked.

"Study lab 4?" she suggested.

"Okay. See you there after dinner," he said and left the classroom.

Marian took two apples—she always took an extra apple—and a sandwich plus a bowl of soup and some fresh bread and two protein pouches filled with a thick, sweet goo that was supposed to be a meal in a hurry. She tucked the extras into the pocket of her smock and sat at the table with her friends.

Charlie was bent over a reader, his concentration astounding. Ashley flipped her red braids behind her back and struggled to peel a banana—one of the newer fruits cultivated in the greenhouses at the capital. Marian didn't care for the funny yellow fruit with the mushy white inside, but it reminded her of the photographs of long extinct animals in what used to be the jungles of the world. She wondered if they would ever be able to resurrect those lost species like they had the plants. If only animals had left seeds scattered for them to discover and nurture back into existence.

Eliza, Emily, and Nick joined them, making the table full and her group complete. Eliza and Emily were twins. They roomed with Marian and 4254 before she was arrested. They were the first to come to Marian and demand answers, help, and a secret alliance against the Leaders. Nick was her first physical fling. She had begun to form an attachment to him when she realized what that would mean—eventual separation and assignment to other partners—and she bailed, explaining to him that it wasn't wise to keep sneaking off together. She didn't want to get caught. She had far too many plans for her life to get thrown in prison like 4254 had. That girl was amazing, a role model for all miscreants hungry to break free, but she was also crazy. Marian was careful.

Nick had been hesitant at first, but agreed quickly when he saw the Leaders in black uniforms storming the school and hauling people away on the train and in large armored trucks. Since then, everything had been discreet and fleeting, just the way Marian wanted it. Exactly the level of fun she could control.

"I don't think you should mess with 776," Ashley said as Marian took a bite of her soup.

"Why's that?" Marian asked.

"Because he's uptight and lame. I don't know why you're so fixated on him. He's prime auto-eye attendant material."

"If that were true, they'd have already sucked him into their program," Marian said.

"I'm going to go with Ashley on this one," Nick said. "He's the kind that would freak out and report you the second you touched his thigh."

Everyone at the table had encouraged Marian's hand on their thigh at one point or another except Charlie. He blushed so furiously every time anything physical was mentioned, Marian didn't have the heart to initiate him in that way.

Ashley leaned in and whispered, "Why him anyway? What does he have that we need?"

Marian was caught off guard with this question, but thought quickly and replied, "He's got experience with the hydroelectric facilities."

"Why do we need that?" Charlie's book was still open, but he had been listening the whole time.

Marian seized her chance to change the topic. "You know what I desperately need right now, Charlie?"

"Right now?" he said, clearly understanding her meaning. "No."

"Yes."

"Marian," he whispered, his eyes pleading for mercy.

She checked the clock. "Right now," she said, and the table joined in smiling at Charlie and patting him on the back. "I predict they are having trouble with external auto-eyes in the front office. Everyone else is busy eating or hiding their dirty deeds. Now is the perfect time."

Charlie rested his forehead in his hands for a moment, then stood up and grabbed his bag.

"You guys are lucky I'm not afraid of the establishment," Charlie said as he made his way out of the room.

Ashley leaned in and said, "I like that kid."

"I do too," Marian said.

"You think he'll get caught?"

"Nope. He's gonna be fine."

"What did you tell him to do?" Nick asked.

"Nothing too bad," Marian said.

"She found this old tradition where they paint nonsense on walls in bright colors," Ashley said.

"It's called graffiti. He's gonna do some artwork for us." Marian smiled.

"Great. He's totally going to get caught. Where did you even get the paint for that?"

"We made it. Combination of fruit juices and lacquer from the woods lab installed in an industrial sprayer."

"Where is he going to do this and not get caught?" Nick said.

"You'll see. I have complete faith in Charlie," Marian said just as Mother 3C approached the table.

"23, there is entirely too much talking at your table. Finish eating and get back to classes."

Marian nodded. "Yes, ma'am."

Then Mother 3C added in a quieter voice, "And for the love of the Leaders, quit laughing out loud. I can't cover for you if you act like outright idiots."

"Yes, Mother 3C," Marian said with a demure nod.

"Cripes, what do you have on her?" Ashley asked as the woman walked away to chastise another group.

"I got her a bottle of lavender oil to help her sleep at night," Marian said.

"That's it?"

"It's not easy to come by, and if you admit you aren't sleeping as a School Leader, they start an investigation. Only the most fit are allowed to administer to our *precious youth*." She finished her sentence with dramatic air quotes and stood to leave.

Nick, Ashley, and Marian all had Herbology together in the school gardens after lunch. As they made their way to the planting beds with gloves and tools, Nick had to cover his mouth and look quickly away from the scene before them.

Several students were staring and pointing at the side of the pristinely white building. Blood red letters, big enough for passing trains to read, covered one wall. They hung like an advertisement for a ghost, declaring:

4254 LIVES!

 Imani

Mother is nothing if not useful. As soon as someone found her an extra pair of boots, she was off and running. She's chatting with strangers and helping to take down tents, fold linens, and pack tools before I know what to do with myself.

I am still trying to process his words when Dr. Bowman catches my eye. He is talking with a guard, crossing and uncrossing his arms.

He's nervous, I think. *I would be too if I swapped teams in the middle of the night.*

"I'll be right back," I say to Thomas and Mother.

I can feel both sets of eyes on my back as I trot towards Dr. Bowman. Thomas calls out, "Imani?"

I turn back to him. "I'll be right back. I promise." I want to smile as I say it, but I don't even have the energy to fake one.

As I approach Bowman, the guard walks away. The frumpy little man looks momentarily relieved, and then he sees me.

"Dr. Bowman, I need to talk to you."

He puts one hand on his forehead and closes his eyes, visibly defeated. "I'm not sure I can help you, but I'll do my best."

"Haman messed with my brain. He didn't wipe it, he just filled it with a massive amount of information. I'm almost to the point that I can control it, but I need to know..." I can't control my urgency. I reach out and squeeze his arm. "Am I going to end up like them?" I nod my head in the direction of the river. "Is my mother going to end up like them?"

Bowman looks me in the eye for the first time. "Are you 4254?"

I shudder at the number but nod. "I was."

He nods slowly. "I don't think your mother was ever experimented on. She was a pet project of Haman's. You are one of very few test subjects who received input without a wipe. The ones who are having, uh, difficulties are subjects who were wiped and input with more than what the Leaders required. A complete Mind Wipe damages the frontal lobe. I was working on minimizing that damage because we hypothesized implantation on top of that is what caused these people to lose their humanity. I don't know the details of the subjects who were input only."

I let my hand drop from his arm and fold mine across my chest, holding myself tightly. "But did you have anyone like me, with only input, who didn't make it? Anyone who went crazy?"

Dr. Bowman looks past me to the river.

"Dr. Bowman, I need to know."

"There really weren't enough subjects to know conclusively. We only uploaded a few memories to members of our own staff and none of them seemed to have anything more than a headache for the first few weeks. I don't know after that."

I nod my head and kick at the ground. This could be all right. If Mother's brain wasn't tampered with and I only had implantation, no wipe, we might be safe.

"They call you Imani now?" Bowman asks.

"Yes."

His face seems sincere. His brow is furrowed, and he isn't fidgeting like he had with the guard. "I know your story. I read your file. I know what he loaded into your mind."

"That makes me feel a lot better." I roll my eyes and kick at another rock.

"Imani." His voice is almost gentle. The phrase *bedside manner* comes unbidden into my mind. I meet his eyes. "He loaded everything into your mind—all of it." His tone is strange, deep and emphasized.

"What do you mean?"

"You are the only person alive to have not only all the knowledge of ancient mankind, but also all knowledge from our recent advances, right up until Haman did the implantation." He taps my forehead with his index finger. "You know far more than I do about Haman's experiments and the results. If you can access the right parts, maybe we can do something about them." He waves toward the other side of the river, too far away for us to see the stumbling wipers.

I stare at him, then close my eyes, concentrating on 699-3244-2578, my mother's identification number, to see what information comes to mind. If he's telling the truth, I should be able to find her medical history, maybe what procedures were done to her...

The previously debilitating pain now registers as brief twinges as I go through ancient information. I've never accessed more recent information, and I frown in concentration as I try to look for something from the last year instead of a hundred years ago. It's like flipping through the world's thickest paper reader. Finally, I latch onto one document: her admittance form to the Institute. There's a picture of her—so frail and sick, her eyes unable to focus on the camera—I lose my concentration, opening my eyes to look at my mother in real time. She's still helping to pack up camp, and I exhale in relief. She's not sick, and if Bowman is to be trusted, she won't go crazy and I won't either.

I ask Bowman, "Do you know how long my mother was with him?"

"I'm not sure. They said she was quite ill when she first came to us. Haman had to call in several favors to get her out of the Shop in your community and back to our facility. He personally saw to her rehabilitation, but I'm not sure if he went beyond simple healing and began uploading."

"He didn't," I say, trying to convince myself. Diving back into my memories, I try to find more about Mother, but I can't seem to access anything Haman did to her beyond restorative medications and nutrients. This might be the first time I wish I had more information stuffed in there than I already do. Then again, maybe she is safe.

I look past the camp to the river. What if what Bowman says is true? What if I do have the solution to whatever ails the wipers crammed in my brain?

Tentatively, I think about the Mind Wipe procedure and am immediately deluged with information—books, lectures, documents, and much more. I shake my head, overwhelmed, but Bowman misinterprets the gesture.

"Imani, it's worth a try. If not for yourself, then for all those poor people across the river, and all the ones in the cities who already lost their lives once and are now being put to final rest."

When he says it that way, I feel like I am somehow agreeing to help the Leaders clean up their streets. But he is right; there is more than just my life or Mother's on the line. I owe it to all of them to try.

I don't look away from the river as I answer him. "Yes, I think you're—"

Methodical pulses fill the air as three giant drones fly low over the tree line, over our camp, over the river, and continue in the direction of the Institute. The sides of the planes bear the painted symbol of the Leaders: a scale surrounded by olive branches.

The guards go into action.

"Get into the trees! Now! Go!"

Men and women run toward the forest. I head for Mother and Thomas, but the commander from the meeting grabs my arm and pulls me away from the clearing.

"No time to go back. They're about to shock bomb us," he yells.

"Shock bomb?" I ask, not believing what I'm hearing. The Leaders swore not to use such weapons after the Great War that destroyed the previous civilization. Bombs are not of use when every hand is needed to build our society. Such death is wasteful. They focused only on the necessities of rebuilding a healthy, self-sustaining society where everyone has a job and a purpose that contributes to the betterment of everyone else. How could they even have them? Why would they? I ask the commander, but he doesn't answer. He's running ahead of me, only glancing back briefly to check my position.

I give up and run with him. Thomas will get Mother to safety, and I'll find them in the trees later.

People file out of the tents behind me, charging into the darkness of the woods as the bombs start to go off. The world shakes, and I stumble as an older man knocks into me. We help each other up and continue running.

I can't hear the cries of the dying and wounded, but I know they exist. Looking back, I can just make out the opposite bank. It is engulfed in flames and still the planes, now hovering over where the Institute must be, drop bombs and fire weapons.

It is an astounding sight. A nation of peace destroying its own citizens.

"I thought this was against the law," I shout. I scan for my mother or Thomas in the growing group of people around me, hiking up the mountainside.

The commander answers this time. "They make up all the laws as they go. Or did you not learn that in Primary School?"

I start to say something rude back to him, but a much larger, closer explosion throws me through the air. Just as I note the sensation of weightlessness, I hit something hard and everything is pain and red, then black.

Charlie didn't get caught. The auto-eyes had mysteriously gone offline on that side of the building during lunch period and no one saw anything suspicious. A search of private living spaces was ordered, and a detail of scrubbing was assigned to students already in need of discipline.

"How did you get up so high?" Ashley grinned at Charlie as they sat in the common area of Dormitory C studying for a mathematics evaluation. Charlie shook his head, indicating he didn't want to talk about it.

"Charlie," Ashley persisted. She was two years older than him and a foot taller, but Marian saw something spark between them when they spoke. Ashley legitimately admired the younger, chubby boy. It was amusing.

Charlie continued to write in his tablet, occasionally glancing at the reader open next to it until he couldn't stand her gaze any longer. He turned to Ashley and put a finger to his lips. "Shhhh." Then he winked.

Marian hid a laugh. She didn't care that he wasn't talking about how he got up that high to tag the building in bright red paint. He'd tell her later. There was no rush.

She packed up her reader and tablet, then stood to go. It was research day. She had a train to catch to the Psychological Studies Center, or PSC. For the past two years Marian had been part of a recruiting and internship initiative for the Mind Wipe program. She had permission to leave campus, often traveling with other officials and Professor 789, her sponsor, to the prisons and care facilities where subjects were studied and treated. The professor taught history classes at the Secondary School, but lately his lectures had been mostly remote, and Marian hadn't seen him onsite at the prison in weeks. He was a gruff man, very serious, and Marian felt he was always on the verge of losing his cool and snapping. But he never had. He was efficient and dedicated, and she had learned much from him, but something was off balance. Marian made sure to keep her distance.

The train pulled into the station outside the Secondary School and Marian scanned her student ID to board. It was a beautiful white machine powered by solar energy like all the family pods and other large buildings in their nation. Its smooth tracks were made from recycled war materials, reclaimed girders and automobile parts melted down, purified, and repurposed to move people and crops from one side of their settlements to the other quickly and with no carbon emissions.

Marian settled into a seat and stared out the window, wondering how a nation could get so many things right this time around but still get so many things wrong. Clean air, efficient use of land and resources, but complete imprisonment of its citizens.

There must be a better way, she thought.

Her stop came sooner than she expected. She exited onto a small platform near a field of velvet beans. Their dark purple flowers were blooming, and the air was full of honeybees. The PSC was an almost exact replica of the Secondary School. The white building, surrounded by a large fence, stood in the center of the community. Fields on both sides of the tracks gave way to white pods, homes for the farm and PSC workers. Marian scanned her badge at the gate, nodding to the guards, and again at the entrance before walking into the building.

Her meeting for the day was on the second floor. A group of past interns, now young research assistants, and doctors in training were seated around a large table. Around the walls of the room sat several doctors. Marian had once been part of a group of ten interns from the Secondary School, but she was the only one that remained. The others had been reassigned for vague reasons, though there were rumors it was because of the recent insurrections. Many students who had been interning off-campus had had their programs cancelled outright, so Marian considered herself lucky.

Marian nodded to those she recognized. She had to be all business in this setting. This was her bread and butter. Secondary School was fun, but this was the rest of her life. If she could get permanently placed here, she'd never be without music and art and, best of all, inside information.

Right on time, Professor 789 walked in the door and took his seat at the head of the table. He looked worn and tired as if he hadn't slept well for several nights. She didn't have to wait long to find out what was wrong.

"I want to thank Doctor 741 and 489 and the rest for making the time to be here." His words were met by disgruntled nods. "There has been an incident at our mountain institute. Security was breached and several of our ill subjects were released improperly."

"I didn't know we had ill subjects there," one woman noted.

"That's exactly why we're having this meeting. Normally my more senior team would manage this situation, but they're already hard at work. As I trust all of you, I've called you here as a secondary team and will explain a few top-secret procedures and form a dedicated team to manage the backlash."

Marian sat taller in her chair. Top secret information was her favorite.

"As you know, this project is my life's work. I believe in the power of usefulness and preserving all resources available to our young nation. In the last few years, our Mind Wipe program has repurposed the minds of several maladjusted citizens, allowing them to continue to be productive, and we are proud of the work we do here. As with any medical treatment, some respond differently, and we have kept these outliers for future study.

Many of these individuals are extremely disturbed and while we have not given up hope of remediating at least their bodies for usefulness, we have had to contain them in a high security setting. They are housed and cared for in the mountain institute. A few days ago, security was compromised and several of our subjects escaped their assigned living quarters."

A murmur passed from chair to chair. Marian kept her eyes on the professor and crossed her feet at the ankles.

"The Leaders have been very lenient with our research, but this incident has brought us into the spotlight. We need to correct our mistakes and gain back their good graces. Does everyone understand?"

The room murmured and most people nodded.

"485, you have a question?" the professor said.

"Was this work sanctioned by the Leaders?" the man across from Marian said.

"All of our work is sanctioned. It isn't all common knowledge. You are the next level of security." He turned to look at the rest of the group. "I'm going to assign you to teams of herb analysis, medicine manufacturing, and outlier research. The doctors present have already been briefed and will lead the teams."

Marian's eyes widened. The escape of these outliers must be a very bad outcome for this much manpower to be moving off psychological mainstream studies and into medicine production. She wondered why she hadn't heard of these studies before and how big this mountain institute was.

A few more logistical questions were asked and answered. Marian was assigned to medicine manufacturing, and she made her way to the labs with the rest of her team. Most of the other twelve citizens had experience creating the assigned medicine, but Marian and two other young men were taken aside by the doctor assigned to their team to receive an explanation of the procedure.

Doctor 741 was an older woman, her silvery hair tied back in a tight ponytail. She walked them through how to feed the pink flowers of a plant called valerian through the expresser machines set up on long tables, and how to treat the clear oil that streamed into a clay pot on the other side. Marian recognized the plant as one of the crops growing outside the PSC.

"How bad do you think this is for Professor 789 to pull us off our projects?" Marian dared to ask the woman.

"Considering I'm in the final stages of anticancer research, I'd say it's pretty bad," Doctor 741 said with a sigh. "I think all of you are ready. Work at this station so I can check the concentration levels as you go." She gestured to a worktable set slightly apart from the others.

Marian was soon lost in the methodical work of extracting the essence of the herb. It wasn't difficult, but it required concentration, and she was determined to be exact in her measurements.

A voice blared over the intercom. "Group B, mountain clean up assignment, please report to meeting room nine immediately. Code Blue Spider is in effect."

Marian's heart raced. She'd heard rumors of the Blue Spider rebels, Professor 789's secret group of closest associates. She wasn't sure what their agenda was or if they were connected with Group B. Normally, she steered clear of eavesdropping on meetings, but this time, with people being pulled off assignments and Professor789 looking so serious, she needed to know what was happening.

She waited a few minutes, then excused herself to use the bathroom and made her way to the meeting rooms. The door to room nine was already closed, but she could see a tall man speaking to the group inside. His voice carried, and, pausing, she found she could make out most of what he was saying. The phrase "leaving immediately" was first to catch her attention. He continued, saying they each had an hour to gather clothing and essential personal effects. She heard chairs sliding and people moving so she kept walking down the hall, annoyed that she hadn't heard more.

As she passed room eight's open door, she caught a glimpse of Professor789 huddled with his closest associates. She walked by casually, then paused out of sight and bent down to pretend to fix her shoe. Someone closed the door behind her as more people rushed by from the previous meeting, but crouched down, she could still hear clearly enough through the gap in the bottom of the door.

"We have confirmation that she is alive and with the mountain people, but we do not know her exact location. The Leaders are dropping shock bombs on our facilities," Professor 789 said. "They don't want to give us time to clean up. We've lost jurisdiction over this particular matter."

A woman came down the hall toward Marian, slowing to reach for the handle to meeting room eight. Marian stood up quickly.

"Just had to tie my shoe," she said and started back toward the work rooms.

The woman nodded and made her way into the meeting with the professor. She closed the door behind her, and Marian rubbed her head, unable to believe what she'd just heard.

Shock bombs?

She hadn't misheard.

Bombs.

As in blow people, animals, trees, and buildings to bits. That couldn't be right. Sure, her nation was screwed up, it wasn't perfect, but they renounced weapons of war. They renounced anything more damaging than a shock rifle. Why did they even have bombs? And what could be happening that would make them renege on the one thing they all agreed on—violence wasn't a solution?

Back at school that evening, Charlie was the first person Marian told about the news she had gleaned. He may be the newest member of the group, but she felt she could trust him and wanted his input.

"Have you ever heard of the Leaders doing anything like this before?" she asked.

He shook his head and scratched his arm. They were in Marian's dorm room, an auto-eye watching them, but no one to eavesdrop on what they said, especially with their backs to the camera.

Marian frowned. "I can't make sense of it. There must be more going on than anyone knows about. Between 4245 kick-starting riots and Haman admitting he screwed up in the mountains, these are big changes."

"True, but do they affect us?" Charlie said.

"I'm not sure yet. I've mostly filed them away as good-to-know." Silence fell as Charlie worked on a problem set and Marian mused. Then she remembered the conversation earlier that day with Ashley.

"So how did you do it?" she asked, smiling at her protégé. "How did you get up so high and paint so quickly? It took them three ladders and half the day to scrub it off, and it's still all smeared up there." Marian laughed remembering the sight as she pulled back into school on the train.

Charlie smiled back, clearly proud of his accomplishment. "I used a garden drone."

"What?" she asked, genuinely surprised.

"I loaded it with paint instead of bug spray, retrofitted and fine-tuned the spray nozzle, and hacked the remote controls. I preprogrammed the movements into it so I wouldn't have to be out there while it did the job."

Marian stared at him. "Charlie, that is pure brilliance."

"I know, right? What a waste," he said.

I taste dirt. My head aches. A sharp pain runs down my left shoulder and into my back. I don't want to open my eyes, but I can't remember where I am. Prison, school, home, and the mountain all run through my mind. My body feels heavy. But I bring my hands under my shoulders and push myself up to sitting, gasping at the pain in my shoulder. I hold my head in my hands and brush the dirt off my face. Small pebbles are embedded in my skin and sting as I run my sore fingers over them, prying them loose. I dare to blink, to look around me.

Damaged trees and rocks and other fallen people surround me. Some forms are moving, most lie still on the ground. A strong pinesap odor laces the scent of smoke and ash. Small fires burn in the brush. Trees have been knocked over, split at odd angles, and different heights of trunks are left limbless. I can't hear the birds or the people crying. My head roars with pain and my ears are ringing. I squeeze my eyes shut and take a deep breath through my nose. Artificial thoughts roll into my aching mind: Men lying in trenches, a firing squad shooting blindfolded people lined up like trees; bombs going off in a city, laying waste to building after building; men in uniforms marching, shooting civilians who oppose them; explosions; children with missing limbs and scars; dead and wounded being moved or buried. Weeping, funerals, scorched earth on every continent…

This is why the Leaders made peace a priority. This is why there are supposed to be no more weapons of war. Shock rifles are painful, but they aren't ever used to kill. This is death unleashed. This is wrong.

A hand on my shoulder brings me back to the mountain. I look up, defensive. It is one of the guards. He is asking me something, but I shake my head. He reaches down and pulls me up by my right arm to speak closer to my ear.

"Are you all right?" he shouts, and I can finally hear him.

I nod my head and try to reply, but my voice sounds funny, far away. I am dizzy.

The guard points to those around us on the ground before making scooping motions with both hands. He needs help getting them up. If we're to live, we need to move.

I nod and take a few tentative steps. More bodies are moving. The past few hours come back to me, thoughts rising slowly just like the people around me.

Mother. Thomas.

I begin to backtrack down the hill and with each step I realize I hurt in other places. The ringing in my ears begins to subside. I pause to help a guard up, then keep going, trying not to stumble.

They have to be here. I just got my mother back, and Thomas... I don't think I can live without him anymore.

I spot my mother first. She is walking up the mountain toward me. Her face is streaked with dirt and blood, her hair tangled and falling out of its braid. One sleeve of her coat is torn, but she is alive. I wrap my arms around her and bury my head in her neck.

"Mother!" My voice is coming back to me. "Are you okay?" I lean back and look closely at her face. She puts a hand to my cheek, her eyes full of tears.

"Yes, I'm fine," she says.

"Where is Thomas?" I ask. "We need to get farther into the woods. The Leaders might be circling back for another run."

"Why would they bomb us? How can they justify this?" she asks, sounding lost. "Or have things changed so much since I was locked away?"

I wonder darkly if this isn't the first time they've used bombs to silence resistors and we just didn't know about it. "They won't have to explain it. No one will know. They lie to the people then do whatever they want," I say.

She nods in agreement then loops her arm through mine and begins to pull me back up the mountainside. "Let's find Thomas. He was ahead of me."

We make our way deeper into the woods. Black patches of smoldering dirt polka dot the hillside where the bombs full impact was felt. How could the Leaders develop weapons like this and keep them a secret? And how could they use them against other humans?

More images of wars long past flood my mind: genocide, torture, chemical weapons. None of this was new for humanity. It sickens me.

"Is that him?" Mother points through the trees to a guard leaning over a body. Thomas's body.

I jog to his side, pain shoots through my back with each step.

"Thomas?" I ask as I come closer. His eyes are closed, and his mouth is slightly open. His clothes are charred black on one side. A matching black hole is carved into the mountain a few feet away.

"Thomas?" I crouch beside him, not sure where to touch him, how to help. Thomas's face is scraped on one side, the skin open and oozing. Forest shrapnel mixed with dirt clings to his skin in random places and has ripped holes in his clothes. There is some bleeding, but not a lot. My biggest concern is the burn on his side.

My eyes fill with tears as I rack my brain for how to help. Possibilities come too quickly.

First aid. Shock victims. Bomb impact. Internal bleeding.

"He's alive, but he's in shock. We need to get him out of here."

I hadn't noticed the guard following us. I nod at his assessment.

"Do you have any kind of medic or doctor with you?" I ask. "What about Bowman? Where is he?"

"The outpost's medic was killed yesterday, and I haven't seen Bowman."

"Can you please go find out? I'll stay with Thomas." I run my hand carefully over his face, brushing dirt and rocks off.

"He's lucky to be alive. If that blast had been any bigger, he'd be dead," the guard says. He's just as shocked as we are.

"Just go get Bowman." My tears threaten to spill, and I am gulping down breaths trying to keep my mind clear.

"I'll help find him," Mother offers as she steps up behind me and puts a hand on my shoulder. "Thomas will be all right. We'll get him out of here."

"We need to start on a cot as well. We're going to have to carry him back," the guard calls back to me as he and my mother walk away.

I walked here from the mine. It wasn't an easy hike. Carrying the wounded is going to make it even harder, impossible if the Leaders come back. I take a deep breath and push my hair back out of my face then keep brushing dirt gently off Thomas, unsure of what else I can do.

First aid.

Images of a red plus symbol, bandages, and tinctures rise above the rush of other information. Maybe I do know what to do.

I close my eyes and focus on thoughts of wounded people, people with burns, and how to save them. All kinds of horrific pictures flood my mind. I push them aside and focus on the ones with doctors and nurses aiding in healing. I try to focus on images like Thomas. Someone alive, but unresponsive, someone you love who is barely breathing after an explosion.

The procedures are there for damage after detonation. I know his body experienced trauma internally. But how major is it? He is unresponsive and the only answers I'm coming up with are from hospitals long gone, machinery lost a century ago, tools and medicines I have no access to. I begin to push away the thoughts of healing and focus on the explosions, the math, the equations.

I look to the charred spot on the hill not far from him. I do the math. It was a small shell. The guard was right—any bigger or closer and he'd be dead. Most likely he had some sort of head trauma from being knocked over, and possibly some organ damage, but I hope not.

I squeeze his shoulder. "Thomas." I press his hands between my own and feel their warmth in the cool air. "Thomas?" My heart tightens as I squeeze again but get no response.

A branch behind me snaps, and I turn to see a new guard carrying some long pieces of wood. "Finn sent me for Thomas. Help me with this branch, and we'll get him loaded up. They will know what to do with him back home." He has two small trees, freshly cut and lashed together at one end. He connects the other two ends to a larger branch. "Tie that one down there." He hands me a piece of rope and then shows me how to balance Thomas's body between the fallen trees in a hasty stretcher.

He doesn't wake when we move him. I run back to what is left of the camp, eyes scanning the sky for more drones, ears tuned for any sound from above, and find a blanket to wrap him in, then help secure him to the cot. Keeping him warm is the only useful information I can act on. Another guard helps us, and the two men pick him up as we join a thin stream of dirty mountain people moving up the trail. My head and shoulder ache, but I push the pain aside, searching the faces around me for Mother or Dr. Bowman.

Mother, Dr. Bowman, and the commander catch up with us after a long, worry-filled ten minutes of hiking. I usher Dr. Bowman to Thomas's side.

"Can you help him?" I ask.

Bowman takes his pulse, listens to his chest, and examines the burns. "He should be all right if we can get him home and stabilized. But I'm not a medical doctor by trade. I'm a scientist."

I push past him, frustrated at his lack of help and signal the guards to keep walking with me.

The commander calls out behind us, "Bowman, see to the rest of the wounded as we walk. Daylight won't wait for us."

Only a handful of the original group stays behind to deal with the aftermath. Everyone else pushes ahead with the most critically wounded in three crude stretchers. A whistle sounds through the trees, a signal from someone ahead.

We trudge through the foothills, taking a different route than I followed. We are higher in altitude and there are more patches of snow and ice, but we also have more cover from trees. A well-worn path marches on ahead of us. It is narrow but makes hiking much easier.

Game trail, my artificial memory says.

Okay then, I say back.

The party is subdued for the first hour. The skies are clear of drones and I start to relax into the steady rhythm of the trail, but my head still throbs and I'm starting to feel the effects of thirst and hunger. Mother asks a few quiet questions about the mountain people—what it is like there, what she should know about their society. She doesn't want to offend her rescuers. I tell her the basics, the strange customs of plentiful food and colorful clothing, how the girls cut their hair as short as boys, and everyone chooses a profession they are interested in instead of being assigned. I also tell her about the music and bathing cave where people aren't ashamed to stand unclothed in front of each other and wash their bodies while others do the laundry, sharing the same natural hot springs to wash away the cavern's remnants.

"I doubt you will offend any of them, Mother. They are a lot like us, only not as strict and the food is much better." I can't imagine my mother ever doing anything to cross anyone. She lived her whole life in the flat lands, home of ultimate good behavior and citizenship.

Once the sun sets, the guards produce portable lights to help us see. Even those uninjured in the blasts feel the effects of our hurried march, but the commander insists we push hard for the mountain entrance.

Our party pauses around the trunk of a large fir tree. Long dead from a lightning strike, its charred top seems to absorb the light from the lanterns. I sit in the dirt next to Thomas's stretcher and wrap my arms around my knees. Mother sits next to me while we wait for the guards to open a hatch hidden near the dead tree. I reach out and take Thomas's hand instinctively.

Mother resumes her questioning, trying to distract me from Thomas's shallow breathing. "These seem like very capable people. Did you enjoy living among them?"

"I suppose so. I was mostly worried about you."

"When did you find out I was alive?" she asks.

"Haman sent a message to me with a photograph of you not long after I escaped the Institute."

Remorse passes over her face. "I was very ill when I first arrived at the Institute. I got better over time, but he kept me medicated and drowsy. There are only a few clear days I remember spending with him. I knew I couldn't go back to our community, but I asked him to help me find information about how you and your brother were doing. I ached to see you, hear anything about you, but he kept saying he couldn't find anything."

I begin to cry all over again as she tells her story. My memories are correct, she was drugged for months, kept like a pet in a box. I think of all the days I sat alone in a prison thinking she was dead and I had failed her, when she was in her own sort of prison thinking of me as well. It is too painful to remember the days we spent just a hallway apart but didn't know it.

"I can't begin to imagine everything you've been through." She squeezes my arm and closes her eyes.

I pat her hand. I want to tell her everything—about school, prison, my escape, Thomas—but this isn't the place and now isn't the time. She has no idea how close to the truth she is—she can't possibly imagine my experiences.

"It's all right," I say. "We will have plenty of time to talk once we are warm and dry and well rested."

I hope I am right about that.

SIX

The halls were quiet. It was getting late. Study lab 4 was in a back hall not far from her dormitory. She had used it many times when she needed some private time with friends or potential allies. The auto-eye in that wing was always on the fritz. The front office admins complained about it all the time.

776 was already there when she knocked on the doorframe and entered.

"Hello," he said. Readers lay spread out around him, and he looked at one with concern on his pale face.

"What's wrong?" she asked.

"I'm working on a problem for the hydro facilities. It's an internship assignment, and it's harder than I expected it to be." He studied the reader a moment longer, then packed up a few things and spread out new ones. "How can I help you?"

Marian knew exactly where to sit so that if the auto-eye was working, the Leaders would have a hard time discerning their movements and conversation. She'd studied the tapes over the shoulders of the admins in the main offices when they hadn't noticed her passing. Just like in her dorm room, she made sure her back was to the camera so that lip reading wasn't possible. Then she put her feet up on a table and smiled at 776, who was straight-backed in a chair next to her.

"I have a proposition for you," she said.

"I thought you needed tutoring."

"I do, but not for nutrition." She watched his face contort and strain. She noticed his hands gripping the edge of the table just a bit. He was nervous, caught off guard.

"What is this about?" He sat back in his chair and folded his arms.

He's nervous but curious. That's a good thing, she thought.

"We're almost to the age of permanent assignment. I'm wondering what your thoughts are on that. Do you have a preference?" Marian tried to make herself seem sincere.

"I suppose so. I'm very interested in working at the dam in community 208, and it's very likely I will be assigned there due to my success in the hydro classes. But why do you want to know?"

"That's probably correct. And that's very far from where I will most likely be assigned," she said and folded her own arms.

"I still don't understand—" he started.

Marian decided to go in full science mode. This guy was as neuroadvanced as they came. Subtlety wasn't going to work.

"I find myself physically attracted to you. I know that these emotions are chemically driven by our minds and developing bodies, but I've thought about it, and while we will most likely be assigned to live our lives far from each other, I'd like to know what it is like to be with someone who I am chemically compatible with before I'm assigned to a mate."

Marian didn't think it was possible, but somehow, he sat up straighter, arms tighter around his chest. He definitely wasn't expecting this.

"That's against the rules. Coupling is for assigned partners only," he said.

"Not necessarily," Marian parried. "I study human psychology and behavioral patterns. There is definitely a difference between assigned mates and chosen mates, and I think it would be a valuable experiment for my work—possibly yours as well—if we were to give it a try." She shrugged as if it wasn't a big deal, just something she was tossing around.

"How does premature coupling help with hydroelectric studies?" 776 was clearly hooked now. His arms had relaxed, and he was leaning forward. She was almost there. He would either stand up in an angry huff and report her or sink into her plan, his curiosity getting the better of him.

"Because humans are electrical beings. You must have studied that at some point in your sciences. We are the quintessential batteries, furnaces, conductors. Our bodies and consciousnesses rely on electricity to function. We produce it and use it and store it; we are both potential and kinetic at the same time. It's completely relevant."

This was the point of no return. The bet had been cast and Marian was nearly breathless with excitement, only she hid it like a pro while 776 listened to her speech and evaluated her offer. He hadn't stood up. He hadn't said no. She just might win this one...

"I'm not sure I follow your argument. And I'm not sure it's entirely legal."

"It's a science experiment. Purely academic."

"It would never be approved."

"Do you get all your research approved beforehand?"

"No, but..."

"Exactly."

Marian was so close. She could see him teetering, almost giving in, his curiosity winning over his intelligence. This was the first step. This was the revolution. One person at a time waking up to their own minds and desires, and Marian loved her role as guide to the unsuspecting.

"I'm going to have to think about this," he said as he stood and gathered his things.

Marian felt the tiniest hint of panic, of failure. By now, she usually had them. He was getting ready to go instead of leaning into her advances and cautiously talking about details. She had to do something to stop him. To show him how important this was for both of them.

She sat forward, putting her feet down on the floor, and leaned toward his pile of materials. She reached for a reader, pulling it away from him before he could put it in his bag. He looked at her, questioning. She slid it back toward him across the table and then beyond, pressing it into his upper thigh, very close to the groin. He didn't move.

"Let me know what you decided." She looked up at him and bit her bottom lip, sucking on it a bit.

He didn't move or reply at first. Just looked at her with those huge blue eyes.

What an absolute child, she thought. *You have so much to learn.*

"I'll think about it," he finally said and took his reader from her hand, stuffed it into his bag, and left Marian without looking back.

She couldn't help but feel this might not have been a good idea. Then again, the best ideas were rarely safe ideas, and she would never admit to her friends that they might have been right.

The next morning, Marian winked at Charlie over the breakfast table. He rolled his eyes and she laughed behind her hand, checking to see if any of the house mothers were watching.

"You're going to get us all sent home," Charlie said.

"But we'll have fun before it happens," Marian said.

"Where did you get it?" Ashley asked.

Nick leaned in to join the conversation while Emily and Eliza walked up to the table with their food. Marian indicated they should wait for the twins before she told her story.

"What's going on?" Emily asked.

"Marian has a gift for us," Ashley said.

"A gift?" Eliza said as she shook a protein drink and then opened it.

"Let her talk," Nick said, clearly the most eager of the group to get up to some trouble.

With talk of bombs and emergency mountain missions, Marian had a feeling she should let her friends in on a secret she'd been saving for them.

"You guys know how they moved all the archives to the capital after 4254 left to keep us safe from our wicked past?" Marian whispered. The rest of the group nodded and leaned in closer as she continued. "They missed a box."

"How did you manage that?" Ashley's eyes were wide and a twitch of a smile was darting across her face like she couldn't decide if this was the best or the worst thing she'd ever heard.

"Admins always love a student who's happy to help. I offered to load one night and snagged a small box, tucked it into a closet while no one was looking," Marian said and smiled her famous toothy grin while flipping her braid over her shoulder.

"What's in it?" Charlie asked. He always cut to the point.

"I don't know. I was waiting for you guys to open it with me," she said.

"But where? There isn't anywhere large enough for us to go without an auto-eye," Eliza said.

"What about the back classroom behind the A wing? That camera went out last week and hasn't come back on. That's why it's been empty," Nick said.

"Yeah, but they will for sure spot a bunch of us walking there and going in with a box," Ashley said.

"I can take care of that," Charlie offered.

Marian patted his shoulder. "I told you guys this kid was golden." She slipped her hand back under the table when she saw a Mother come into view, and the whole table was suddenly very interested in chewing their food.

Once the room was clear again, Charlie said, "Just meet me outside dorm A tonight an hour before curfew and I'll get you in."

Everyone nodded. That hallway would be busy, and it would be easy to get lost in the shuffle of the nighttime routine.

On the way to her room, Marian ran into 776. She nodded to him but didn't speak. He returned her nod and her silence but joined her as she walked. The hall was quiet for the most part. Marian was thrilled when he looked around and, seeing no one was there who would report, whispered, "I've thought about your offer."

She raised her eyebrows. "And?"

"And I'm curious as to the details of your proposal."

Marian beamed. *Got him*, she thought.

"Just a meeting now and then to talk about possibilities and try out a few of them," she said. Her pulse was racing. The anticipation was a main part of the fun. She didn't know why this boy interested her so much. Maybe it was because he was seemingly unattainable. Or because she liked the challenge? Maybe it was those blue eyes? It could also be a simple matter of pheromones. That gave her an idea.

"You should do a little homework first," she whispered without turning her head.

"What's that?" he asked.

"Research pheromones," she said.

"I've already studied that in botany."

"Not in plants, in humans." She winked at him and let her hand brush against his as she passed him at the entrance to her dormitory. "I'll be in touch."

He blushed violently.

Got him, she thought again.

Charlie waited for them in the corridor like the clockwork machine he was. The others were slowly trickling up in pairs. Marian walked with Ashley. She had the box in a gray satchel she used for hauling projects around the school. It was brown, unmarked except for a number code on the side. Just like any other box in the school, except this one wasn't supposed to be in the school.

Charlie nodded once they were all there and typed a few things into his reader. Some of them stood across the hall and a couple stood by Charlie. Several other students filed past in their uniform smocks, chatter hushed, faces tired. Finals were coming up again soon and projects were due. The school was a whispering hive of activity and stress.

"Okay, we're good for fifteen minutes," he said without looking at his friends. "Let's go, but spread out."

They did as the younger boy said and made their way down the hall then turned left into a deserted corridor with lights off. Once they came upon the classroom they were seeking, Nick pulled a metal tool out of his pocket and slipped it between the handle and the door casing. It was a trick he'd learned so that the admins couldn't track their badges to opening the lock.

He wiggled the tool then slipped it up while pushing down on the handle and it popped open soundlessly. They filed in while Nick held the door and Marian stood guard, waiting to enter and latch the door behind them.

The twins looked like their faces would split with excitement. Everyone gathered around the table where Marian set the box. She held her hand out and Nick placed the tool in it. They were close enough that she could lean over and kiss his cheek, so she did.

"Thank you, darling," she said. Nick blushed and Ashley looked a little annoyed. Marian looked at the rest of the group. "Are you guys ready?"

They nodded in unison. Marian slid the sharp end of the metal tool into the taped opening of the box and sliced the seal. She was then able to pry the lid off and everyone peered inside, their breath held.

Several small paper readers, a stack of cards with brightly colored pictures, a silver music disk labeled *Sawdust by The*

Killers, and a strange blue and silver object. It was rectangular and made of stacked pieces of metal bolted together with spaces between. On top were inscribed the words *Fender Blues Deluxe Harmonica.*

They took turns removing each item and handling them as if they were made of glass. Passing each one around the table, flipping through the pages of the readers, pointing out interesting pictures from the stack of cards.

"What do you think this is?" Eliza said as she examined the metal rectangle.

"No clue," a few of them murmured and she passed it along.

"These are all about food," Charlie said rifling through the paper readers. "Something called cookbooks."

"They used to make their own food in each family pod," Marian said.

"What a waste of resources," Emily said. "Look at this though." She held up one of the cards. Most of them were ancient buildings and landscapes but this one featured a scene with flowers of all colors and a river with a tall-legged mammal standing at the bank drinking. It had soft brown fur and a slender tail curved to one side. "Do you suppose that's a real animal?"

"Looks like a real photo, but they were good at altering images. It's hard to tell," Charlie said.

"That's a deer," Nick said. "I've seen drawings like that in History of Fauna."

"Huh." Emily continued to gaze at the image.

"I think those are personal letters," Marian said as she picked one up. The backs were inscribed with handwritten notes. She read aloud:

Dear Flynn,

It's amazing here but I miss you. I wish you could have come with us. The weather is beautiful and the food is to die for. See you soon!

Love, Gwen

"Wow, love, huh? No wonder they hid these," said Ashley. Love was not *of use* in their community.

"Food to die for? Sounds terrifying," said Nick.

"Hello there," Marian said as she pulled a paper reader from the pile of cookbooks. "This isn't about food."

The others paused to look at the reader in her hands. It was thicker than the others, the pages faded brown with age, torn and dog-eared in some places. The cover was off-white and featured an artist's rendition of a group of young boys. They were wearing black jackets, white shirts and blue pants, their hair was slicked back and some curled at the ends. *The Outsiders by S.E. Hinton* was written in large red letters.

"What is it?" asked Eliza.

"It's a novel," said Charlie. "A work of fiction meant solely for entertainment."

"Not just entertainment," said Marian. "Sometimes they were a covert means of teaching lessons and morals."

"How is it covert?" Eliza asked again.

"They hide some tale of doom in between the pages of a made-up story meant to teach you to avoid the doom," Marian said, trying to get it on Eliza's level. She was bright enough in math, did an excellent job on Marian's homework when she was in a pinch, but sometimes needed things spelled out.

"Sounds like a roundabout way of getting something simple done," said Emily. She was just as smart as her sister academically but a bit quicker when it came to common sense.

"You don't have to read for the sake of the moral. You can just read for the sake of the story. It's entertainment. Totally not *of use*," Marian said.

"Here's another," said Charlie, handing Marian a paper reader titled *Fahrenheit 451 by Ray Bradbury*. She flipped past the boring red, black, and white cover and began to read the printed synopsis on the back.

"Guy Montag is a fireman. In his world, where television rules and literature is on the brink of extinction, firemen start fires rather than put them out. His job is to destroy the most illegal of commodities, the printed book, along with the houses in which they are hidden.

"Montag never questions the destruction and ruin his actions produce, returning each day to his bland life and wife, Mildred, who spends all day with her television 'family'. But then he meets an eccentric young neighbor, Clarisse, who introduces him to a past where people did not live in fear and to a present where one sees the world through the ideas in books instead of the mindless chatter of television.

"When Mildred attempts suicide and Clarisse suddenly disappears, Montag begins to question everything he has ever known."

"Whoa, let me see that," Nick said. "Was that guy some kind of mystic prophet? I want to read it."

Marian handed the book to him. "Dunno, but I want it next."

"Then me," Charlie said.

"I like those names, Clarisse and Mildred. We should give them to someone," Emily said.

"We can all take turns passing the novels around," Marian added.

"Not me," said Eliza as she leafed through a cookbook. "I want these."

"I don't think you should take them all," says Emily. "It would be hard to hide." There were eight cookbooks total, and though they were small, they made up the bulk of the box.

"Yeah, but how do I choose between beef Wellington and streusel? I need to know what this stuff is," Eliza said as she held a book up in each hand.

"Time's almost up," Charlie said.

"Thank you, Charlie." Marian smiled at him and set her book down. "Which reminds me, before we go back to our cells, we really need to catch up on our amorous endeavors." She took a step toward him.

"I'm good," he said and blushed heavily while the rest of the group laughed.

"Well, I'm not," Emily said. "I need some arms around me."

Marian held up her own arms and offered an embrace to her friend. Emily gladly slipped in and pressed herself against the older girl. They held each other and squeezed, their heads even enough to rest on the other's shoulder. Then Marian leaned back and pushed a stray hair fallen from Emily's braid out of her eyes.

"You are a beautiful person, you know that, right?" she said.

Emily responded by kissing her on the lips, a slow lingering kiss to be savored for several days until another opportunity of privacy and willingness was available.

When they parted, they were both flushed and smiling. Eliza smiled too and hugged Marian next but forwent the kissing. Nick and Ashley were much more intense in their physical displays of affection than they had been in the past. Marian thought it was almost like animals, the way they held and practically swallowed each other. But she remembered a time when Nick was like that with her, and she remembered how good it felt, his hands running along her body under her tunic. She looked back at Emily and they smiled at each other before one more round of kissing. This time Marian lets herself go a bit more, sinking further into Emily's soft lips and wet tongue, synching their breath and urgency, her hands wandering.

"You sure you don't even want a hug, Charlie?" Eliza asked.

"Nope. I'm sure. I'm good with those rules. But I wish we had some way to play this music disc. I'm going to hold onto it and do some research in the laser labs. Maybe I can build something. Hey, you guys, for real, peel yourselves off each other. We need to go."

The frantic couples separated, laughing and wiping their mouths. Lingering hands rubbed backs and arms as their thoughts turned from lust to the night ahead and the next day.

"We have twenty minutes to curfew. Let's head out," Eliza said.

"Ashley and I will go last. I need to make sure the door locks behind us," Nick said, a funny grin playing on his swollen lips. "You can turn the lights out."

"You guys are gross, you know that?" Charlie said.

"Don't knock it till you try it," Marian said as she slipped a couple of cards in her bag with *The Outsiders*. She stuffed the rest of the contraband back in the box offering it to the others to share.

"Whatever." Charlie pulled out the Fender Deluxe Blues Harmonica and stuck it in his pocket, then shut the door behind them as the rest of the group headed to bed.

Marian looked back at the closed door and wondered for a moment if her friends would be discovered. She felt something she thought might be jealousy and wished her newest recruit would have jumped on the bandwagon earlier. But there was time for that. She'd have her own nights alone in dark rooms with boys and no auto-eyes soon enough. She'd make sure of that.

Thomas's mother, Maire, is waiting for us when we finally enter the mountain. The hatch leads to a concrete passageway, not the rough-hewn stone I've seen before. I hesitate at the entrance. I've never been here before. It's so much like the prison I have to remind myself that I'm not walking back into jail. It helps that there are medics and supplies waiting for us as well as loved ones.

"Where's my boy?" Maire is grief stricken and searches the faces as we pass. Someone must have run ahead for help.

"He's here." I wave her down and she makes her way to us, skirts bustling, sweat rolling down the sides of her face. She must have run all the way up the mountain to get here.

"Joseph! Alan! Over here," she shouts at two men carrying bags of supplies.

The guards carrying him lay his stretcher down. The two men rush forward at her command and begin to assess Thomas's broken body, applying salves and washing what can be cleaned in the passageway. They seem optimistic, and the heavy weight of dread lifts from my shoulders.

Once he is treated to the satisfaction of the medics, we resume our march, Maire bustling away now that she knows her son will survive. She's not the head of the council, but everyone in the mountain listens to and respects her, and I hear her voice giving orders long after she's out of my sight.

A boy hands me a canteen of cool water and I take it gratefully, offering it to Mother first. She takes a few sips then I drink the rest down.

Artificial lights hang overhead, filling the air with a chorus of electric thrumming under the chaotic rescue chatter. Soon we are all moving deeper into the earth through these strange new tunnels.

As we march, I note doors along the way. Some are labeled with numbers, some with antique plaques—*Munitions, Control, Storage*. One door is open far enough that I can see inside to a bank of machinery, lights flashing, a man sitting at a desk staring at a black screen full of green characters.

It's so foreign, like something from Secondary School come back to haunt me, although much older. This facility was built before the Great War. It has none of the sleek whiteness that the Leader's modern buildings have, and none of the homemade qualities of the mountain people's dwellings.

A group of guards jog past us going the opposite direction as we near a door with a bright yellow sign. Three black triangles surround a small black circle in the middle that reads *Caution, Radiation Area*.

I immediately comb my implanted memories for a reference. *X-rays, laboratories, bombs*. There are so many possibilities. I keep an eye on Thomas and continue to search for more clues as we rush forward.

"What is this place?" I venture to ask the woman in front of me.

"It's the forbidden wing. Not structurally sound. We never should have come in this way, except it was an emergency. Take a good look. You won't be back."

I do look. Then I wonder why there is a man and functioning machinery left in a *structurally unsound* underground bunker.

The passageway widens and we're suddenly in a high-ceilinged room with what feels like everyone from the mountain outpost milling around. Mother is breathing heavily and my head feels like it's about to split. Now seems like a good time for a break. The commander and Maire speak to one side, and I help position Thomas and Mother near them so I can overhear what's going on. The two seem to have a mutual respect even though Maire doesn't wear a shock rifle or any sort of uniform. Dr. Bowman stands uncertainly behind the commander.

Maire stops a young girl with short-cropped red hair and a yellow dress carrying a basket of canteens. "We need to meet with the council immediately," Maire tells her. "Run ahead and tell them to assemble. I'll get these poor folks situated." The girl hands off the canteens to a medic and sprints ahead, disappearing around a corner.

The commander steers Dr. Bowman toward Maire. "This scientist needs to be seen to as well. We pulled him out of the raid. Says he has information that can help us." Maire nods and waves down a guard. They exchange a quiet conversation I can't hear, and then the guard takes the doctor in the same direction the girl disappeared.

Maire turns to us next. "Come on, lass, let's get you and my dearie out of this mess." She hoists up one end of Thomas's stretcher, a guard takes the other, and we follow the rest of the group. After a few yards we turn to the left and step through a thick metal door. The artificial walls morph into the more natural rock walls I'm used to. A few more twists and turns, passing mining shafts where workers are changing shifts, and we are finally in the part of the mountain I recognize.

"You doing all right, Imani?" Maire calls back to me.

"Yes," I say. I wonder how much she knows about what happened and why Thomas was out there. I wonder if she knows they never intended to save my mother. That's when I remember she hasn't met my mother yet.

"Maire, this is my mother," I say, indicating Mother as she walks behind us, almost stumbling from exhaustion.

"You look like you need a good meal and a rest," Maire says. "I'm glad you're here with us. We'll have time to chat later."

"Thank you," Mother says, unable to keep the weariness from her voice. "I'm grateful to be here. Let me know how I can help with the wounded."

"Same goes for you, Imani. You need a good night's sleep, I expect," she says and then stops us. "I'm going to settle Thomas and I'll be back. Head in there." She points to the room where the council meets. Inside, we find seats in a corner and lean on one another while a boy passes out bread and warm tea to everyone returning from the exhausting march.

"He's going to be okay," Mother says.

"I hope so," I say.

As the room fills with community members, Mother leans over to me, wide-eyed. "So many colors."

I had forgotten the awe I first felt when I entered these walls full of freedom. It's nice to see it on her face.

Joe leads the procession of council members. Though I saw him only two days ago, his hair looks more gray, his face more lined. His robes are a somber brown, a dark contrast to the bright colors around him. He looks at me but doesn't say anything. I see no kindness or concern in his features. He is hard, ready for action. I wonder if I'll get a chance to tell Thomas about his unwanted proposal in the kitchens the night I left. The thought of potentially losing Thomas makes me want to tell him everything all at once.

I can't lose Thomas.

The meeting is called to order. Everyone takes their seats. People crowd in on small stools or lean against the walls. Once Maire takes her place at the table, Joe begins to speak.

"Reports from the guards?"

A man I recognize from the mountain outpost gives a detailed account of the last week there, including the attacks. Council members take turns asking questions. A growing sense of dread fills my stomach. Finally, a woman in a plain blue dress says what I fear the most.

"They were after her." She points a long slender finger at me. "Why are we still protecting her? People are dead because we didn't hand her over when they asked. We should not be involved in this conflict at all."

An angry murmur rises around me. Some glance in my direction, and my mother puts her arm on my back. I stiffen at first, still unaccustomed to any affection, then relax into her embrace. It feels so right even in the midst of all that is wrong.

"Because we are decent folk, that's why," Maire booms above the din. "We don't leave anyone out and we don't flinch when the Leaders or anyone else comes knocking at our doors." Maire pauses with a deep breath. "This would have happened one way or another. I think it's better to end this ridiculous sham of an arrangement we have with them. When's the last time they shipped us any grain? Look what they did to our folks living in the village. Our brothers and sisters and mothers and fathers are out there wandering mindless because the Leaders couldn't leave us in peace. I say we take this spark and fan it into the flame it should be. Finally claim our independence."

"I agree with Maire," Joe says. "Blame can't be placed on one girl or one rebellious act. This is the catalyst we've been waiting for. We finally have a reason to strike back."

"But what if they bomb the mines?"

"They outnumber us a hundred to one!"

"What about our camps?"

"They know where to find us. We'll be sitting ducks in here."

Everyone is talking over each other, and I clutch at my aching head. Joe bangs his hand on the table to quiet them.

"I have been working with a special detail of guards over the last few years," Joe says. "I knew this day was coming and I wanted to be prepared. We don't need more people. We need not fear their bombs. Our home is secure. We have a weapon far greater than anything they could imagine."

Another low murmur rolls through the room. Everyone is looking at Joe with puzzled expressions, including Maire and some of the other council members. I can't help but think, *If he says love, so help me, I will walk out of here and never look back.*

"And what weapon is that?" Maire asks, arms folding across her chest.

"Are we prepared to discuss the forbidden tunnels?" Joe looks around the table at the other council members who then look to each other, some nodding, others confused. Minerva, a member of the council who I have never gotten along with, scowls, her long face getting longer, and shakes her head.

"This is not the place for that," Minerva says.

"Spit it out, Joe. We don't have time for this," Maire says, and several people around her agree with murmurs and nods.

"Joe, move on. This is not the time." Minerva is insistent.

Maire stands up. "Since when do you make those calls, Minerva?"

"Ladies." Joe holds up a hand and Maire steps back but does not sit down. Minerva pinches her lips tight and folds her arms.

"For the sake of those new to this information, a few years back, while mining in the north passages, we discovered a bunker made by our ancestors to protect against war and famine. It is filled with machinery and supplies. I have overseen the research and testing of these passages. We have determined they are safe to inhabit, and in the last few months we made another discovery. The facility was built for offense as well as defense. A missile silo was dug into the mountain and is fully stocked and operational. One strike will end all of this madness."

Joe looks pleased with himself as the room erupts. Approval and horror mix on the faces around us. My mother squeezes me tightly. I glance at her as she asks, "They wouldn't do that, would they? Fire on the Leaders?"

"I don't know," I say slowly.

"The Leaders aren't right about everything, but I don't believe violence is the answer. Why go back to that?" Mother wonders out loud.

"I'm starting to think it's just how humans are wired," I murmur.

"Wiring can be manipulated."

She is right. For a moment I can picture her beside me changing the circuitry in the Secondary School, helping me to project music and art to the students. She would have been smiling if she'd been there then.

She isn't smiling now.

Joe bangs on the table again, but in the momentary silence, a man on the council cries, "You will make us as bad as them."

"I told you they weren't ready," Minerva says.

Joe holds a hand up and speaks to Minerva. "I knew this would be a controversial topic. I knew we would spend hours and even days arguing the pros and cons."

"As we should," interrupts Maire, red-faced. "We forsook a life of war and weapons long ago. Just because they act violently toward us doesn't mean we should respond in kind." Several people around her nod in approval while others shake their heads, fists pounding palms.

"That is exactly the kind of fool's logic that will get us enslaved or wiped out. We don't have time to hesitate or gather dozens of opinions for a consensus," Minerva says.

"Yes we do," Maire says. "These are the kinds of things we *make* time for."

A tremor shakes the room, growing to a rumble, then subsiding again.

In the shocked silence, Joe nods as if satisfied. "It doesn't matter. I've already given the order to fire."

Ashley was out of breath as she sat on Marian's bed describing the details of her night with Nick. Marian was jealous all over again as the pretty red-headed girl explained how they'd explored each other's bodies and how thrilling it was, how it made her feel.

"We almost went ahead and copulated," she squealed then remembered to lower her voice. "It was amazing! But I stopped him in time. I mean, other stuff happened, but I didn't want to risk a pregnancy."

"That's amazing," Marian said and forced a smile. "I'm so glad you had fun." She had researched methods of preventing pregnancies from the ancient times, but none of the herbs or medications or tools were available to them now. They were expected to only have sex when a child was needed.

"That's just the thing, Marian." She looked at her hands and smiled. "I think it's more than fun. I think I've developed actual feelings for him."

Marian sat up straight. "That's not good, Ashley. You can't get attached. That's the first rule of our group. Enjoy, explore, cause a little trouble, but don't get attached and don't get caught."

Ashley looked annoyed. "What about your obsession with Mr. Blue Eyes?"

"What about it?" Marian asked.

"You haven't even kissed him and you're already attached." Ashley folded her arms and raised her eyebrows.

"I am not attached to him."

"Then why do you keep working on him? He's not the right fit. He's going to blow our cover and get us all kicked out. Then it won't matter where we go or what we do, we won't be together."

"We're not going to be together after next year anyway." Everyone in their group except Charlie would graduate the following year and be assigned to work duties in different communities.

"But I don't want to be on sewer detail for the rest of my life," Ashley said.

"Then you better be more careful about your sexual rendezvous," Marian said, matching Ashley's folded arms and scowl.

"You're always taking chances, Marian. You really can't lecture me about that."

"Hey, let's stop." She was tired of the argument and just wanted her friend to be happy again—even if she was jealous. "I'm sorry. You're right." She motioned to the bathroom. It was the only room in the dormitories where the auto-eye wasn't allowed to pry. Ashley got up and followed her into the private room. Once inside, they embraced, and Marian kissed her quickly on the lips.

"Forgiven?" she asked.

"Of course," Ashley said.

They hugged again and made their way back to Marian's quarters.

"I'm supposed to meet with 776 this afternoon," Marian said as she gathered her things for their classes.

"Where? Do you have a safe spot?" Ashley asked.

"He actually suggested an engineering lab in C wing where the eyes are down."

"Good to know. Stay safe and bail if he's even slightly off, okay?" Ashley said. She really was concerned.

"Of course. Safety is my middle name." Marian smiled and they left her room.

Later that day she was surprised to find 776 waiting for her in the lab. She was a bit early and wanted to get settled before him, catching him off guard. But he had done just that to her.

"Hello," she said and smiled in greeting.

"Hello," he said, his tone somewhat stiff and formal.

Marian pulled out a chair and sat next to him, facing the door. She set a writer in front of her and her gray satchel on the floor. She had her copy of *The Outsiders* and an apple in it along with an electronic reader filled with contraband information she'd gathered over the years.

"Are you ready to get started?" she asked.

776 slid his chair slightly away from hers. He wasn't expecting her to sit next to him; the element of surprise was back in her corner. He nodded and she continued.

"Did you do your homework?" She opened the writer and pulled up a fresh drawing screen.

"I did. I spent some time reading about human pheromones and hormones."

"Extra credit. Excellent!" she said. "And what did you think?"

"I think it's fascinating that the chemical makeup of our brain can control so many functions in our bodies. Most of which are especially useful, others not so much," he said.

Marian nodded even though she didn't agree, then said, "My theory is that all of our natural pheromones and hormones are useful. Otherwise, why would our bodies have them?"

776 got out his own writer. She watched him write down the date and a couple of notes. Then she said, "What about the appendix? It doesn't have a primary function."

He shrugged. He wasn't getting her point. She would have to kick it up a notch.

"Can I show you something?" she asked.

"Of course," he said.

She held up her hand, spreading out her fingers. "Don't worry. This won't hurt, I just want to demonstrate something purely scientific."

776 looked anxious as she slowly placed her palm on his thigh just under the table. *He looks like an Ethan. I wish I could just give him a name,* she thought, but she knew it was too risky. He needed to be converted first.

"How does that make you feel?" she asked.

His quadriceps stiffened under her touch, but he didn't move. He was stronger than she first anticipated. He must come from a manual labor community.

"It's uncomfortable," he said, but he didn't move her hand.

"How about this," she ran her hand farther up his leg toward his tunic and wondered if it was hiding a muscular chest. The boys from the farms were usually in very good shape.

"I'm not sure what you mean for me to feel," he said as he swallowed, a red creeping up his neck and onto his face.

She pulled her hand back quickly and wrote a few meaningless things in her notebook. When he tried to speak again, she held up one finger indicating he should be quiet until she was done. He obeyed.

"You are a fascinating partner. I've been studying human chemical makeup and brain receptors for a couple of years now, so I'm more sensitive to the feelings that come with physical touch. I'm hoping to get data on interactions with someone whose pheromones so strongly compliment my hormones."

"And that's me?" he asked.

"Yes," she said.

"How do you know?"

"Because when I look at you, when I smell you," she leaned in and breathed deeply from the air around his neck, "I feel a lot of things at once."

The red blazed brighter on his cheeks and Marian became very serious. "This is all strictly for the sake of my research. Tell me, do you feel anything when you smell my aroma?"

"I've never really thought about it before," he said. "I suppose not."

She leaned in. "Well, how about now?"

He met her halfway and took a deep breath next to her ear. She picked up her writer and feigned recording his response.

"Now?"

"Yes, I feel something in my gut when I am close to you, and I can smell something sweet, almost food-like."

Marian had rubbed almond oil on the nape of her neck just before leaving to meet him.

"Very interesting," she said and scribbled a bit more. "Ready for stage two?"

"I suppose," he said.

"You're fond of that phrase," she noted then put her hand on his thigh again.

He swallowed and breathed through his nose.

"Do you feel anything now?" she asked.

"Yes, I'm guessing it's a combination of the scent and the contact?"

"Exactly. On a scale of 1 to 10, 10 being the greatest thing you've ever felt, 1 being nothing, how good does this feel?" She rubbed his leg slightly, up and down.

"I'd say a four?" it came out as a question instead of a statement.

He was nervous. She bet if he put his hand on her bare back his palm would be wet with sweat.

"I'm going to come closer now." She leaned in, their faces inches apart. "Let me know how this feels." She gently rubbed her nose on his and squeezed his thigh.

"Five," he said.

"And this?" she asked as she leaned in even closer and pressed her lips against his, making sure to breathe with his breath and only just touch the tip of her tongue to his bottom lip.

"Seven," he said.

His eyes were closed. She ran her hand farther up his thigh and put her other hand on his face. "Do what I do, and I'll take notes as soon as we're done," she whispered and opened her mouth slightly more, sucking on his lower lip, a hint of blond stubble teasing her skin. He reciprocated, his breath coming faster. His movements were awkward, stilted. She moved her tongue carefully along his lip in her mouth and he attempted to copy her movement but jerked his own tongue back into his mouth as soon as it made contact with hers. Marian felt her own stomach filling with dopamine. She enjoyed it for a very short moment before he yanked his head back and put his hands on the table in front of him.

"Stop," he said. His blue eyes were wide and alarmed.

She picked up her writer as if this was all part of the plan and wrote a couple more notes.

Subject noticeably disturbed. Physical contact has had a definite effect. Suggest exploring dopamine levels.

She would never look at her notes again after this night, but she knew he was reading them over her shoulder. She had to make it look good.

"How was that?"

"I don't think this is right. I'm sure the Leaders have already studied these hormones and their effects."

"But we haven't," she said. "What number rating would you give that interaction? It's called a kiss, by the way."

"A kiss?" he asked.

"Yes. Did you like it?" she said.

"It's not a matter of *liking* anything. It's a matter of what is *of use* and I can't see how triggering extraneous hormones can be *of use* to the community as a whole."

"Well, that's why we're studying it," she said, her eyes innocent and wide. "I thought you understood. If you're not up for the research, I understand, but I definitely think we're on to something. I felt an 8, which is more than I've felt with anyone else, to be honest."

"You've done this with other people?"

"Every study has to have multiple subjects."

"I'd like to see your data at some point. I'm curious about your findings," he said.

"I'll let you know when I get them complied."

Everyone is on their feet and shouting. Maire is up first and giving orders to two men and a woman by the door with shock rifles. "Do whatever you can to stop this."

They rush out at her command. A few more people hurry into the passageway. The council members are all on their feet arguing while Joe remains in his chair, a smug grin on his face as another rumble follows the first.

"You're going to kill us all, you stupid bastard," Maire says as she charges toward him.

A flash of fear crosses Joe's face before he hides it. "I made sure our people were all gathered in the mountain before the attack was launched."

"What about those at the outposts?" a council member asks.

"They are well out of range. We are going to be fine. We will be better than fine. We will finally be free of the Leaders' tyranny." Joe is completely confident in his choice.

The signs I'd seen on the walls of the strange passage come back into focus. With each rumble of ancient machinery and gears moving deep in the mountain, realization sinks deep into my gut.

He's destroying it all. He's killing all the people in the flat lands—the communities and towns, the Secondary School and the capital.

Flashes of wars past fill my mind. People screaming in the streets, being crushed by their own homes, limbs lost, bodies burned, secondary fires and explosions taking the lives of the survivors, radiation poisoning, cancer, famine.

Hiroshima, Nagasaki, Iraq, London, Aleppo, Palmyra, Tokyo, Israel, Palestine…

Rocking back and forth I clutch my head. "Stop, stop, stop!" I moan. "Stop fighting. Stop arguing. There are people dying out there. People I know and love."

Mother reaches for me and we embrace, tears wetting our faces and shoulders. She doesn't have to speak for me to know we are feeling the same thing, weeping for the same thing: all those lives lost.

I think of my father, working in the forests of our small community in the countryside, his calloused hands accessing a reader each night for personal study time. I think of his soft face and gentle nature, the way he always followed the rules and tried to make sure I did too. He never let any sort of anger or disappointment cross his face when I was disobedient.

I think of the twins, their thin frames the last time I saw them in Secondary School, the way they looked exactly the same but were so very different from each other. I think of their huge smiles and wide eyes when I shared my food rations or helped them with assignments. I think of their disappointment when the guidelines changed and their grades began to plummet along with their health.

I think about Marian, my first real friend, the girl who showed me the ropes at Secondary School, who broke the rules for me. Who knew everyone and everything and how to get what she wanted from the system without betraying herself or her friends. Her calm smile and rebellious attitude toward the Leaders. The way she never admitted to helping me but did so all along. Her beautifully braided hair and easy way with every- one she met.

Faces flash through my mind—all the other girls from my residence hall, all the students from my classes, all the profes- sors I actually liked and the ones I didn't, the house mothers, the people from my community living in the pods next to ours. Where are they now? Are they alive? Suffering? Where is my brother?

Even though he was a double-crossing traitor, I still wonder if he died quickly or is witnessing others suffer and die. Is he able to help anyone or do anything to help himself?

I can't let this go. I let go of Mother and stand on my stool.

"The Leaders may have been wrong about a lot of things, but this isn't one of them. Violence is wrong in all its forms," I cry, and to my amazement, the people still in the room turn to listen.

"If those are nuclear missiles, you've not only doomed everyone in the towns and cities, but also all of us. Those ancient symbols on the wall mean radiation poisoning. That affects water supplies, animals, the ground we grow crops in. It causes cancer, birth defects, all sorts of atrocities. In killing his enemies, Joe has doomed every living thing within hundreds of miles."

"I couldn't agree more," Maire says.

"You don't get to agree. You aren't in charge," Joe says.

But Maire is ready for him. "Neither are you anymore." She balls up her fist and punches him in the face, catching him off guard and sending him stumbling backwards.

"Maire!" I shout as two council members and a guard make their way to Joe's side.

"Sorry, love. Been wanting to do that for a long time." Then she adds, "Violence is wrong, very wrong."

"Sometimes a good whack is necessary," an older woman says.

"Yes, Joanne, but so is self-control. Take him to a cell," Maire says to a guard. A few onlookers, who must have been in on Joe's plan, rise to stop the guard, but Joe holds up his hand, bloody from where he wiped a split lip.

"I'll submit to discipline until my decision is vindicated. I accept the consequences of my actions."

Someone bumps me and I almost fall from where I stand on my stool, but Mother balances me. Minerva, slinking for the door.

"Take her too!" Maire cries, and two more mountain people take her by the arms. Both her and Joe are escorted from the room.

Maire stands at the front of the group, her voice booming. "Until we know the extent of what Joe has done, we need to stay underground. Please check in with your families and be sure your emergency bags are ready to go if we need to evacuate on short notice." She turns to me. "Imani, I'd like you to come with me to the missile rooms. Your mother is welcome to come as well."

I still feel sick to my stomach as Maire leads us down the halls back to the missile rooms.

"You need to help me understand exactly what we're looking at down here, lass. Anything you can dig out of that head of yours to help, I will take." She doesn't mention my disappearing with Thomas, but I'm sure she hasn't forgotten. There are much more immediate concerns.

I don't try to hide anything. I've already been focusing on missiles, especially ground launch versions, clean up, first aid, and what we can expect. It's a gruesome collection of images and so much information it could be overwhelming but I'm handling it. The pain isn't an issue right now. My pain is the least of my concerns.

As we enter the bunker section of the passage the signs are before me, I explain what they mean to Maire. "There's a chance we can't go outside for several days. We need to find out what was launched and what damage has been done."

We make our way into the control room with the ancient screens and buttons I had seen earlier. There is a buzz of people talking and arguing. Two guards have a man cornered, firing questions at him as he holds up a binder like a shield.

"Joe gave me the coordinates and I put them into the machines," he's saying as we approach. "I followed the instructions, there was a lot of movement, but nothing happened."

"They didn't fire?" Maire says as we join the group.

I can almost taste the hope welling around me.

"No, I couldn't get them to work. I followed the instructions here…" The man lifts the binder, then rubs his eyes, which have dark purple crescents under his eyes. He looks at Maire with confusion. "You didn't know about this? Joe told us this was a council-approved retaliation."

"How could you have thought that?" the guard asked.

The man's jaw tightens. "Those flatlanders have been telling us what to do long enough. I can't stand it anymore and neither should you. We should be able to live outside and make our own rules. They took my Nelly after the raids, and you didn't do anything about it. Just hid us all down here. I wanted to do something. When Joe asked if I could do this, I didn't ask questions. I was relieved the council was finally moving!" The man is crying, big racking sobs that wet his face and shake his shoulders.

Maire shakes her head. "I miss Nelly too, but next time use that head of yours, Marcus. Radiation poisoning and thousands of corpses is not good retaliation. Until we get this figured out, you'll have to be in lockdown." She gestures to two of the guards awaiting instruction. "Take him to the cells with anyone else who feels like blowing people up is a good idea."

"You'll regret this," he yells at Maire as he's taken from the room. "The time will come when you'll wish we had blown them all away. You'll be pushing the button yourself before the end of the season!"

The room empties until only the original people Maire sent here, two men and a woman, remain along with Maire, Mother, and me. I take a moment to breath. Is it true? The missiles weren't fired? I look at Maire and shock and relief cover both our faces. Hers breaks into a wide smile.

"I can't believe this," she says. "That arrogant blowhard didn't even know what he was doing." She laughs and it sounds a little crazy. Mother hugs me.

I pick up the book the man dropped when the guards took him and start flipping through it. There's too much to go through without some serious concentration.

One of the guards pops back into the room and proffers a sheet of paper to Maire. "He had this in his pocket. Looks like a list of coordinates."

"Thank you," Maire says, then surveys the room full of machinery and lights. "I suppose we better figure this out before anyone else decides to end the world. Imani, can you help me decipher this mess?" Then she asks Mother, "Would you mind checking on my Thomas for me?"

"Of course," Mother says.

"Do you have a name?" Maire asks.

"I did once. But it was given to me by someone who didn't have that right. I'd like to pick my own name this time."

"Sounds reasonable. Let me know when you do." She turns as Grimley enters. "Just in time, Grimley. Would you mind taking this lady back to the medic hall?"

It's the man who helped Mother on the mountainside. He nods and holds out an arm to Mother, who takes it even though she doesn't need support to walk anymore. They leave the room, and I turn back to Maire, who's already working on a map and speaking to another guard.

"Thank you," I manage to say. "Not just for today, but for everything."

Maire waves me over. "Jim, one of our best engineers, found a book with a detailed list of the silo contents. Can you get in there and figure out what we're dealing with? I don't want anyone getting hurt if we can manage it."

I nod and join Jim at his table where he has a stack of books.

He looks up at me skeptically. "I can't make any sense of these names. I studied engineering but nothing like this."

I set down Marcus's book and look over the inventory in front of Jim. Letters, numbers, names I don't recognize, but with such specific terms, I'm able to locate the information in my mind rather quickly.

"These are surface-to-surface ballistic missiles with a long- and short-range capabilities." I point to a different batch in the row. "These are ballistic missiles as well, but with different warheads. They hold a higher payload and split into multiple smaller bombs once the target is in range."

"What does that mean?" the man asks, bewildered.

"I'm not sure, give me a minute." I close my eyes and let images of schematics and warheads run through my mind.

It's easy now. There's no pain. The stress of the situation and urgency have pushed me into a new realm where I know I can do this. The information is mine, and for a moment it feels incredibly freeing to have so much knowledge at my command. And I can use it for good.

Only the answers are not good.

"Each one of these bombs carries multiple warheads. Essentially we're talking about weapons that can wipe out three hundred square miles around any coordinate it touches."

"Wipe out?"

"Gone off the face of the earth."

Maire is behind me, looking over my shoulder. "That's a lot of firepower. Is it nuclear?"

"No, the bombs themselves aren't nuclear, but there must be components in the silos that are, otherwise they wouldn't have warning signs everywhere."

"Well, that's relief number two for the day. I want you to spend every minute figuring out how to disarm these bombs," Maire says.

I know how important this is. Our whole civilization could be wiped out—again. But with the immediate crisis over, I want to see Thomas, and I need to search my implanted memories for ways to help my mother and the wipers. If I can just figure out the right thing to search for, the right terms...

Maire is waving her hand in front of my face. "Can you do that?"

"Yes," I say. "Of course I can."

Marian made her way off the train and into the PSC labs. She swiped her badge and joined the group working at her new assignment. She was surprised to find the room buzzing with activity. More than twice the number of people from last week were in white coats loading expellers with velvet bean plants and collecting oils, and a distilling tank had been set up in the back room. Doctor 741 was walking around checking each station and giving orders. She saw Marian come in and waved for her to follow.

"This way, we need you down here," she said.

Marian followed her to another large room with the same set up. A man was coming out of the door with a metal cart full of bottles of a translucent green-brown fluid.

"We've set up two more rooms for this project. You'll be here processing expeller refuse today." Doctor 741 pointed to a table with only one assistant managing the expeller machine and its byproducts.

"This is a lot of medication," Marian noted.

"We have a serious situation on our hands," she said.

"What is that?"

"It's a need-to-know basis. You do not need to know. You need to get to work."

"Fair enough." Marian shrugged and got to work, the expeller machine familiar to her now.

She knew the tech she was working with today. He was young, just coupled with a partner, and they had their first child on the way. He was generally in a good mood and didn't cause any issues. He also liked to gossip.

He greeted Marian and looked over his shoulder to see if their team leader was within range. Then without turning his head toward her, he began to speak while he worked. "There's been a breakout in the mountain facility. Apparently 789 had some special project going on up there and it's gone wrong."

"I heard about the shock bombs and escaped patients," Marian murmured.

"That's just the beginning. The patients weren't part of the Mind Wipe. Turns out he was trying out a new form of memory erasure with a chemical base instead of electrodes."

"Like, medication to wipe their minds?" She piled freshly squeezed stalks of valerian into the hopper for another round of pressing.

"Apparently so, but it didn't go the way he planned. Then the security went haywire, which no one has been talking about because they are worried about a bunch of disturbed citizens attacking towns. I heard someone from the mountain people broke into the facility and kidnapped a bunch of doctors."

"Wow, that's kind of unbelievable," Marian said.

"Right? It has to be rumors and lies."

Marian nodded and kept at her work. This was *a lot* of medicine for a rumor.

On the train ride back to school she shuffled through the possibilities and how any of this crisis could work to her advantage. She didn't want to do field work yet, especially if it meant being sent to the mountains to wrangle a bunch of escaped subjects. But she also didn't want to miss a chance to shine should it come up. She decided she should talk it over with her group and get their ideas.

She also wanted to see 776. When she wasn't thinking about conspiracy cover-ups, she thought about him. She couldn't help it. She would try to push him out of her mind and focus on something else, but her homework was mundane and expelling oil from pink flowered plants wasn't exactly stimulating. Her bench partner had run out of things to gossip about and continued to talk about the *fascinating* changes in his pregnant partner's body. Marian ignored him.

Instead, she thought about 776 putting his hand on her stomach. It was slightly round, just the right curve to fit a large palm—and he had large ones. She thought about the last class she'd seen him in, how he was so focused on his work, so intent on getting the answers right, on impressing their instructor. He was so serious. Definitely not a good candidate for their group, but something still drew her to him. Maybe it was the challenge. Nick had been easy, so had Ashley. The twins were in before Marian even had an idea of what she was doing, and Charlie was just the best.

776 was different. His work in class was brilliant. He was brooding and quiet. He often squinted at blank walls, so deep in concentration that he couldn't hear the instructor or a fellow student talking to him. She wanted to be inside that space where he went when the rest of the world melted away, a nonentity for him to stand on. She wanted to stand there too.

Ashley wasn't around when she made it back to her quarters. The twins were gone too, most likely studying somewhere or working on a project. Marian put away her things and changed into her gray school smock then headed for the common room to study. 776 was already there.

"Hi," she said, eyes wide and wondering what he was doing in her common room.

"Hello," he said and stood, wobbling a little bit then dropping his reader. He bent to pick it up.

"What are you doing here?" she asked.

He straightened and ran his hand through his stubbly hair. "I wanted to talk to you, but you weren't in any classes."

"I had labs all day today."

"That's what 12 said." He looked nervous.

"What's wrong?"

"Can we go back to the lab?"

"Sure." Marian's heart was thumping hard. "Let me get my things."

She took a deep breath and calmed herself as she gathered her writer and bag—her pretense for research. When she returned to the lounge he was already out the door and waiting in the hall. She stepped over the threshold and he strode ahead. She had to quickstep to keep up.

"Is there something wrong?" she asked but he didn't answer.

When they reached the lab, he held the door for her and checked the hall before closing it. Marian shifted gears. It was time for official mode.

"776, this is highly irregular and unprofessional. I would appreciate an explanation," she said and folded her arms, her bag still slung over one shoulder.

He was quiet as he took a few steps closer to her, his eyes focused somewhere on her neck. She wasn't sure if he was going to attack her, speak, or pass out. He was so nervous he didn't appear to be breathing.

"I want to do more research," he finally said. It was just a whisper, but it was all Marian needed to hear. She immediately relaxed and let her hands fall to her hips.

"You could have told me that in the dorms," she said.

He looked at her face for a moment then back at her shoulder. "I can't stop thinking about you," he said. A crimson wave rushed up his neck and onto his face.

He was taller than her. She could look up at his strong jaw line where a hint of a beard was starting to show, an afternoon shadow they used to call it. Only his was blonde, golden, like honey or sand sprinkled on his chin. She reached up and touched it.

"Pheromones are real, and they are powerful. How does this make you feel?" she said.

"Good," he said.

"And this?" She put her other hand on his other cheek. The heat from his skin warmed her palms, then dripped down into her chest.

"Very good." He looked at her face again. Drops of sweat were starting to form on his forehead.

"Close your eyes," she said.

"What for?" he asked but did it anyway.

She stood on tiptoes and pulled his mouth to hers. Her warm lips against his, firm and pinched closed at first, then softer, relaxing, finally parting as she pressed her body against his and slowly let her tongue glide across his bottom lip. She sucked on it a bit and then stepped back down.

"And that?"

He opened his eye, this time meeting her gaze directly.

"Indescribable."

"Should I take a few notes so we don't forget?"

"No," he said. "What's next?"

ELEVEN
Imani

After another two hours with Maire and her team in the bomb rooms, explaining what I recognized to them and going over the files and manuals, I fold up the notes left by the angry tech and go to my room, absolutely exhausted. I plan to rest for a few minutes, maybe bathe, then go see Thomas.

It seems strange, being back in the mines. I don't know why, but when I left to free my mother, I didn't think I'd ever come back. Maybe I assumed I would get caught or never find my way back. Either way, I am here now, and my room hasn't changed. I slip the papers into my trunk, all the same items waiting there for me—a blue sweater, two multicolored skirts, and some soft cotton undergarments. The scent of clean linens wafts up and wraps itself around me, cutting through the stink of sweat and dirt clinging to me from the past few days.

I need a bath. I need to sleep. But more than all of that, I need to see Thomas.

Someone left a pitcher of water and a bowl for me. I strip down, sponge off, put on fresh clothes, and then tie my hair back. The medical rooms aren't far. Mother will already be there. Hopefully the three of us can talk through this.

People don't stare at me anymore as I make my way through the corridors. Only a handful stare at my hair, a long black braid swinging behind me. I'm one of the only grown women to have long hair in the mountain. Everyone else keeps theirs short-cropped and out of the way. I like having my hair long. It's just one thing that sets me apart from the rest, even though part of me would love to get lost in this crowd, settle down in a little house and raise a baby, like women used to do.

Thomas is sitting up when I get to the infirmary. My mother is sitting next to him on a stool. They are chatting genially. His head is bandaged and so is his arm. Two or three pillows support his head, and he is smiling.

"You're awake!" I cry and take three big steps to his bed.

"He is," Mother says, "and he's doing really well."

"Never met a bomb that can take me down!" Thomas is cocky and confident. I like this side of him. This is the side that doesn't give up, that broke into my cell at night to give me a kiss on the hand. This is the Thomas that will help me figure my mess out.

"Mom, do you mind if Thomas and I talk alone for a few minutes?"

"Sure," she says. She stands, pausing to give me a kiss on the cheek, then hesitating. "It's so wonderful that we don't have to hide from cameras here."

"Yes, it is," Thomas echoes and winks at me. He's going to be fine.

Mother steps into the hallway and strikes up a conversation with a nurse. I can hear her asking about all kinds of things, from Thomas's health to the daylight reflection lamps lining the halls. I sit by Thomas and take his hand.

"Your mum is lovely," he says and pulls my hand to his mouth, pressing a sweet kiss to my fingers before setting it back in his lap.

"She really is," I say, and I want to go on, tell him more, but I can't. He looks so tired and worn. Bandages everywhere, his face puffy and distorted. "How are you feeling?" I ask instead.

"Like a truck ran me over and left me for dead," he says, wincing as he shifts positions.

"What did the doctor say?"

"Says I'll be fine. Just gotta take it easy for a while."

I nod. There's not much more to say.

"Are you okay?" he asks.

"Yes and no. Looks like there's no worry about us being able to stay."

"That's good," he says. "Why so certain?"

I guess Mother didn't tell him anything. Probably didn't want to worry him, but I know Thomas can handle it. "Because they need me. Joe found a whole room full of bombs and was going to launch them, but they couldn't figure out the sequence. They want me to disarm them before anyone starts a war."

I explain the rest of the situation to him, the secret military tunnels from the old days, the coordinates and how devastating the attack would have been.

"Golly Moses. It's a good thing he had a team of dummies in there, and it's a good thing we've got you to sort it out."

"That's just the issue. I have so many things to sort out, I don't know where to start," I say and put my head in my hands.

Thomas shifts on the bed and leans forward to put his hand on my head.

"I'm afraid my mom is going to end up like a wiper," I say, then the tears come. "I have to figure out the bombs and the science behind what Haman did to her… and to me. What if I become like that too?"

"Love, that's not going to happen. Whatever he did to those poor bastards, he didn't do to you or your mom."

"We don't know that for sure," I say.

"Actually, we do. I'm guessing that's what you talked to Dr. Bowman about. And you've been fine all this time. Let's put that aside and worry about shutting down bombs and taking care of you for a bit. I think you need a good night's sleep in a real bed. Maybe with a pair of loving arms wrapped around you."

"You're too good to me, Thomas. I came here to check on you but you're the one consoling me." I sigh.

"Hey, it's what I do best," he says, his lopsided grin a bit more lopsided than usual under the bandage. "I'll be up and moving soon. Probably tomorrow."

"Imani?" A man's voice is at the entrance.

"Who's askin'?" Thomas barks back.

"You're needed in the council room," the man says.

"What now?" I groan and wipe the wet off my face quickly.

"The shock bombs The Leaders dropped triggered some sort of seismic quake and our water supply is damaged. They said you could help with schematics?" he says, looking like I might kick him for his bad luck as messenger.

I put my head back in my hands.

"Do you need to sleep some first?" Thomas asks as he brushes my hair with his fingers.

"No," I say and lift my head up again.

"They really do need you now. Apparently, there's a leak in the lower shafts. Evacuations are in progress down there," the man says.

"I'll be right there," I say and wave the man off. "Thomas, I just don't know…"

"First things first, go save the world and I'll be there to kiss you as soon as possible."

I lean forward and kiss him gently, the feeling so wonderful I don't want to leave.

"You're right. I just need to sleep. I'll come back tonight. I'm sure no one will care if I do it here." I indicate the empty sick bed next to his.

"If they do, they'll have to answer to me."

"So scary coming from the guy with bandages all over his body." I laugh a bit.

"I think the old times called that a mummy and they were terrifying," he said.

"Touché. You can be terrifying when you want."

TWELVE
Marian

"776 is in," Marian said to her table at lunch the next day. "What do you mean? How do you know for sure?" Charlie asked.

"He's as stiff as a board. Are you sure you didn't mistake a coma for interest?" Nick said.

"Funny," Marian said, narrowing her eyes. "We had a really great study session last night. We broke some new ground and had a good chat."

"I'm still skeptical," Ashley said.

"Just relax and don't make him feel weird," Marian said and nodded toward the food line. 776 was gathering his meal and heading their way.

"Hello," he said as he approached their table.

"Hi. Sit here." Marian scooted closer to Emily so there was room for him to sit between her and Charlie.

"Welcome, 776," Nick said. An air of mockery played behind his straight face.

"Thank you," 776 said. "23 says you are all research partners in her studies?"

"Yes," Charlie answers. "You could say that. In an unofficial capacity, of course."

Everyone was sitting up straight, eating quietly, on their best Leader-approved behavior.

"Do you have any findings ready for presentation?" 776 asked.

Emily and Eliza exchanged glances with Ashley as she took a bite of her apple. Ashley wasn't going to speak to 776. It made Marian giddy to see her friends all side-step her newest recruit. They were always careful when someone joined them, feeling the other person out, making sure they were a good fit. Charlie had fit in perfectly, but 776 would take more time. She was okay with that. Their skepticism came from her training, after all. Still, she couldn't help but wish they trusted her judgment a bit more.

"We are getting together later today to work on some new findings. Would you like to join us?" Marian asked 776.

Nick glared at her and rolled his eyes. She knew he didn't like this guy. Was he jealous or just scared? Maybe both.

"That would be very interesting. I would like that," 776 said as he sipped legume soup from a spoon.

Marian stuck her apple in her bag next to the extra packets of protein gel she had forgotten to put in the drawer of her quarters, then let her hand brush across 776's thigh under the table. He stiffened and his eyes grew wide, but he coughed it off and continued to eat. Marian couldn't help but smile. Ashley was staring her down, but she made a point of not looking in her direction.

"What field do you work in?" Charlie asked.

"I'm in hydroelectrics. I'll be stationed at the lake next year."

"That's a lot of engineering, right?" Nick asked.

"Electrical mostly. I'll get into structural once I'm assigned."

"We have a full house here," Marian said. "One from each discipline."

"Ahh, that makes sense now," Charlie said.

"What makes sense?" 776 asked.

"Nothing, sorry. I have to go. See you guys later." Charlie stood to leave.

They had planned on meeting that night to talk about their paper readers and other contraband. Everyone had been excited until Marian told invited her new recruit.

"I'm not going to be able to make it," Ashley said.

"Why?" Nick looked surprised and said the word a bit too loud.

"I have an exam in fauna I need to study for. You guys can catch me up later."

"Do you need help?" Nick asked.

"Maybe." Ashley smiled and stood as well.

Nick didn't come that night. Marian knew exactly what kind of fauna the two of them were studying, but she didn't care. She had her own distractions to lose herself in now. Charlie had rigged the cameras again and she and 776 slipped into the un-used classroom where they'd met the first night they opened the box. Charlie was right behind them.

"Where are the twins?" Marian asked.

"They had something pop up for another group project," Charlie said.

Marian frowned. "That's irregular."

Charlie shrugged. "What are we going to go over tonight?"

"I thought you could help me brief 776." Marian smiled.

"You sure?" Charlie looked from Marian to the tall boy standing next to her. His hands were shoved in the pockets of his trousers. He looked nervous and uncomfortable.

"Of course," Marian said. "You ready?"

776 nodded and they all sat down.

"Let's make this quick. I have stuff to do too," Charlie said.

Marian was annoyed with her friends but plunged ahead anyway. Explaining how after 4254 had sabotaged the school's audio-visual equipment and everything had been reordered—

some sanctions lifted while others were put in place—she and her friends had started doing research.

"We feel the Leaders may be too conservative in their definition of what is *of use* or not," she said.

"We mine any area we feel it is safe to research for more useful ways to benefit our society," Charlie added.

"What do you mean, any areas?" 776 said.

When Charlie had been at this point, Marian explained everything in depth, but now that she sat with Charlie on her side of the table facing 776, she started to talk and Charlie cut her off.

"You need to prove your dedication to the project first," Charlie said.

"How do I do that?" 776 said.

Why does he always look so confused? Marian thought.

"We will give you a task to complete. If you are successful, you'll receive the rest of our debriefing. If not, you can go your own way," Charlie said.

"That sounds ominous," 776 said.

"It's really not. It's no big deal, right, Charlie?" Marian said.

"What's my task?" 776 asked.

"The group will decide and get back to you later," Charlie said.

Marian didn't like how this was going. Since when did Charlie take over and get so cocky? He'd only been officially inducted a few days ago.

Before she could say anything, he was standing from the table.

"I have to go," Charlie said.

"Where?" Marian asked. Her group was slipping through her fingers.

"I promised my bunkmate I'd help him finish his ancient civ homework."

"On a meeting night?" Marian raised her eyebrows. She didn't believe him. Why had her friends bailed on her? Why didn't they trust her judgment?

"Yeah, sorry," Charlie said and shrugged as he left.

Marian was only upset for a few minutes. Then she realized they were alone and 776 had his hand on her leg.

"Can you tell me anything else about this group?" he asked.

"We have names," she said.

"Names?"

"Yes. Mine's Marian." She couldn't stop looking at his blue eyes. He was so nervous and shy and brave all at once. She couldn't help herself.

"Marian," he said. "That's…"

"It's hard, isn't it?"

"What?"

"Finding the ancient words for description."

"It is," he said.

She put her hand on his arm and faced him. He leaned in and kissed her. They practiced and laughed and talked through an hour of kissing the day before. She would stop and write down various things, more for her own memories than any sort of science. He asked her questions and she answered, but mostly they kissed, their hands exploring each other's bodies over their tunics. Tonight was no different, except Marian slid her hand onto his bare skin under the gray cloth that separated them. He tensed then relaxed, breathing deep.

"Do you want a name?" she asked as their lips parted for a moment.

He nodded, his lips never leaving hers, his hands tracing the skin on the small of her back.

She pulled him close and whispered in his ear, "Ethan."

"That's…" He faltered.

"I know," she said.

THIRTEEN
Imani

The council room is in an uproar again. Maire spots me as soon as I walk in.

"There you are," she says. "Can you verify this map? Tell us if it is accurate and up to date? You have maps in your head, right?"

"Yes, I do." I look at the black-and-white drawing on the table and the room quiets down. As I focus on the shafts and passages, I can see the duplicate image in my mind, only there are things missing from the paper copy on the table.

"Give me a writer," I say.

An older woman hands me one from her pocket and I begin to scribble on the map, filling in everything that has been left out. Some of it looks like it was not part of the initial design and some was never built, but none of that matters. I can read the copy and compare it with the pictures to see how the tunnel system is supposed to work.

"There!" a man calls out as I fill in a missing passage and door. "That must be it."

"I agree. Get a team down there right now, let's get this done."

"We're running out of manpower," a woman says. "I just sent the last of my crew to evacuate the secondary levels."

"We'll have to find someone from somewhere."

"There's a unit in the woods still, a full staff in the hospital wing, those we lost and those with children. Almost everyone else is in the shafts…"

"That are about to fill with water!" Maire shouts. "I don't care if you send Joe, get someone who knows what they are doing down there and get it under control."

"I can go," I offer.

"I need you back in the bomb room figuring out those books," she says. "Can you get down there?"

"Yes," I say. "I can find my way."

The bomb room is empty now. Maire left one guard outside in case of trouble, but inside it's just me and the machines and manuals. I take a seat in the only chair with a cushion that isn't cracked and disintegrated. The thick binder labeled *PROCE-DURES* is laid out in front of me and I start thumbing through the section on detonation. There must be something about disarming if there is a whole section about blowing them up. As I skim, I realize what the tech did wrong. He put in coordinates and failsafe codes, but there are two buttons to press in order to activate the launch. You need two people to do it. My artificial memories confirm this and soon the manual is lined up with the information in my mind—word for word. I close my eyes and skim through the pages in my head much faster than I could in the binder, reaching the disarming instructions. I open my eyes and turn to that page in the binder on the table, wanting to be sure the information I'm accessing is accurate.

An alarm cries from somewhere deep in the corridors. I hope they're containing the water leak and that nothing else has gone wrong, but I can't worry about that now. I have to focus on this, then I can help my mother and hopefully the rest of the wipers as well.

Footsteps echo down the hall coming towards me. Someone is running. The guard outside the door calls out, "Hey, how did you—" but is cut off by a loud grunt and a thud and clatter.

I stand to face the opening and two men rush in, slamming the heavy metal door behind them and locking it.

"What's going on?" I ask.

They face me, out of breath and angry. One of them is the tech who was here before, the one who couldn't figure out the launch sequence. My stomach clenches.

"How did you get here?" I step behind the table full of machinery.

"Marcus, it's the flatlander girl," the other man says.

They are both sweating and breathing as if they have run a long distance. More footsteps, muffled by the closed door, echo down the hall.

"Good, we can use her. Get that binder and help me make this work before they get back in here," Marcus says.

"You can't be serious. Why are you doing this?" I ask, trying to block the other man from picking up the binder.

He's much bigger than me, and before I can react, he knocks me away like I weigh nothing. I hit the edge of the adjacent table. A crack rocks through my midsection and pain cuts off my air.

Marcus is at the computer as I struggle to my feet and launch myself at him.

"Stop! Don't do this," I say, trying to gain a hold on him any way I can, but my injured right arm is clenched to my side, holding back the pain, and my left is useless against two men.

Both men turn on me. Marcus pushes me back this time. "Have you ever lost someone you love? Have you been chased into a tunnel and made to cower like a rat for months? Have you been starved, digging in the rocks day after day for minerals that will go to the people who stole your family?"

I stand up to him, head pounding and ribs screaming. "Yes, I have! That doesn't make me a killer."

"I'm not a killer either. I'm going to stop the cycle and you will either help me or get out of the way." He shoves me again and I fall to the floor.

"Marcus! This is it! I found it. The binder was opened to exactly the page we needed."

My stomach twists in shame under the physical pain. *I left the book open.*

"Please don't do this," I say. Begging seems to be my only option as Marcus heads back to the computer. "Please, no." I try to get up and stop them again. I have to do something. I can't just lie here and let them destroy our civilization. I put a hand on the other man's lower leg.

"Shut her up," Marcus says. "I'm done with her."

The man next to him moves too fast for my pain-racked body. His foot smashes into my face. My head shatters with pain, there is a moment of light and ringing and then nothing as I fall back to the floor.

FOURTEEN
Marian

Marian had to control herself. She couldn't stop smiling on her way to nutrition class. She and Ethan had reached a new level of connection she hadn't felt with anyone else. She knew she had to remain impartial and to stay unattached. She agreed with the Leaders—love wasn't of use. But every time she thought about the way he was unsure but pressed forward, his hands finding their way to new places under her clothes, their breathing in rhythm as they finally gave up and just laid on each other on the floor. She didn't want to leave him. His questions were sweet and shy, his hunger for her insatiable. She couldn't believe the rush of emotions and hormones she felt—pure endorphins—and she had to admit, she loved it. Maybe this was what the phrase "falling in love" meant.

She scanned her card at the door to her class and looked around the room for his sandy blonde head. He wasn't here yet, but that didn't matter. There were two seats together in the middle. He would be there soon enough.

She sat down and greeted the students around her. Then waited for Ethan to arrive. She could truly call him that now. In fact, she had whispered it over and over in his ear the night before and it seemed to thrill him, lead him on.

Finally, he appeared at the door, his head down, bag over his shoulder. He looked serious, but he always looked serious. It was a good reminder to Marian to get it together and stop grinning like an idiot. He looked at the empty seats as the professor came in behind him then sat in the closest one, on the opposite side of the room from Marian.

This troubled her before she realized he was being careful. They shouldn't be seen sitting together too often. They needed to play it cool and keep their distance until it was appropriate. That's how everyone else in the group behaved. Why was she forgetting her own rules? She made a note in her writer to study the effects of dopamine on rational thinking.

The professor began his lecture on lipids and fatty acids. Marian was genuinely interested in diet and nutrition and how it affected human cognition, but she couldn't concentrate. Her mind kept drifting back to the abandoned classroom. To Ethan's hands, to his hot breath on her neck and his trusting eyes.

She shook her head but found herself staring at him a few minutes later. He was taking notes, his eyebrows pinched together and his tongue ever so slightly poking out the side of his mouth while he concentrated.

That tongue… she thought.

"23?" The professor was calling her number.

"Sorry, yes?"

"Can you perform this function for us?" he said as he indicated a formula on the board.

Marian stood and walked to the front of the class. She hadn't been paying attention, but it was a simple caloric compound formula she had covered in another class. The people she wrangled into doing homework for her thought she struggled with math, but really, it bored her and she felt she had better things to spend her time on.

She finished and turned triumphantly to the waiting professor and class.

"Excellent. Please take your seat," he said.

She tried to catch Ethan's eye as she walked back to her desk, but he didn't look up, just kept typing notes from the board to his writer. She felt a twinge in her chest, and she caught her breath a little then shoved the unfamiliar feelings away and sat at her desk.

He was very good at this.

At lunch she sat in her usual spot. Ashley and Nick sat very close, their legs touching under the table across from her. She was jealous of them. Ethan hadn't come to lunch yet. He'd left class too quickly for her to catch him in the hall. She was starting to worry, but then she reminded herself she wasn't the jealous, worrying type.

"How did it go last night?" Ashley asked.

"Fine," Marian answered. She definitely wasn't going to give them any details. If they wanted to know they should have come.

"Hi," Emily said as she and Eliza sat next to Marian.

Charlie was headed to the table as well when she spotted Ethan across the room. She sat up straighter and smiled, then remembered herself and looked at Ashley, trying to make her face blank and uninterested, but she could still see him out of the corner of her eye. He was walking straight to their table.

"What's wrong, 23?" Charlie said as he sat next to Nick and pulled out his ration of cheese and bread for lunch.

"Nothing." She looked at Charlie and forced a smile. As she glanced back at Ethan, she noticed for the first time that he was not alone. Two guards in black uniforms were following behind him.

"That's her. Right there," he said and pointed at Marian. "All of them are guilty, but she's the only one I have a recording of."

Marian stood, knocking her chair backward behind her. "What the hell are you talking about?" she said.

"You are under arrest for the harboring of contraband knowledge, for distribution of the forbidden, as well as food hoarding and possession of forbidden items," one guard said as the other pulled a wrist tie out of his uniform pocket and made his way toward Marian.

For a long moment, she stared at Ethan. How had she missed this? Her friends tried to warn her, but she didn't listen. How had she been so wrong? His face was stone, his arms were folded—those warm arms that held her last night and did their best to make her feel all the things she was longing to feel.

Charlie was on his feet too, "This is ridiculous. 23 is an exemplary student and member of the community. What possible recording could he have of her?"

"Save your breath, kid. We searched her room," the other guard said. "We found ancient readers and enough food for several days." He held up a black bag that had been camouflaged by his uniform before.

Marian looked from the guard to her friends. The twins were looking down, clearly terrified, Ashley was furious, probably with Marian for not listening. Nick was on his feet and about to speak.

She shook her head at him. *No*, she mouthed. It wasn't worth getting them all dragged in for her mistake. Instead, she looked from her friends to Ethan.

"None of that is mine. He must have planted it in my room," she said, her gaze steady and sure.

"That's not true. I've never even been to her room," Ethan said, shocked.

"You've been to my dorm and you have the electrical experience to tamper with auto-eyes," she said. "I'll go with you, but I would like to file a formal complaint against him as well."

"What would that be?" the guard asked.

"Premature coupling," she said and didn't blink.

The guards looked at each other and then at Ethan. "Is this true?"

He was conflicted, she could tell. He wasn't used to lying. He didn't know how. "No! It's not true. It was her idea."

"So you have?"

"Yes," Marian said. Charlie rolled his eyes and put his head in his hands. They all knew what she was doing. "I can prove he tampered with the auto-eyes in order to make our meetings private. He blackmailed me into it."

"Okay," said the first guard as he lashed Marian's wrists together, "You're both going to come in until we can review the tapes and a judgment can be made." Then under his breath, "Stupid hormonal teenagers."

"This is not right," Ethan said. His face flushed and his hands balled into fists. "She's the one who's causing trouble here. She's the one spreading mutiny in our school."

The guard came closer to Ethan, his hands held out with another wrist tie to strap his wrists together as well, but he jerked back and stumbled into a chair. "I'm not going with you, you can't take me!" he shouted, frantic to get away.

"Sure they can, 776," Marian said and stuck out her tongue in a suggestive way. She'd never been this angry before. Her mind was sharp and focused. No more haze of passion or dopamine. She hadn't worked so hard to get to this point to have one bad choice ruin everything. She studied people who underwent the Mind Wipe, she didn't become one.

"I have recordings of her," Ethan persisted. "I can prove it. She can't prove anything about me."

"Just come with me and we'll sort it out," the guard said but Ethan lashed out at him, swinging awkwardly with his fist and missing. He stumbled again and fell backwards. The guard started to scramble after him and Ethan scooted on his back under a table. The guard holding Marian pushed a button on his uniform and spoke into the mic on his chest.

"Back up to the cafeteria." Then he looked at her and said, "Don't move, okay? It's better for you in the long run if you stay still."

"Sure," she said.

He jogged to the other side of the table where the first guard was trying to get ahold of Ethan.

Charlie was around the table and at her side just as quickly.

"How do we get you out of this?" he whispered.

"I'll be fine," she said. "Just get the others out of here. You don't need to be involved."

"23, don't be stupid. We're in this together," Charlie said as the guards continued to scramble after Ethan.

"You're in this precisely because I was stupid. Now get back to the table or to your rooms."

But they didn't have time to do either. At that moment, everyone was thrown to the ground. An explosion rocked the building, sending bodies, furniture, debris, and food flying all over the cafeteria. Marian was knocked into Charlie and they ended up sprawled on the ground, ears ringing, vision blurred, pain and confusion spinning around them.

Marian's hands were near her head. She tried to wipe the dust from her eyes but felt something wet smear across her face instead. She pulled her hand back, blinking at the fingers in front of her. They were dripping with blood.

FIFTEEN
Imani

I wake up in the hospital wing, my vision blurred and my head throbbing. Someone is talking—Thomas, Maire, Mother, and someone else.

"She's awake," Thomas says at my side. "We have to move you, love. How's your head?"

My head feels like someone cracked it open with a hammer. Breathing hurts, blinking hurts, my nose feels broken. I reach up to touch my face but cringe as the pain intensifies.

"Imani," Maire says. "If you can walk, we need you to walk. We have to evacuate."

The last thing I want to do is get up, but Maire's tone scares me.

"What's happening?"

"The mines are flooding. Joe's goon set off the missiles after he knocked you out and they shook everything up. The lower levels are already full of water," Thomas said. "We're heading back to the village."

It took me a minute to realize what he had said. *Set off the missiles...*

It's hard to focus but I need to help. "The coordinates and plans are in my room. I left them in my trunk."

"I can go get them for you, but first let's get you and these other folks out," Maire says.

Looking around, I see a dozen other people on beds, waiting to be helped. Several are being supported as they limp from the room. One is on a stretcher being carried out by two men. Everyone is rushing, grabbing supplies and bedding.

"Daughter, let me help you up," Mother says. "Can you walk?"

"Yes, I think so." I sit up and the room shifts around me. I squeeze my eyes shut and hold my head for a minute while I get used to the sensation. I want to stand, but I'm not sure my legs can hold my weight. Instead, I rest my spinning head on my mother's shoulder.

"Good then," Maire says. "Thomas, you help them too. We'll be out of here in a jiffy." She tends to some other injured people, then makes her excuses and heads to check another part of the mines.

"Thomas, your mom runs this place," I say.

"She always has," he says. "Can you manage the stairs?"

"I can try."

Mother puts her arm under mine and helps me get to my feet. Thomas braces me from the other side. He is moving much slower than his normal brisk pace. My face throbs and stings with each step. As we leave the infirmary, the chaos intensifies. People carry bags and baskets, pulling little ones behind them. Everyone is heading for the exits.

We make it to the stairs Thomas and I once used to sneak out. They are packed with people moving single file much faster than us. We wait for a break in the flow, then start our ascent. I have to stop and lean against the wall every few feet. The people backing up behind us get impatient. There is no room to pass easily but some shoulder by anyway when I close my eyes and tip my head back.

"We need to keep going, love," Thomas says. "I'd carry you, but at this point I'm barely staying on my feet."

Mother rubs my back and urges me to move on as well, but my head is throbbing and my vision swims. I'm afraid I might pass out when a man calls to us as he approaches.

"Grimley," Mother says.

"Is she okay?" the man asks. "Thomas, how are you?"

It's the same man who helped Mother before, showed her around, and somehow managed to get past the line growing behind us to help now.

"Let me get her, we need to move out of here as quickly as possible."

Grimley gathers me into his arms like I weigh nothing and starts plodding up the stairs at a rapid pace. I look back at Mother and Thomas as they try to keep up, the congestion behind them easing.

"Take her to our place, Grimley," Thomas says as we reach the door to the outside.

The wind is blowing icy and strong. In the distance we can see huge clouds of smoke rising above the tree line.

"Mercy," Mother says.

"What is that?" I ask. "What's on fire?"

"Our whole civilization," Thomas says.

Then I remember—the bomb room, the manuals, how angry those men were. I left the answer to complete their plan open on the table for anyone to read, and now it's done. It's all done.

Visions of war and devastation flash across my mind unbidden and I moan.

"Imani," Mother says. Grimley sets me down.

I crumple in a ball, weeping uncontrollably.

"It's my fault. I did this. I left the manuals open," I mumble. "All those people—"

Thomas is at my side. People move around us in groups and alone, carrying things and empty-handed. Some stop to look at the smoke darkening the skies, others move ahead, the village their only goal.

"Imani." Thomas's voice cuts through the sound of feet and voices in the forest. "It's not your fault. We didn't know what they would do. Someone released them to help with evacuations and they broke free. They knocked you out, love. I know you never meant for this to happen. It's not your fault."

I am shivering. The cold cuts through my skin to my bones, and Thomas's words bounce off me. My gut is clenched, my mind reeling. All those people…

I think of the fire power, the bombs, the ability to annihilate everything, everyone. I think of my father, my friends from school, even my brother. I wonder if any of them have survived.

I think of the twins, of Marian.

I killed them all.

SIXTEEN
Marian

Marian couldn't see. She could feel Charlie underneath her, but he wasn't moving. Another explosion rocked the ground, but she could only feel it. The sound around her was blocked by a shrill ringing in her ears. Her hands still zip tied, she rolled off Charlie onto the debris-covered floor, bits of rock and dirt falling off of her, and propped herself up on one elbow.

She blinked several times and coughed. Dust filled the air, glimmering motes muting the sunlight that bathed everything around her. The artificial lights were gone. The ceiling was gone. Everything was smashed and thrown out of place. Marian couldn't figure out how they had survived being crushed until a strong breeze ran over her, blowing the dust away and revealing a large ceiling beam above them, fallen onto and held up by two tables. The beam had protected them from larger falling debris that now lay around them or leaned against the beam.

"Charlie?" She looked down at her friend. Her voice sounded muffled and distant, like she was underwater. She nudged him with her shoulder. As she processed more of the scene around her, she noticed other spots of blood on his clothes. He must have hit his head when they went down and shielded her from hitting her own, though she couldn't see any injury except for a cut on his cheek.

She nudged him again and got closer to his ear. "Charlie!" she called. Unable to check his pulse, she lay her head on his chest. His heartbeat was steady. He was still alive. She shifted onto her knees and closed her eyes for a moment, taking a deep breath. The acrid air—a mixture of dust and smoke—burned her throat and lungs, and she coughed. Fires burned in patches around them. She could see the copse of trees that grew behind the school—all the walls were leveled.

"How in the hell…" she started.

Charlie shifted next to her, moaning. His left arm was twisted and pinned underneath him at an odd angle.

"Hold still, I think you broke your arm." Her hearing was starting to clear a bit, and she looked around for something to sever the tie around her wrist. It didn't take long to spot a piece of broken metal jutting from the table next to them. She slid her wrists over it and turned back to Charlie. He cried out as she lifted his body as much as possible and gently pulled his forearm out from under his back. It was bent and swollen at the wrist.

"That doesn't look good. Are you hurt anywhere else?" she asked.

Charlie shook his head and it occurred to Marian again that it was a miracle they weren't both dead.

"Actually," Charlie said, "my head feels pretty horrible." He kept his eyes closed while he talked.

"You were knocked out. I bet you have a concussion."

"Where is everyone else? What happened?" he asked.

"I don't know," she said. She hadn't thought far enough ahead to check on their other friends yet. She didn't even know if she could stand.

A cry rolled through the mess from their left, then another small explosion.

"What is going on?" Charlie asked.

"I have no idea, but the school is gone. It's been," she paused, trying to find the right word, "destroyed."

Charlie used his good arm to try to prop himself up but stopped with another moan. Seeing him in such pain filled her heart with agony. But there was no time to be sentimental.

"We need to get up and help if we can," Marian said. "I don't see anyone else moving." As she said this, she realized she couldn't see anyone else at all. Had they all been crushed?

She shifted to her hands and knees, dizzy but stable. "I'll find something to splint your arm. Can you sit up?"

"I think I can. Give me a hand," he said.

She sat back on her heels and pulled on his good arm.

"My head feels like it's going to explode." Charlie closed his eyes and coughed with his head bowed forward.

Marian scanned the area where her friends had been sitting. The end of the beam that had saved them was resting on their lunch table. Piles of debris covered everything else around them. She stood and began to pick through the plastic, wood, and wiring that covered the places where her friends were sitting a few moments before. She picked up a piece of metal that used to be a ceiling light and saw blood on the underside. Below it was Eliza's head.

Marian sucked in a breath and looked away. There was no need to check for breathing or pulse. Eliza was dead.

"What is it?" Charlie asked.

"Eliza…" Marian couldn't finish. She heard a moan from deeper in the rubble. She tried not to look at her friend's decimated body while she dug for Emily.

"Emily?" she said. "I'm coming. Don't move." She pulled off more debris and carefully stacked it on top of Eliza. She didn't want Emily or Charlie to see what she now had seared into her mind. She choked on a sob but sucked in and steeled herself. She could see Emily's tunic and her black hair. She was half under the table, half pinned by rubble.

"Let me help," Charlie was up and at her side, his left arm held against his ribs as he tried to pick wires and wood off Emily. He swayed and Marian had to stabilize him.

"Just stay still. You don't want to make the concussion worse by falling."

She heard another moan and moved faster to clear Emily's torso. Luckily the pieces were smaller, and Emily seemed to have fallen mostly under the table, which had protected her from bigger pieces. She had to get on her knees for the final pieces, but a few minutes later had her friend free. She slid out from under the table, coughing and blinking.

"What happened?" she asked.

"Some sort of explosion. Are you okay?" Marian was still trying to hold back tears over Eliza. She knew Emily wouldn't be able to handle it, but they had to keep moving, keep helping other people.

Charlie started to move one of the boards Marian had placed over Eliza.

"Stop," Marian said. "Just sit down. Both of you. Emily, are you hurt?"

"I don't know. Everything hurts, but I think I'm okay."

Marian looked the girl over and didn't see anything more than superficial scrapes and bruises. Her tunic was torn, and she was bleeding from her head, but the wound was small. She tore off a piece of her under shirt and wiped at Emily's head.

"Marian," Emily said as she pointed at her stomach.

Marian looked down. A bright red stain was forming on her own tunic. Blood was seeping from somewhere on her torso, soaking her shirt. Marian pulled up the gray cloth to examine herself. There was a piece of metal stuck in her gut. Marian was astonished she hadn't felt or seen it earlier.

"Adrenaline does amazing things for our pain thresholds," Charlie said.

Marian pulled the shard out and pressed her shirt into a wad at the opening, soaking up more blood. A corner of dusty cloth peeked from under an overturned serving tray, and she squatted to pull it out. After a few good shakes and careful folds, she tied it tightly around her abdomen, holding her wadded shirt in place over the wound. It wasn't a large cut. It would heal on its own. Marian had much bigger issues to deal with.

"Where's Eliza?" Emily was looking around the heap now. "Eliza?" she called, completely forgetting the name was forbidden. "Eliza?" She was on her feet, frantically digging through the rubble.

"Stop!" Marian said, grabbing Emily's arms. "She's gone, Emily. She's dead."

"No, no, no, no…" Emily's thin, dust-covered face lengthened in shock, her eyes opening wide. "Where is she?"

"You don't want to see," Marian said and with one arm drew her close, still holding her shirt to her gut wound. "Don't look, just catch your breath and help me figure out what to do next."

Emily shook her head, then her whole body began to shake.

"She's going into shock," Charlie said.

"We need to find somewhere for her to lay down, but good hell, there's nowhere." Emily was limp by her side, her silent tears leaving clean trails in the dirt on her cheeks. Marian squeezed her and looked at Charlie. "Can you walk her that way?" Marian pointed to the far side of the cafeteria where a wall used to separate them from the gardens outside. Beyond the rubble of the cafeteria were wide-open fields of brown winter grass, dormant fruit trees blown over in the blast, and cold spring sunshine.

"I'll try," Charlie said. "Come on, Emily." He had an arm around her and, leaning on each other, they started to pick their way through the mess to the field beyond.

Marian would have to do the rest on her own. She steeled herself again and looked to the opposite side of the table where Nick and Ashley had been sitting. She'd been jealous of them a few minutes ago. Now they were covered in a pile of crumbled building.

She made her way over to them and moved a few pieces of debris. A hand came into view first. She could see a tunic underneath. They had been blown sideways, their chairs knocked out from under them. She moved a large board and tried to lift a light fixture, but it was too heavy. She shoved and a tear fell on the silver metal by her hands.

"Ashley? Nick? Can you hear me?" she called.

A few other people were starting to stand, a student, a house mother. Not nearly as many as had been eating before the blast hit.

"Ashley?" she whispered and shoved at the light again. Something under it gave way and it lurched far enough over that she could clearly see their bodies pressed together, a mix of blood and wood and metal tangled together. Ashley's head was at a strange angle on Nick's chest and his arm was severed at the shoulder.

"No!" Marian cried.

They were both dead.

"No, no, no…" She echoed Emily's words as she looked around at the war zone that was now their school. Who had done this? What force on earth was powerful enough to do this, and why would they do it to her school? She sobbed openly. Damn the rules, damn the Leaders. Where were they now? Where were the black suits when they needed them? When they needed help?

"23, are you okay?"

The voice behind her was familiar. The touch on her shoulder was gentle, unsure.

"Are you injured?"

Marian shrugged him off before turning to face him.

"No, I'm not okay, *Ethan*." She spit the name out with disgust. "My friends are dead and you're alive."

SEVENTEEN
Imani

The village is soon overflowing. The mountain people have only been living underground for two years, but in that time they have grown in population. Children are bigger, more have been born, and refugees from the flat lands have joined their cause. Each house left standing is full to capacity and several groups are working to make more shelters and repair the ones damaged by the raids.

Spring is here but the air is still crisp and biting, especially at this altitude. Crews of men and women make their way back into the mines to assess the damage and retrieve needed items. Maire meets us at their old home where we crammed in with her children. Mother and I set up makeshift beds in the store front and the rest of Thomas's family set up places to sleep in the other two rooms. It is tight, but everyone is on their best behavior.

Thomas has been helping since the night we arrived, although the strain of the situation and physical demands are taking a toll on his recovering body. I am no use at all. For a full day, I sleep and sip water, getting up only to use the bathroom. Maire has given me that one day to recover, but now she enters the store and heads straight for me. She has the papers I'd left in my trunk.

"Are you feeling up to a little work, deary?" she asks.

I sit up and lean against an empty shelf that used to hold canned goods. "Yes."

"Good. Can you tell me exactly where that nutter sent the bombs?"

She hands me the papers I hadn't had a chance to study in depth. The first page is a list of unlabeled coordinates. I close my eyes and focus on the first one: 35.2271° N, 80.8431° W. My head still aches, especially my nose and eyes, but I am still able to sort through information.

The maps in my mind swirl until one comes to the surface. I can see the lines of latitude and longitude, the communities and farms spread through our land, the capital and small towns around it. The first set of coordinates aligns with the capital. I look at the next and see a smaller town to the east, then one to the west. It's clear he planned to systematically take out one major concentration of people after another. Our people aren't nearly as numerous as our ancestors who once lived here, but two days ago we were an impressive, thriving band of survivors. Just not big enough to withstand an attack like this.

The fifth set of coordinates line up with the Secondary School. My stomach clenches as does my fists. I have to bite my lip and hold back tears as I realize the sixth set matches my home community.

For a moment, I think of my dad, then I shake it off and keep going.

Maire hands me a writer and I record my results. Mother leans over my shoulder, sees the names, and puts a hand to her mouth.

"All those places?" she asks.

"Yes," I say but don't look at her. I just keep writing. Twenty targets in all. One for every community. Our whole budding civilization, wiped out.

I hand Maire the list.

"Good glory be." She mimics my mother's gesture with her much larger hand. And in a beat, she was back to business. "Right then, we need a plan. How much damage do you think those bombs did?"

I thought back to the manuals I'd read, the signs on the walls, the information I'd already gathered.

"Those were military issued T.E.A.N.C.U.M. bombs—Tactical Earth to Air Neutralizing Critical Utility Missiles. They also called them the War Stoppers. They were designed to take out entire cities with one rocket breaking into hundreds of high efficiency explosives several hundred feet above the target. They aren't precise, but they are devastating."

"Given this list, I'm guessing if the bombs worked, there isn't much left down there," Maire says as she bites her bottom lip, her face strong and focused.

"What about the farmlands?" Mother asks. "Won't those be intact?"

I shake my head. "Every community was targeted. Even the farming and logging settlements."

"But that doesn't mean the fields and forests are gone. There could still be food there for us." Mother is avoiding looking at me. I know she is thinking of our farming community, of Father. I wonder if she is also thinking about my brother, who was studying in the auto-eye program at the capital.

Maire nodded her head. "I'm going to talk to the other council members—well, the ones that are left."

"What happened to Joe and Minerva?" I ask.

"They are being held in a dry portion of the mine for as long as possible. I'm not sure how long that will be though. The water caused a cave in on the central floors. There's no telling how stable the other shafts are. Flooding is still an issue and we are low on manpower. It's not practical to have guards watching over people who've already done enough damage to change the course of history, but it's necessary.

"Given our situation here, and the mess down there, I think we're going to have to move down the mountain and help the survivors. It's the only way we'll all make it. No one is going to be delivering supplies up here. Do you feel like you could come with me to a meeting tonight?"

I start to nod my head then wince at the pain and say, "Yes," instead.

Thomas comes in the door. The usual bounce in his step is gone and his shoulders droop like the bags under his bruised eyes. He walks carefully, careful not to twist his burned torso, and sits cross legged on the floor next to me and puts a hand on my hair. "How's my girl?" he asks and kisses my forehead. Apparently, the end of the world means no more pretense or hiding how we feel about each other. This is a relief.

"I hope you weren't out there overworking yourself," Maire says.

"Never, Ma. Why would I do something as stupid as that?" he says and winks.

It is so good to have him at my side. I love his jokes and the way he has of making me feel like I am part of something special, not just a girl trying to hack it on her own.

Mother puts her hand on my arm. It is shaking slightly. Her face is pinched and she is breathing deeply, showing what the rest of us are feeling.

"All those people…" she says.

"Yes," says Maire. "And I intend to help the ones left."

Mother and I put our arms around each other and squeeze. I look up to the ceiling, then catch myself. Will I ever be able to enjoy a moment of affection without looking for an auto-eye? How long will it take?

The remaining members of the council meet in the center of town around a bonfire. Benches and chairs have been brought for the older and injured attendees, but Maire stands at the front of the group, her body outlined by the fire behind her. She reads out the list of locations that have been bombed, she discusses the rations they were able to salvage from the food stores of the mines before they flooded, and she lays out her plan for moving down the mountain to lend aid, regroup, and reorganize whatever is left of the flat lands.

"The good news is that Imani was able to verify the bombs weren't nuclear, so we don't have to worry about radiation."

"There's not much sense staying here and starving to death. We should head for better soil and get the new year's planting started," says one woman.

"True. We might as well plant down there. Better soil and irrigation," says Thomas's sister, Adelaide. I haven't seen her since returning from rescuing Mother. She glares at me when she catches me watching her. The past three days have aged her.

"We could start gathering early spring berries as well," says a man.

"I don't think we all need to leave right away. I propose we assign small groups to head down to the different vital locations and then report back."

"That could take weeks," says the woman. "How much food do we have?"

"Not if we use the old radio communicators," Maire says.

"Do we have any that are functioning?" asks another man.

Thomas chimes in. "Our last group to check the mines brought back a crate full of antique crank radios and receivers. They don't need electricity to operate and we can communicate if we stay on the same frequency."

Maire nods decisively. "Good. Let's get the groups made and get everyone trained on how to use them."

"We also have two hand cars from primitive days. We can move them to the tracks. Then we won't have to hike," Grimley says.

"Excellent idea," Maire says as the rest of the crowd nods in agreement. Everyone seems glad to have something to do in the face of incomprehensible destruction. I'm less optimistic thanks to the pictures of in my head of what those bombs can do. But good moral is a start. *Maybe this is possible,* I tell myself.

"You're going to need weapons as well." The familiar voice speaks up from the back of the group. Dr. Bowmen steps through the crowd and into the firelight. "There are still wipers out there."

With all the drama of the bombs and betrayal, I'd forgotten about the original threat: our own people gone mad and blood-thirsty.

"We have a few shock rifles, but that's it," Thomas says.

"That won't be enough," Dr. Bowman says.

"What are you talking about?" Maire says.

"If the power has failed, all the facilities are unlocked. If they weren't destroyed by the blasts, the occupants are now free to roam."

"Does anyone know the status of the Institute across the river?" asked a woman.

"We didn't bomb it, but it could have been bombed in the drone strike," I say.

"We'll be crossing the north bridge anyway if we're taking the tracks. We'll avoid that area—" said the woman.

"Wait," Maire cut her off. "Dr. Bowman, what do you mean *facilities*?"

"Haman had three different locations where he was holding test subjects. Almost all of them in electrically locked cells."

"Where are these facilities and how many wipers do you guess are out there?" Maire takes a step toward him, angry, like it's his fault this new obstacle is in our way.

"Obviously, the Institute, the lower floors of the main pris-on outside the capital, and the Psychological Studies Center." Dr. Bowman puts his hands in the pockets of his brown trousers. He looks like one of the mountain people now, a beard sprouting on his face, his clothes are colorful and dirty, but he still wears his glasses and the far away stare of high intelligence. "And those were just the ones I know. But I've heard rumors of the Blue Spider rebellion reaching as far as the capital."

"Well, the capital is most likely gone now," Thomas says.

The group is quiet for a moment, taking in all that has been revealed and all that lies ahead.

Suddenly, I know a way to combine what they want me to do with what I want to do. "What if we can help the wipers," I say into the silence.

"What do you mean?" Maire asks.

Adelaide huffs and says, "Ridiculous."

"What if I can find a cure, an answer to what's happening to them?"

"I'm not sure that's possible," Dr. Bowman says.

"They were created before I was taken by Haman. So, the knowledge must be somewhere in my head, right? How did this happen? Maybe there is information on how to stop it."

"I'm not sure that's the best use of your time and resources, Imani," Maire says.

"If we are down to a handful of people left to start over, doesn't it make sense to try and save everyone we can, including the ones Haman took advantage of? They could be your missing relatives."

"True, but we don't have any resources to develop a cure and they are violent. They attack without provocation," a man on the other side of the campfire says.

"I'm afraid he's right. We don't even have a way to gather them back up. We'll have to send a shock rifle with each group and hope for the best. I'd like to take advantage of any resources in the unbombed areas. Could you possibly find some information about that, Imani?" she asks.

"Sure," I say. But in the back of my mind, I'm already looking for Haman's research. What did he do? What exactly caused this, and how can I help? I need some quiet time.

"Right then," Maire says. "All that's left is to assign groups and organize our supplies. Johnson, are there any other areas of the mines with resources we need to evacuate?"

They continue planning and I let my mind wander. I glance at my mother, her face unreadable in the firelight. I wonder if she is thinking of my father and brother. Is she worried about them? Is she glad to be alive?

I would have to ask her later that night when we were alone. For now, I have to dig through my subconscious and find Haman's tracks.

EIGHTEEN
Marian

Night was falling. The handful of students and instructors who survived the bombings were huddled around a fire on the edge of the gardens. They had waited for support, medical aid, the black suits to show up in droves, but no one came. They pulled all the survivors they could find from the rubble, but those were few. One girl sat with her bunkmate and held her hand as she died under a pile of metal and wood. Most had died on impact or soon after. The cries of some could still be heard, but they were beneath such large pieces of debris that, despite best attempts, nothing could be done to save them.

Small fires still smoked around the campus and before the dark settled in, they could make out smoke on the horizon in several places. They waited expectantly for the evening train. Surely that long white bullet would pull into the station with support and information. It never came. So they gathered all the blankets and food they could safely pry loose, wrestled firewood from the rubble and embers from the explosion, and built a fire to settle in for the long, cold night.

Marian sat next to Emily, clinging to the black confiscation bag the guard had taken from her quarters. It was filled with apples, protein packets, and her book, *The Outsiders*. She'd managed to get it out of the dead guard's grip and out from under him before they gave up searching the rubble. Charlie sat on Emily's other side. They shared two blankets, one over their shoulders and one over their legs. Emily was shaking and still cried intermittently. Marian was amazed that she had any tears left. She'd been crying for hours. Charlie had his arm tied in a makeshift sling now, but the grimace on his face told Marian he was still in a lot of pain.

Survivors included a male instructor, a house mother, and two office workers, along with five other students of varying ages, including 776. He sat on the opposite side of the fire, alone and without a blanket. One of the adults was sobbing uncontrollably while two others tried to calm her. The fourth was still digging through the rubble in the dark. What he was searching for, none of them knew.

No one was being reprimanded for showing emotion. There were no write ups for tears or for comforting those in pain. At one point, Charlie started throwing up, symptoms of a concussion from hitting his head, but there was no medic to help. There were no auto-eyes, no guards, no Leaders, only smoke, debris, and death.

Marian knew it was a freak accident that the beam hadn't crushed the tables when it fell and taken them out too. But she couldn't entertain this thought for very long. She couldn't waste time being angry at 776 either—she was done calling him Ethan. Marian was formulating a plan.

"Emily, Charlie, listen to me," she said, her voice a raspy whisper. "We need to take care of ourselves. Clearly this is bigger than just our school, otherwise help would have come by now."

Charlie leaned forward so he could see Marian's face in the firelight. "What are you thinking?"

"Given the lack of response, and the smoke on the horizon, I'm guessing multiple targets were hit today."

"Yeah," Charlie mumbled.

Emily didn't say anything.

"The closest facility that I can guess would have any sort of bomb-proof planning is going to be the PSC."

"How do you figure that?" Charlie asked.

"Because it's a pre-war building. They just added on to it when reconstruction began. If it made it through those blasts, it had to have made it through these. Right?"

"Possibly. It's not a bad theory," Charlie mused.

Marian was relieved that his logical side was kicking in. It helped her to talk through problem solving.

"If we follow the tracks it should only take us a day to reach the facility. Hopefully, there will be more answers there, supplies, people who know what's going on…" She trailed off as she noticed 776 watching her. She glared at him and he looked back at his feet.

"What if it's gone too?" Charlie asked.

"I don't know," Marian said. "What are our other options?"

"Good point. I mean, we could stay here and see what happens," Charlie said.

"True," Marian said.

They all grew silent as the sun fell behind the horizon, blood red from the smoke. Marian felt like it was about time this day was over.

Emily began to shiver and sob again. She hadn't spoken since she found out her sister was dead. Marian put an arm around her and pulled her close.

"We should probably try to get some sleep," Charlie said.

"Emily," Marian said. "Do you think you can sleep? Put your head on my shoulder and close your eyes. Let it all go for a while. Let yourself forget."

A tear welled up and fell down Marian's face. She wiped at it, smearing it across her cheek with the back of her hand as if it had done something wrong, as if that droplet of salt water was to blame for all this loss.

Charlie put his good arm around Emily and scooted closer. The instructor across the way was sobbing loudly now. Marian wanted to tell her to shut up but knew that wouldn't help anything. Instead, she held Emily closer and rubbed her back, trying to get the younger girl to stop shivering. Eventually, her sobs subsided, and her breathing became even and still. Marian chanced a glimpse at Charlie. He had leaned forward, his broken arm cradled against his chest, his good arm propping his head up. His back was rising and falling in a slow rhythmic pattern. Marian laid her head on Emily's and closed her eyes. The last thing she saw was 776 laying on his side close to the fire. He'd found a blanket and rolled himself up in it. His eyes were closed but they opened while she studied his features, as if he could feel her pupils reaching out to him.

She looked away, angry with herself for letting him take up any of her time. He might as well have died in the blast as far as she was concerned. She'd learned a valuable lesson from him, but she didn't owe him anything—not even a glance.

Marian woke up shivering. The fire had died down and the cold night air was creeping into her bones. She was chilled deep in her spine and feet. Emily shivered next to her as well. Only instead of from shock, this was from cold. She had no idea what time it was. Countless stars still salted the deep blue sky above them. Marian rubbed Emily's back and her own leg, trying to warm herself up. It was soon clear that wouldn't help. She could make out Charlie's form in the dark. He'd rolled away from them and was curled in a ball without a blanket, closer to the dead embers that kept them warm earlier in the night.

The moon was waxing in the southern sky. There was enough light to see outlines of the plants and rubble around them. An urgency to get up and move filled Marian with dread. She couldn't sit here and shiver, doing nothing to help herself. So far, the adults in their party had been useless except for gathering supplies, and the other students were all in shock, huddled in little groups of blankets. Finally, she couldn't take it anymore. She shook Emily.

"Hey, we're going to get out of here. It's too damned cold to stay."

Emily shuddered as she woke but didn't answer. She leaned back onto her own weight and rubbed her forehead. Her hand was trembling.

"Get up," Marian whispered as she stood up. "We need to move, or we'll get hypothermia."

Emily didn't argue. She reached for the hand Marian was offering and stood next to the older girl. Marian pulled the blanket up that was slipping off Emily's trembling frame then she wrapped the other blanket around herself holding the folds close to her chest. She walked to Charlie next and bent down, shaking his shoulder. At first Marian was afraid he had died in the night. He was cold to the touch but also trembling.

He moaned and shifted so she whispered, "Charlie, we need to get up and move. It's too cold to sleep."

He looked up at her, his eyes still half closed.

"Charlie, get up," she said and looked around. Packaged food rations sat in a pile on the other side of the fire. Blanketed lumps indicated the adults and other students. One student had rolled up in three blankets initially but had rolled out of one. Marian took her own blanket off, the night air attacking her bare arms and neck. She wrapped it around Charlie and hissed at him again, "Get up, Charlie. We're going for a walk."

This time he sat up and Marian took the opportunity to make her way to the other sleepers and grab a blanket for herself from the boy who'd taken three. She carefully maneuvered around a couple of other bodies on the ground and pulled two water packs and a handful of protein gels from the pile of supplies. She recognized the 776-size lump as she made her way back to her friends. She wanted to kick him hard in the gut as she walked past, but she didn't. She blew her held breath out in a determined stream and took Emily by the arm. The girl was staring at the ground, still shaking with cold and, Marian guessed, realization that this nightmare was real. She stuffed the food and water into the black confiscation bag and slung it over her shoulder, using it to hold her blanket in place around her body. She motioned for Charlie to follow and pulled Emily into the night.

There was enough light that she could see the contours of the ground when she concentrated on it. The train tracks weren't far. She'd taken this route several times over the years—walk out the school, take the train heading to the left. Get off at the PSC station. It couldn't be much harder by foot. The land was cleared and neatly maintained by the tracks. There were farms along the route. Maybe there were farmers out tending to their crops early. Maybe they would have information.

"Do you think they'll worry about us?" Charlie asked Marian waited for him to catch up.

"Who?" Marian asked.

"The other survivors," Charlie said.

Survivors—that's what they were now. That's what they'd always be as long as they could find shelter and answers. Marian didn't know if she liked the idea of being a survivor or not.

"I don't think they'll care. It's not like I took all their food or something."

"Right," Charlie said, and they tromped on in silence.

Once they reached the tracks, they made a left turn and walked between the rails. There were bits of debris all along the way—paper blown by the wind, chunks of buildings hurled by explosives.

"Who do you think did this?" Charlie asked.

"No idea," Marian said.

"I thought we were beyond bombs and guns and global warming," Charlie said.

"Apparently not. I wonder if humans will ever evolve beyond killing each other to solve problems."

"We have viable evidence against that theory," Charlie said.

Emily didn't say anything. She walked silently alongside Marian, head bowed, arms crossed over her chest, blanket ends tucked between them. Marian looked at her once in a while but wasn't sure what to say. As long as they were moving, at least she knew the girl wouldn't freeze, that she hadn't given up.

Marian was starting to feel better. Her feet were defrosting, she could feel her toes, and she had stopped shivering. She listened to their footsteps fall on the rocks and dark wooden ties, alternating *crunch* with *plod* in obscure patterns. Crickets were singing from the grass on the sides of the rails. Bats swooped over their heads and a night bird sang from a tree sheltering a water stop for cattle. If it weren't for their situation, Marian would have enjoyed this walk. She'd never been outside at night like this before.

The sounds of nature fell into step with their march, darkness slowly fading into pink-yellow morning. Marian stopped to pull out a protein pack. She hadn't eaten since lunch the day before and she was starting to feel it. Charlie and Emily stopped next to her as she reached in her bag and pulled out three packets, one for each of them. But the sound of footsteps didn't stop.

Marian immediately looked down the tracks to see a solo figure stumbling along behind them. She was tense, ready to run, unsure of what this meant. Then she realized the sandy blonde hair was familiar. The lumbering gait was slower than she was used to seeing, but it was definitely 776 following them.

Marian swore under her breath. "What does he think he's doing?"

Charlie held a protein pack to his lips and followed her gaze. "Is that Ethan?" he asked.

"776," Marian corrected him. "He doesn't deserve a name."

"Huh," Charlie said. He seemed to be out of energy for the situation.

Emily didn't acknowledge their follower or the food Marian tried to press into her hands.

"Whatever," Marian said. "Let's just keep going. Emily, you're going to have to eat pretty soon. I'm not carrying you; I don't care how tiny you are."

NINETEEN
Imani

Dr. Bowman sits on a bench by the fire, his head bowed, elbows resting on his knees. I approach him slowly as the others leave. I sent Mother and Thomas on without me, claiming I needed a minute alone. This is true. I need time to think, but I also need more clues. I have all the information I need in my head—more than I need—but I don't know how to isolate the information I need. I need a springboard to point me in the right direction if I am going to find answers to help the wipers—and possibly me and my mother—anytime soon.

"Doctor Bowman?" I ask.

He looks up for a moment then back down at the ground. "Yes?" he says.

"Can I ask you a few more questions?"

"I'm not sure I can help," he says. "But go ahead."

"I need to know more about the regressing subjects. It started about two years ago, correct? Do those patients have anything in common with each other? Do they come from the same region? Have the same assignments? Was there anything to link them together?"

He looks into the fire, and its red flickering tongues reflect off his scratched and bent glasses. "Yes, two years ago and one year before I started working with Haman. There didn't seem to be any connecting variable. I wasn't working in that sector though. My main focus was pre-procedural health." He sounds tired, but he isn't leaving so I pressed on.

"Did you see every subject before they were treated?" I ask.

"Nearly. There were quite a few toward the end. Seemed the Leaders were having a hard time controlling some of the younger citizens. Their emotions were getting in the way."

I sort through lists of subjects in my mind, quickly glancing at dates and numbers. I wish there were some way to see commonalities, some way to search more quickly or specifically, but I verify what he said and keep shuffling through information while he talks.

"The only subjects I never saw were like your mother, the ones rescued from the Shops," he says.

The Shop was a place in every community where uncomfortable issues were *dealt with*. If you were ill and beyond the age of medicine, like my mother had been, you went to the Shop and came back cremated in a small box for your end-of-life ceremony. I had no idea anyone ever left there other than in a box.

"There were more than just her?" I ask.

"Yes, there were many. All of them ailing, some beyond medical care, but most just needed medicine that the Leaders were denying them—insulin, antibiotics, etc."

"Where did you get the drugs?"

"Haman set up a black market. Small operations the Leaders didn't know about for producing most major health needs. We were running in two other communities. The right hand never knew what the left was doing. We only made what we couldn't justify in subscribing legally."

"This is much more complicated than I thought."

"Corruption always runs deep. One of Haman's pet projects was a super shot. One to heal and vaccinate at the same time. He said the final product would prolong both the length and quality of a subject's life. That's why he wanted the sick people from the Shops—perfect subjects for his experiments."

I frown and ask, "What was in it?"

"I'm not sure. Once again, it wasn't part of my assignment," he says and shrugs.

"So, they were rescued from the Shops, rehabilitated with the super shot, then you saw them to prep them for the wipe?" I clarify. I hate the word *subjects*. These are people.

"Yes. Personally, I was responsible for dealing with the more aggressive or unruly subjects who went directly to the Mind Wipe. The other subjects were adopted into our group as anonymous contributors. We tried to help reassign them or kept them in our facility to work and live,"

"Did any of them try to go home?"

"Not many, and if they did, we just wiped them."

I shudder at how casually he uses the term. Taking away someone's identity and memories shouldn't be an easy thing to do or talk about.

"Dr. Bowman, were these people connected in any way? Any pattern at all? I need your help finding the right trail of information in my mind." I'm focusing on the sorting process. There isn't much documentation on the subjects from the Shops.

"The ones from the Shops weren't part of my—"

"I know, not part of your duties. But you're a smart man. There has to be something. Did any of the ones you send back into the communities lose their minds?"

"No, they were all…" He pauses, finally looking up from the fire to meet my eyes. They are wide, reflecting the firelight. "Imani. You've found it."

I bring myself out of the information. "What? What is it?"

"None of the subjects sent back into the community were turned. It was only those kept in our organization who went mad—the ill patients or the ones working for us as volunteers."

Implications run through my head. "That means it's not just the Mind Wipe machine that did this. It has to be something on the other end of the procedure. What exactly did you do when you made examinations?"

"No, that's just it. I didn't do anything. It was the ones coming from the Shop who were treated by Haman. That's where he administered his black-market medications and the super shot. He called it the One Shot."

I nod, encouraging him to go on as I search for anything about this One Shot in my artificial memories. Hundreds of documents rise above the others. I look at several records—all who received the One Shot started regressing.

"Imani…" he says.

"I know. I think we have it. I just need to search now." Need to confirm our hypothesis.

He looks like he just received a second chance at life. "If we can make it right, help those people instead of killing them..."

"We should," I say.

"Yes, we should," he echoes.

Back at Thomas's house I hug my mother. I can't contain my joy. When she asks me why I am excited, I start to tell her, then stop.

My mother came from the Shops. She received the One Shot. This revelation with Dr. Bowman confirms that she would soon fall to the disease. My wonderful news is now my mother's death sentence.

Her face falls, mimicking my own.

"Imani, what's happened?" She reaches up and touches my cheek. Her hand is trembling. I clutch at it. Why is it trembling?

I can't tell her. I have to save her.

"I think I know where to find food and shelter in the flat lands. We should have a decent shot at resettling down there." I cringe at the word "shot" but she doesn't seem to notice.

"What about the wipers?" she asks.

"I'm not going to think about them," I say and lay down on our mat in the front aisle between shelves.

"We have to. Especially if you are going with them. Is there any way you can get a shock rifle or some sort of weapon to defend yourself?"

"I'll check in the morning." Then I think of something else. "Mother, I think you should stay here."

"I'm not sure I want you to go out there on your own again." she says.

"I think it's safer up here and there's a lot you can help with."

"I think I'm still your mother. I'm going with you."

I close my eyes tightly and take a long deep breath. I can't cry. I have to focus. Have to keep searching my memories, but first I have to ask.

"Do you think Father and Brother made it?"

She is quiet for a few moments, then says, "I don't know."

"Do you miss them?"

"Yes."

"Do you ever wish you had died?" The words came flowing out on their own; I can't stop them.

She is quick to answer this time. "No. Of course not." She put a hand on my arm and rubs. I can feel it trembling through my shirt.

I have to find a cure before she changes her mind.

TWENTY
Marian

The sun was close to the top of the sky when Marian, Charlie and Emily finally sat down for a break under a tree on the side of the tracks. Marian didn't want to stop, didn't want 776 to catch up to them, but Emily was slowing down and clearly needed rest. The chilly night had warmed into an unseasonably hot day and all three travelers had pink faces and sweat dripping down their brows and wetting their tunics.

Charlie had been carrying Emily's blanket and his own in his good arm for the last few miles. Marian tucked hers into her confiscation bag. She took it out now and spread it on the ground before laying down, her arms and legs wide. The cut on her stomach throbbed, but it was tolerable. She would inspect it again when she had a chance to clean it. Down the tracks, 776 was still walking toward them. As she watched, he stopped and made his way to the other side of the tracks.

At least he doesn't want to be by us either, Marian thought. *But why is he following us at all?*

Charlie spread out both blankets. Emily curled up in the middle of one, and he sat next to her. She began to cry as he pushed hair from her face with his good arm.

"We have to get her to drink something," Marian said. She had given up trying to get Emily to talk, but she wasn't going to let her dehydrate and die.

"Emily," Charlie said in a soft voice Marian hadn't heard him use before. "You need to drink something. You've been sweating and crying and you're going to get very sick if you don't eat and drink."

The small girl's fists were balled and pushed up to cover her eyes.

"Eliza wouldn't want it this way, Emily. You know that. She would want you to get it together and kick some ass." Charlie's voice was still sweet and calm, but his humor laced it now.

Marian watched him watching Emily, coaxing her, stroking her hair back from her sweat soaked face with his good hand.

What would it be like to have someone care about you like that?

She couldn't help it. She looked back in Ethan's direction, but he was down the hill on the other side of the tracks, beyond her line of sight.

"Hey," Charlie said. "Look at this."

Marian looked. He had a water packet up to Emily's dry lips and she was drinking. Tiny little Emily sips, but it was a victory.

"Nice," she said. "You've got the magic touch, Charlie."

From the other side of the track, they heard a cry, shock and pain rolled into one long utterance.

Marian was on her feet, ready to sprint in any direction necessary, but the disturbance didn't repeat. She looked in the direction of the wail.

"What was that?" Charlie remained hovering over Emily, who'd stopped drinking from the pouch but hadn't opened her eyes.

"I don't know."

"That came from Ethan's direction," Charlie said.

"776," Marian corrected him again.

"We should see if he's okay." He started to get up but struggled with his broken arm.

"We don't owe him anything. He was going to send us all to the wipe. He's not worth our energy. We still have a few hours to go before we get to the PSC. We don't have time for a traitor who's sprained his ankle."

Another cry came from the same direction, followed by a shriek.

"I'll go," Charlie said as he made it to his feet. But Emily was holding his arm, clinging to him.

"Ugh," Marian groaned. "You stay here and keep her alive. I'll be right back." Marian scanned the area and found a thick stick the length of her arm before she started walking toward the commotion. Glancing back at Charlie and Emily, she called, "I'm not going to get too close if I can help it."

"Sure," Charlie said.

Marian didn't care for his answer, but this wasn't the time to pick a fight. She continued down the track, and the closer she got, the easier it was to distinguish other sounds and then movement in the long grass on the hillside ahead.

The embankment sloped from the track to the fields below. A fence separated railroad land from farmland to keep trespassers out and animals in. As Marian approached the spot where she'd seen 776 go out of view, she realized there was more than just one person howling. Two bodies were tangled in the grass, wrestling, snarling, and fighting for what seemed like their lives.

She broke her own promise and rushed closer, trying to see what was happening and who was fighting.

776 was definitely one of them, his blood- and dirt-stained tunic flashing between limbs and grass. The other person was a large man dressed in an all-white tunic. Marian had never seen all white outfits except at Haman's facilities. This was a Blue Spider patient.

She rushed forward. The man had 776 pinned to the ground and looked like he was trying to bite his face. 776 pushed him back with both arms as the man flailed and snarled, drooling and snapping his jaws like a wild animal. Marian didn't think. She took three brisk steps down the hill. When the raging man noticed she was there, it was too late. She swung her stick as hard as she could, hitting him in the face and knocking him backwards.

776 scrambled away from the man writhing next to him. He was on his feet and reaching for Marian's stick before she had a chance to strike the downed attacker again. The boy went after him with a brute force Marian hadn't ever seen before. He swung at the man's head and chest until he was a bloody pulp, no longer reaching for him.

"What was that?" Marian said, shocked by both the attack and 776's brutality.

"I don't know, but I don't want to deal with it ever again," he said through deep heaving breaths as he swung a final, needless blow before throwing the bloody branch over the fence.

"Where did it come from?"

"I don't know. I sat down and closed my eyes and he was on me." He wiped his brow and leaned forward, trying to catch his breath.

"Well, you're alive. I'm leaving," Marian said and started walking back up the hill.

"Marian," he called after her.

She ignored him.

"Thank you," he said. "I know you didn't have to help me."

She stopped just before reaching the tracks and turned around, hands on hips and scowling. "You're damned right I didn't have to do that. You should thank Charlie. He's the one that wanted me to save you." she said, hands on hips, scowl on face.

"I will be sure to thank him."

Marian couldn't help thinking he looked genuinely sorry. Maybe that's what two life-or-death ordeals in twenty-four hours did to a person.

"Kind of ironic considering Charlie didn't want you to join our group in the first place and I did." She folded her arms for emphasis.

"You were breaking a lot of rules," he said and stood up straighter.

"You've got to be kidding me," Marian said and turned to leave again.

776 jogged up the hill and caught her. "You expected me to let you take all those people with you? It was a game to you, but you were ruining their lives. I realized it that night. You didn't really care about what you were studying, or what the results were. It was all a game, and that was too much of a risk for me to take. I decided I had to turn you in and that would put a stop to all of it. It would give the others a chance to stay out of prison."

Marian walked faster. Her face burned and her eyes threatened to water, but she wouldn't let them fill with tears. She steeled herself, then turned on the boy following her.

"It is *not* a game to me," she said, her voice low and furious. "Don't you think we all knew how serious our situation was? Don't you think we all knew what risks we were taking? Our risks were calculated. We knew what we were doing, we had a plan. If you'd given us a chance to explain you would have understood. But no. You called the Leaders in and sold me out."

"You have to understand that was the right choice from my point of view at that time," he protested.

"No, I don't have to understand. You think I don't care, but you're the one who turned me over without a second thought. You basically handed me a death sentence because you didn't agree with my methods."

"Marian… wait," he said as she walked quickly away from him again.

She felt strange hearing him say her name like that. Somehow all those feelings from two nights ago—was it only two nights ago—came rushing back. When he held her in his arms and they smiled and enjoyed each other, whispering forbidden things to each other. Especially their names, repeated over and over again until exhaustion settled in and they knew they had to part.

"I did take it seriously. I took you seriously," she said as she continued to walk away, not caring if he heard her or not.

"Well, none of that matters now. The government is likely gone, there are crazy people attacking us on the road, and we have no food and water. Don't you think we should work together to survive?"

"No," she said and turned around one last time. "I don't think we should."

TWENTY ONE
Imani

The floor is hard, making it impossible to get comfortable until late into the night. I tune out the sound of Adelaide, Maire, and Thomas discussing rations and who should be assigned what tasks for the following day. I should have joined them, tried to help, but I want to spend my limited energy searching for answers in my artificial memories.

I mentally follow the trail Dr. Bowman gave me and begin going through the information on Haman's One Shot. There are logs of people, listed by numbers, who had received medical procedures after they were rescued from being put to final use. A few lines in, each one started to receive the One Shot as well, but there is little follow up as to how they improved. Only notes on whether they died or not. There are plenty who didn't live. I shudder as I wonder what Haman did with all those bodies. Would we find a pit somewhere full of bones and gray tunics, or did he burn them and spread the ashes somewhere? And how had he done all of this without the Leaders finding out? It was a huge operation. So many parts to the puzzle, so many people involved in each step of the process. It's amazing that I ever thought I was the only one who was unsatisfied with the status quo.

Exhaustion overtakes me, as do dreams of unmarked graves and needles full of green liquid lying in stacks in a warehouse. Sleep is short lived. A voice, closer than Thomas and his family, wakes me. It is Mother. She's moaning and muttering. I sit up and look her over. Her hands and arms shake, and she seems to be repeating the same sequence of numbers again and again. I lean closer, trying to make them out.

"Five, three, one… eight... zero, zero, eight…" She moans and rolls over, her back to me now, only to start again. "Five, three, one… eight… zero, zero, eight."

I pull her blanket up over her shoulders and wrapped my arms around her, hoping the tremor was from the cold, not anything else. Please, not anything else.

I wake with the first rays of morning spilling into the window. Dust motes dance over my head. Mother trembles next to me, her whole body quivering. It feels like I haven't slept at all, but I have to get up and move. I am the only one who can help her and all those other lost wanderers. Because deep down, past all my denial, I know she's starting to change. She is losing her mind and her humanity.

I wonder where Haman is, if he died in the bombs or if he's battling his own monsters. I feel angry all over again but as I cover Mother with another blanket, I hear Thomas come in.

"You ready, love?" he asks.

"No," I say.

"How's she doing?" he asks.

"Not well. She was talking and moaning most of the night. The tremors are worse."

Thomas nods. "I'm going to talk to Adelaide about watching over her while we're gone."

"I'm not sure Adelaide is the best choice," I say.

"I know you two don't get along, but she's a good egg. She'll do right by your mum."

He takes me in his arms and holds me tight. I press into his warmth and lose myself in his musky smell. It's been ages since either of us has had a proper bath, but somehow it doesn't bother me. There is so much more to worry about than being clean.

Thomas pushes me back and holds my face as I keep my arms around his waist. He looks into my eyes for a moment and smiles. "It's going to be all right, love. You have to hold on to that."

"I'm not sure," I say. "Things are pretty bleak, Thomas."

"But not as bleak as a few months ago. At least now I can hold you and kiss you without sneaking into your prison cell at night." His grin is devilish and infectious. He leans in and I'm lost in his warm lips and sweet breath.

Moments like this are what keep me going. He fuels me. We are going to be all right.

"Please. You two are disgusting. People are dead and dying out there, and you're making out with her mom right there." Adelaide walks in the back door and stands with her hands on her hips, evaluating us.

"You're just jealous, little sis," Thomas says.

"Not hardly," Adelaide says as she walks to a shelf and grabs a brush then pulls it through her growing hair. I realize she hasn't had it cut short like the other girls. It now reaches her chin.

"I know you'd love to get your hands on a girl like Imani, but she's all mine."

Adelaide glares at Thomas before stomping out of the room. I look to him with my eyebrows raised in question.

"She thinks no one knows why she hasn't accepted a betrothal yet. But I know her better than she knows herself. She fancies the girls."

"How do you know that?"

"You watch a person long enough, grow up with them every day, and you get to know the little things that even they can't see."

"I suppose that's true." I wondered what I know about my brother that he didn't know about himself... and Mother? What do I know about her? "Can we move her into the bed now that everyone else is up?" I ask.

"Of course."

I stoop and squeeze her shoulder. "Mother, we're going to move you."

She doesn't respond.

"Mother?" I try again.

Thomas squats beside us and feels her forehead. "No fever, but she's clammy."

"I don't think she's going to wake up," I say, my gut clenching.

"Let's just carry her in there," he says, not speaking the thought that is on both of our minds.

She is too light, I think as I pick up her feet. Thomas takes her under the arms, and we carry her to the bed in the next room. A few of his smaller siblings crowd around, scrambling to clear a path through their blankets scattered on the floor.

We settle her on the large mattress and pull the covers over her. The young ones offer their own blankets and scraps to keep her warm. I thank them and add them to the pile, hoping to warm her up, to chase away this nightmare.

"What's the trouble?" Maire asks as she walks in the room.

"It's Mother. She's not conscious."

"Oh, blast it, I'm sorry, Imani. Let's get Dr. Bowman in here. I need both of you out at the fire pit this morning for assignments," she says, her face drawn in a pattern of worry and anxiety. "Marsha, watch her and come get us if anything changes."

One of the little girls stands straight and nods with importance, then takes her place by Mother's side—a little sentinel standing guard.

I hesitate to follow Maire outside, glancing back to Mother. She seems still now, the trembling subsided. Thomas takes my hand and we continue to the fire pit.

The community has gathered once again. A stump has been procured for Maire to stand on so that all might hear as she reads names and gives assignments. Adelaide stands next to her holding a stack of papers with lists of names and jobs. Most will stay, tasked with repairing village homes and working to keep extracting supplies from the mines, and bodies when possible. Several died in a collapse on the lowest level when the waters rushed in unannounced. It seems devastation is around every corner.

Thomas leans over and whispers, "You know the lower entrance we came in after the little boat ride?"

"Yes." The hole in the side of the mountain face is covered by bushes and hides an entire society underground.

"It's pouring out water like a spigot now," he says.

"That means the main levels are flooded as well," I say, shocked. "The main hall and our quarters."

"Not completely. There's still access to them, but there's a good two feet of water in there. It's not safe to rummage around in without an extraction rope."

I have a hard time picturing the underground city under water, but I don't have to work at it long. My name is called with a group that will stay and help with strategic planning and offensive initiatives.

I look at Thomas. "When did you decide this?" I ask.

"Last night. We need you here to keep that noggin pumping out information for us."

"We've been through this before, Thomas. I'm not going to sit around like someone's database and watch you go off to fight wipers. Plus, I'm close to connecting some very important dots. If I can get back to the flat lands and see what's still intact, it might help me untwist the facts in my head about wipers."

Thomas studies me. "We'll have to talk about it later. I'm going to help get the hand carts up and running. At least those will make the journey faster." He kicks at a rock. "As long as the rails are still passable."

There are a few requests for changes, but no complaints about assignments. Maire and the remaining committee members know their people well. They have assigned them to help where they had strengths and would be comfortable. I feel strange complaining about their desire to keep me safe and with my Mother, but I need to get back to the flat lands. The answer isn't up here on the mountain.

There are other reasons I don't want to stay, but I can't admit them to myself or anyone else yet.

Adelaide is handing out papers when I see Thomas take her arm on his way to the hand carts. They speak briefly. She looks in my direction and nods, then goes back to work.

Thomas walks back to me, smiling. "She's gonna keep an eye on your mum."

"Thank you, Thomas," I say and kiss him quickly on the cheek.

"Anything for you, love. I'll see you at lunch." He walks back the direction he came from. He used to jog everywhere he went, always in a hurry for life to keep going. His injuries have slowed him down, but at least they haven't stopped him.

All the people around me seem to have purpose and jobs. I'm supposed to report to a building on the far side of the village. But I need to be alone. I need to keep thinking, keep digging. I'll take a few minutes to sort through maps and plans of the communities, find locations that would most likely still have survivors and supplies, but then I will focus only on Haman's work. If he'd known about this problem for over a year, then he had to have been working on a solution. Haman was a jerk, but he wasn't completely callous. His goals were to set our people free, not to make them into monsters.

I make my way up the mountain east of the meeting spot. It is brisk and sunny. There is an abundance of plants sprouting in the damp spring soil. Birds sing and small creatures crawl over fallen logs full of insects. The whole forest is alive and humming its own song. I soak it up, breathe in the cool air. My ribs still hurt and every step sends a thrum through my head, but I push on and hike until my lungs are burning and my legs sore. The summit clearly in sight, I sit on an outcropping of smooth boulders and lie back to look at the sky. I should have brought a coat or a blanket. My sweater isn't thick enough to keep the cold of the gray stone off my body. There's no time for that though. I let the sun warm my face, sweat evaporating off my skin, a gift to the universe around me. I close my eyes and I remember things I've never seen before.

It doesn't take long to lose myself in the information. The leaves moving in the early spring breezes, the birds and animals, the smell of damp loam and metallic dirt—all help guide me to the answer, which I find, finally, in Haman's private logs. Haman was working on a cure to the madness caused by the One Shot. He tracked the illness to his own medications, tied together in the One Shot, and was working on isolating each one to determine which strain caused the mental decay of those subjects when he uploaded the database to my memory. He'd thought he found a solution. I found the records of a few trial runs that look promising, but then the trail stops. He must have been in the middle of his tests when he uploaded them to my memory.

I need to find the rest of his research in real life—or find him. His logs mention a place called the Psychological Studies Center as the location for the production for the cure. Bowman also mentioned this place, and I quickly locate it on a map. It is on the train line, surrounded by farms with potential food, and is one of the largest holding facilities for Haman's *subjects*.

The place will be crawling with wipers.

TWENTY TWO

Marian

The four students made their way down the tracks in silence. Marian had given up trying to keep Ethan from walking with them. Charlie was showing obvious signs of fatigue. Marian worried about his broken arm and if it would need more than the splint she'd cobbled together. Despite his pain, Charlie peppered Ethan with questions and what seemed to be genuine welcome. Emily didn't register his presence at all. Her walking coma state hadn't changed, but at least Charlie had been able to get her to drink and eat a little.

They all kept a vigilant watch for more people like the man who had attacked Ethan. For the past few miles they hadn't seen anything, but Marian wasn't about to let her guard down.

"It shouldn't be much farther," she said to no one in particular.

The sun was sinking toward the horizon on their left, blood red again from the smoke on that side of the fields.

"They must have bombed community 219," Ethan said matter-of-factly as he gazed in that direction.

"Were you familiar with that place?" Charlie asked.

"Yes," he answered. "I grew up there."

"Oh, I'm so sorry," Charlie said and shook his head. "Do you think they bombed every community?"

"I don't know. I can't imagine who *they* even are," Ethan answered.

"Yeah, who would do this?" Charlie asked.

"It doesn't matter," Marian said. "We need to find food and shelter. That's what I'm worried about."

"There's smoke ahead," Charlie said.

He was right. Beyond the hill in front of them smoke billowed up in great plumes. The wind had picked up and they could smell decay, dust, and ash making it all the more real.

"Do we have food for tonight?" Charlie asked.

"Yes. As long as you don't mind protein shots," Marian said. She didn't look at Ethan but asked, "Don't suppose you brought anything?"

"Actually, I did. I grabbed water and some bread and a few protein packs."

"How much of each?" Charlie asked.

"Five," Ethan said. "And one loaf."

Marian stopped and looked at him incredulously. "Where are you hiding all that food and water?"

Ethan patted his legs and the blanket he had slung over his shoulders. "I have hidden pockets and I rolled the rest in my blanket."

Charlie laughed. "You were right, Marian. He's perfect for our group."

Marian scowled and kept walking.

"What's that?" Charlie said and pointed his good arm to a large building close to the tracks but ahead about half a mile.

"It's probably an outbuilding used to store farm equipment or for animals during a storm," Ethan said.

"Let's check it out." Marian said.

By the time they got to the barn, they could see the outline of a bombed building on the horizon to their right and the remnants of a community. The shards of white family pods lay in burning black heaps. The fields of bright green wheat, bean flowers, and valerian shoots were untouched, dancing in the smoky breeze.

"That's the PSC," Marian said.

"Doesn't look like it's in very good shape," Charlie said.

"Why are you heading here anyway?" Ethan asked. "What's the point?"

"It's a pre-war building. It's bound to have bunkers still intact and supplies."

"I'm going to check the barn while we're here," Ethan said and jogged down the hill to climb the fence into the field. The others waited on the tracks.

"Emily," Marian asked her friend who stood still next to her, unblinking. "Are you ready for more water?"

Emily kept her gaze on the horizon, silent and unmoving.

"Charlie, can you try?" Marian asked.

"Emily." Charlie put his good hand on her shoulder. "I'm going to put the water container to your mouth, and I want you to drink."

Emily didn't move but Charlie did as he said and lifted the water container to her mouth. She drank without acknowledging him.

"I guess you're officially in charge of feeding and watering her now," Marian said.

"It's got to be a mental breakdown," Charlie said.

"It's shock and a break, most likely. If we can make a home out of the PSC, we'll be able to help her more. We just need to get there."

Ethan called them from the small building. "It's got a tractor and a loft. There's some hay. Might be a good place to sleep tonight."

Charlie looked at Marian. "That's not a bad idea. We should go check it out."

Marian was trying to decide if she wanted to quit here for the night or go all the way to the PSC when she realized Emily had moved.

The girl lifted her right arm and pointed ahead of them on the tracks.

"Charlie, get out of here," Marian pushed Emily and Charlie down the hill toward Ethan, stumbling as they went.

"What's wrong?" he asked.

"No time." Marian looked back at the tracks where Emily had pointed. Charlie followed her gaze as they tripped down the hill to the fence. A large group of people walked toward them, all in dirty white uniforms. They weaved and stumbled as they made their way toward the kids. A couple of them trotted, the movement uncoordinated, but the majority slowly crept down the track. It was more of the people like the man who attacked Ethan, and they were heading right toward Marian, Charlie, and Emily.

"What's wrong?" Ethan said. He hadn't seen the mob.

"It's more of those killer people—a lot more. Can we hide in here?" Marian called as she climbed the fence and ran past Ethan to look for herself. It was bigger than she expected, and the hayloft was far above with a rope ladder. It could work.

Outside, Ethan and Charlie were trying to get Emily over the fence, but Charlie wasn't much use with one arm broken and Emily wasn't cooperating. She could walk, and point out attackers, it seemed, but she wasn't able to save herself. Finally, Ethan climbed over to her side, picked her up and hoisted her over. She landed in a heap on the other side. Then he gave Charlie a hand as he made his way over the bars. Marian joined in and the three of them got Emily up and dragged her to the ladder inside.

"Oh, hell. How are we going to get her up there?" Marian said.

"You and Charlie go first. I got this," Ethan said.

Charlie stared at the rope ladder. "I'm not sure how…"

"Use your elbow," Marian said and demonstrated with her own arm before jumping back to the ground. Her side wound twinged, and she ground her teeth together to stop the gasp of pain from escaping. "It's going to hurt, but it will work. I swear we'll get you pain meds as soon as we are safe at the PSC."

"I'm not sure we'll be safe anywhere," Charlie said but did his best to climb the wobbly ladder while Ethan held the bottom steady for him.

Marian scanned the walls for tools or weapons and settled on a rake and a length of rope. She got both and brought them back to Ethan. "Will these help?"

"Yeah," he said and tied the rope around Emily's waist. He padded the rope loop with their blankets, trying to make it more comfortable for the small girl. "Can you get the other end up to the top for me?" he asked.

Marian didn't answer. She made a slip knot out of the other end and looped it over her head and one arm, and her black bag. Then she hooked the rake through the loop on her back and started to climb after Charlie. It was slow going even with two hands and two feet. Charlie was doing his best, but he was taking too long. A trickle of blood down her side told her the cut had reopened.

"Charlie, you've got to move faster," Marian said. Scuffles and moans drifted in from outside. It was eerie and terrifying. Marian had experienced several nerve-wracking moments in her life, but nothing like this. Never anything like the last two days.

"I'm almost there." Charlie had his good arm on the top now and was hauling himself over the edge. "Remind me to go on a diet when this is over?" he said, voice weak.

Marian was too busy concentrating on how far off the moans sounded to answer or laugh. She wondered if they would ever laugh again like they used to.

"They're coming. Hurry!" Ethan called as he started up.

Marian was at the top, but with Ethan climbing instead of holding the ladder steady, she was thrown off balance. The rake banged against the boards lining the opening and she cried out.

"What are you doing?" Charlie called, eyes wide. "You can't leave Emily!"

"Just go!" Ethan cried. "Get up there!"

Charlie reached out as best he could to help pull her into the loft. As soon as Marian got her knees on the platform, she slipped the rope and rake off her back and looked up. She finally understood Ethan's plan. The rafters were an arm's length above her. She tossed the end of the rope over the nearest one and caught the other end, pulling it tight.

Ethan was next to her in an instant, pulling as hard as he could. Charlie looked down the ladder and said, "It's working! Her feet are off the ground."

Ethan and Marian pulled as hard as they could, their faces red and sweating, every effort feeling like a new hole in her gut.

"She's pretty heavy for such a little thing," Marian said.

"It's the friction from the rope on the boards, and the fact that we're exhausted and malnourished."

"Thanks." Marian wasn't in the mood for facts.

"They're here! Hurry!" Charlie was frantic. "Pull harder! The fast one is about to get her."

Marian and Ethan doubled their efforts and strained to pull their friend out of harm's way. But Charlie let out another gasp.

"What's happening?" Marian shouted.

"Where's the rake?" Charlie was digging through the hay and finally put his hands on the wooden handle then flipped the rake around, so the prongs were pointed down.

"Charlie, what's the matter?" Ethan asked.

"He's climbing the ladder," Charlie shrieked then started poking the rake into the hole and grunting with one arm. "Ugh! Why didn't I pull it up?"

"You got this?" Marian asked.

"Yes, go help him," Ethan said.

Marian took the rake from Charlie and surveyed the situation. Emily was almost to the opening, and the creature below her was slowly making headway up the ladder.

"This isn't going to do anything. Help me pull the ladder up. Maybe he'll fall. He's not very sturdy." Then she saw the rest of them. They must have figured how to climb the fence or broken it down because they were flooding into the building, jostling each other and moaning.

Ethan heaved on the rope holding Emily, pulling her closer to safety. Marian and Charlie, with his good arm, tried to shake the ladder. It jiggled the man, but he didn't fall, just held on tighter and moaned a sickening gargle at them.

"What the hell is wrong with him?" Charlie asked.

"I don't know. There's so much I don't know," Marian said. "Just keep helping me. Wait till he lets go with one hand, then we'll yank again." She shouted over her shoulder, "Ethan, can you tie her off and help us? She's high enough they can't get her now."

Ethan nodded and sidestepped to the slope where a cross beam was exposed. He tied off the rope and came to the hatch, grabbing part of the ladder with two hands. Emily hung like a rag doll, unaware of anything going on around her.

"Wait till my signal," Marian said.

It took a moment, but finally the creature started to tackle the next step while hordes of others crowded around his feet, possibly hoping for their turn. The noise was almost unbearable.

"Now," Marian cried as the man let go with one hand to reach up and grab the next rung. They pulled with all their might. "Drop it!" Marian cried and the trio let go. The jolt was enough to knock the wild man off his balance. He fell into the crowd below.

"Pull it up!" Ethan cried, and they did just that.

Once the ladder was secure, Ethan and Marian pulled up Emily while Charlie guided her with one hand onto the platform, trying to keep her from getting scraped.

Marian shoved Emily out of the way as soon as she was lying on the hay covered floor. She slammed the trap door shut then dropped to her knees. Her face felt hot and her heart was racing. She was riddled with adrenaline and was having a hard time breathing in the dark dusty loft, but the worst of it was that her eyes were watering. She couldn't hold back anymore. She fell forward, burying her face into her hands, and wept.

Marian couldn't remember the last time she cried. She had never cried like this. Not ever. She never wanted to cry like this again, but for the time being she gave up and let it out.

A hand rested on her back, but she ignored it. Then a body was beside her, warm and soft, an arm around her while she sobbed. She pictured sweet Charlie's face hovering over her, and she was glad she wasn't alone.

"What can I do?" It was Ethan who spoke, so close to her ear she could feel his breath.

She wiped her face on her sleeve and sat up. She could do this. She wasn't going to fall apart, and she certainly wasn't going to let him comfort her.

"Hey," Ethan said, searching her face for an answer. "We made it."

"I'm fine," she said. "And I'm not sure you can say we made it anywhere. We're alive. That's it for now."

"But that's a good thing," he said.

Since when was he so positive? she wondered. Then she looked at Charlie and Emily. They lay curled up in the hay. He was holding her with his good arm and whispering to her. Emily was stony faced, blinking occasionally, and then slowly closed her eyes. It reminded her of the last time she and Ethan were together alone.

"I don't understand you," Marian said to Ethan.

"Why?"

"You make no sense. We have a connection; we are attracted to each other. Then you turn me into the black suits and claim I seduced you. And now you want to be my friend?"

"There have been some pretty major changes between each of those instances," he said.

"Not the first."

"I had my own reasons for that, and I've explained them to you. If you'd rather not be friends, that's fine, but I'd like to survive, and that means working together. Besides, we're a good team. We're both smart and strong, and together I think we can get Charlie and Emily to safety."

"Working together is fine. I don't really have any other choice. But that's as far as it goes. I can't trust you," Marian said. She felt like a petulant young one, but she couldn't help it. "Please, just leave me alone now."

She crawled over to Emily and Charlie and started to untie the rope that was still around her midsection. The blankets had helped to pad her body and protect it from bruising, but she had a rope burn on her arm where it had rubbed every time she was pulled a few feet higher.

Marian made a makeshift pillow in the hay and stuffed it under Emily's head then covered her with a blanket. The girl began to sob again, a sound Marian was sorry she had grown used to. Charlie was curled up next to her and closed his eyes, so Marian put a blanket over him as well.

"Marian?" Charlie asked.

"Yeah?"

The sound of tortured people rumbled beneath them, impregnating the pause between them.

"I don't know," he said.

"I don't know either," Marian said. "You want some water?" She dug in her bag for a packet. Her hand fell on the novel she'd saved from the rubble and carried all the way here. She'd forgotten about it.

"No, save it," Charlie said.

"How about a story?" Marian asked and pulled out the book.

"Sure," Charlie said and closed his eyes again.

Marian opened it up and began to read. "When I stepped out into the bright sunlight from the darkness of the movie house, I had only two things on my mind: Paul Newman and a ride home. I was wishing I looked like Paul Newman—he looks tough and I don't…"

"What is a Paul Newman?" Charlie asked.

"I'm not sure. Probably a person from back then," Marian said.

"I don't look tough," Charlie said.

"But you are tough," Marian said. "I bet Paul Newman never ran away from a hoard of killers and climbed a rope ladder with a broken arm."

"True. We should look that up when we're safe," Charlie said.

Marian didn't want to remind him that the archives were probably destroyed by the bombs, so she continued reading and everyone fell into a quiet reverie. Her voice drowned out the sounds below them and eventually, after two chapters, she put the book away and took a blanket for herself. She moved to the far end of the loft by an air vent. At least there she could hear the wind occasionally and not just the sound of the people below, moaning and scraping, trying to climb the walls to get them. With the occasional breeze came the smell of smoke and something she couldn't place, something foul yet sweet.

She looked out the opening. From here she could see the PSC. The walls were rubble, just like the school had been and like the community next to it. In her small range of vision, more bodies wandered the tracks and fields. She couldn't make out their features, but by their awkward movements, she guessed they were suffering from the same malady as the people below.

How did this happen? What in the world is wrong with them? She remembered reading fiction novels from the archives about mindless wandering humans who ate each other—zombies, she thought they were called. Was that what these people were?

She lay down and pulled her blanket over her head until all she could smell was the soft wool and the scratchy hay and her own sweat.

TWENTY THREE
Imani

I open my eyes and sit up. The sun is well on its way past noon. I've been gone too long. They are probably looking for me. I hurry down the mountain. No time to enjoy the animals or the sun. The answer is clear and must be delivered.

Maire meets me on the outskirts of the village, trailing several people who are asking questions.

"Imani, we've been looking for you," she says, voice on the edge of irritation. The people around her quiet.

"Sorry, Maire. I needed some quiet time to sort through the information."

"Next time you go off, you need to tell someone." She is frustrated and sweaty in spite of the cool weather. She finishes pointing out instructions on a paper for the man standing next to her.

"I need to go to the flat lands," I say when she's done. I hope she'll agree, and we won't have an issue.

She raises her eyebrows. "You're needed in logistics. We can't risk losing you or your information, especially given the way things are blowing up around here."

Her tone is final. There isn't going to be an easy way around this.

"Maire, I'm not staying here. I'm going with Thomas. We need to find the Psychological Studies Center. I can answer any questions you have from the road with the radios."

She eyes me.

"What's so important about this center that you have to be there in person?"

"It was Haman's main research facility. He was working on a cure for the wipers. He found it just before he implanted my brain but hadn't had a chance to distribute it to the people who needed it yet." I don't mention that I'm not positive it's the cure. It's our best bet—our only bet—and I need her support.

"And how are we supposed to do that? Even if there's anything left down there, how are we supposed to get medicine in all those crazies? I've heard what they do, I watched them stumbling around on the shore of the river. My main concern right now is gathering survivors, supplies, and shelter, and defending us from those crazies." She shoos away the people around her, and a couple give me disgruntled looks before they head in different directions.

"But the wipers are survivors. And if we don't help them, they will continue to attack us. This is just as important, but anyone else going there won't know what I need. I have to go." I follow her as she walks down the path to another building turned into a workspace and home.

Crews are at work on repairs, patching roofs and mending windows. Men and women build on new homes as well, starting by clearing foundations of the ones that burned so many years ago and scouting for trees to be felled for walls.

"Imani, I don't doubt that you have good intentions. Maybe if we didn't have so many other things to worry about, this could be a priority. But it just can't be right now. Plus, you need to stay and help with your mother. She's still not out of bed."

She says this like I should feel guilty, like it's my fault Mother is shivering and muttering. But she's wrong.

"Maire—" I say, then stop. This means too much to me, and my emotions are rising in my throat. My eyes sting with tears. Countless moments of reprimand come to mind. These are my own memories. When I was a young one in the community with my parents. When I wasn't allowed to cry or show emotion of any sort, where Mother and I had to hide in the bathroom for a goodnight hug and kiss. I never learned to control myself back then, but I can control myself now. There will be time for crying later.

"I can't stay here and watch her turn into a monster."

Maire looks at me, searching my eyes and face as if she's considering me for a portrait … or punishment.

"I watched her die once. I can't watch it happen again," I say, quietly but firmly.

She is quiet for a moment as we walk side by side down the trail. "What do you need from this building?"

With an internal sigh of relief, I tell her my plan.

Mother is trembling constantly now. Thomas's sisters, including Adelaide, took turns watching her through the day. They spoon fed her water and tried to get her to eat some broth, but only succeeded in making her pillow and shirt wet.

I lean over and kiss her forehead. "I'll be back soon," I say, not sure if it's the truth.

"We'll take care of her," Thomas's smallest sister says. She reaches up and holds my pinky finger, her warm little hands squeezing and releasing with no pattern.

"Martha is a great nurse," Adelaide says from the doorway. I hadn't heard her come in the house.

I look up at her, she nods to me, almost with kindness.

"Thank you," I say.

"Just don't let my brother do anything stupid."

"I won't," I say. "If she is turning into a wiper, you'll have to lock her up somewhere. She won't be safe to be around."

"We know," Adelaide says. "At least if she changes, she'll eat and drink again."

I can't see the good side of this other than she might live long enough for me to get the meds and get back to her. That is only if the meds work.

"I have to go help with at the strategic center. Thank you for taking care of her," I say. Then I add, "And me. Thank you for taking care of me."

Adelaide shrugs and turns her back to me as I head to the outside. We might never be friends, but at least she isn't actively sabotaging everything I do.

I spend the rest of the afternoon at the strategic training center, an old log home turned into a makeshift war room with beds pushed up against the walls and two large tables pushed together in the middle, mostly covered with maps.

They ask me questions about locating fuel cells, food, agricultural products, how they could find reliable weapons, tools, and materials. The answers come easily when they ask the right questions. I make a note to have Thomas ask me about Haman's work. I wonder again where Haman could be, if he survived. I realize with a twinge of remorse that I only care because if his cure isn't real, I'll have to find him and figure out a way to continue his research. Haman couldn't have known what was coming. No one but Joe and his group knew about the missile silos hiding deep in the mines. Haman is probably just as dead as the rest of them.

By evening, we have everything packed and ready to go. Food, tools, camping gear, although we don't know if we will have the opportunity to pitch a tent or build a fire. The hand carts are old fashioned, clearly pre-war. Two people stand on either side of a large handle and take turns pushing their side up and down, propelling the large flatbed car down the train tracks. There is an emergency brake as well, but that is all. Basic technology at its finest.

Mark, the technology person assigned to our mission, shows me and the others in our group—a strong older woman named Sam, a man with a full dark beard named Josh, Thomas, and a vaguely familiar guard named Jason—how to use the radios for communication. Despite Mark's attempts to make it complicated, it's simple: hold it upright and press two buttons at once, then give your call sign to identify yourself to the receiver.

"We'll try to get a tower up," Grimley says as we put the last of our gear on the cart. "That will make the signal stronger." He's been quietly involved in every step of each process. I've seen him in logistics and helping grease the carts and pack provisions. He is calm and strong. It reminds me of my father. Except Grimley speaks and smiles more.

"We're leaving tonight," Thomas says. "No sense in wasting the travel time. We can take turns pumping the gears and manning the brake while three of us sleep."

"What about the other hand car?" I ask.

"It's not ready yet. Needs the brake system fixed before it will be safe to move down the mountain. They'll get it ready for another group to follow us if we find anything promising." He is a natural leader. People listen to him and look to him for advice, just like his mother.

"Are you coming with us, Grimley?" I wasn't sure who'd been assigned to our detail.

"No. I have business here," he says.

I nod and watch as the familiar man, Jason, slings his pack on our car. I know him, but it takes me a minute to place the memory. My gut clenches as I realize he is one of the guards who was supposed to save my mother but never left.

"Who assigned him?" I ask, not bothering to keep my voice down.

Thomas looks at Jason then back at me. "Most likely Ma," he says.

The guard sees us looking at him and approaches me. "You're Imani, right?"

"I am," I say, folding my arms, preparing to tell him what I think of his cowardice.

"I need to apologize," he says as he takes a few steps closer.

The statement is almost as surprising as seeing him. I'm not sure how to respond. He seems to sense that and continues.

"For a long time, I thought Joe knew what was best for us. I've known him since I was a boy. I kind of idolized him, if I'm being honest. When he told me about his plan, I figured it was just another way to keep our people safe. I've been taking his orders for several years and I needed a break. The idea of a few days off the radar on a fake rescue mission sounded pretty amazing."

"I bet it did. I'd love a few days off the radar," I say, unable to keep the bitterness out of my voice.

"What I'm trying to say is that I'm sorry. I hope your mum is all right, and I'm glad you didn't die. I hope this mess isn't my fault for listening to Joe."

He seems genuine. I'm going to be traveling with this large man and his shock rifle for the next few days, trusting him to have my back. Can I trust his apology too?

I don't have time to respond. Someone on the trail to the mine calls out, "They're coming. Prepare the way."

I look to Thomas and he shrugs. For all the things he knows, there are a surprising amount of things he doesn't know. It didn't take long to clear the confusion, however. Behind the man who called to us are two guards followed by Joe, his hands shackled together at the wrists. Minerva and two others I recognize from the council, a man and a woman, follow behind Joe, then two more guards.

It's a slow procession. Joe looks straight ahead, his fists clenched and his jaw set. I shudder as I remember that face being too close to mine in the kitchens late one night; the suggestion that we couple and the lies about my mother.

Minerva is disheveled and gaping at the crowd, so different from her normal prim coldness. She is searching each face for… what? Sympathy? Rescue? She won't find it in mine.

The group passes by, making its way to the clearing. Maire is approaching as well. She stands on her tree stump and calls everyone to order. Then she pulls out a piece of paper and begins to read, her soft lilting accent now harsh and unrelenting.

"Joe of the house of John, you have been found guilty of mutiny against the council, inciting unrest and war, and mass murder. What do you have to say for yourself?"

Joe draws himself up and takes a deep breath, looking at the crowd surrounding him like a fence.

"I happily face my judgment and punishment. One day you will remember me and how I changed our world and you will be grateful. My name will be whispered with reverence and statues will be built in my honor," he says, his chin jutted out and his eyes aflame.

"Fat chance," Thomas murmurs.

I elbow him and can't help but laugh. It's a serious moment, I remind myself. This man is about to face severe punishment, but what? I don't know the traditions of the mountain people in this circumstance.

"Thank you for your thoughts. Guards, remove the prisoner." Maire waves her hand.

Joe is unceremoniously taken to one side and Minerva is brought forward.

"Minerva of the house of John, you have been charged with the crimes of conspiracy against the council, inciting unrest and war, and treachery most high. What have you to say for yourself?"

I lean in and ask Thomas, "They are both from the house of John, does that mean they are related?"

"They're brother and sister," Thomas says. "Their pa was a pain in the arse as well."

I wouldn't have guessed this connection, but now that I study their faces, I can see a slight resemblance. Minerva holds her mouth tight like Joe; her jaw set in much the same way. The shape of their eyes is similar, only Minerva's look wild and she refuses to speak.

"So be it," Maire calls, gesturing for her removal.

The other two are arraigned in a similar fashion, only for slightly lesser crimes.

"Where are the men who set off the bombs?" I ask but I think, *The ones who kicked my face in.*

Thomas grows somber. "Drowned. We chased them until they were swept away in one of the floods."

"What's going to happen to Joe and Minerva?" I ask.

Thomas nods his head toward Maire. "Watch."

"Due to the severity of your crimes and the state of the world that you have left us in, we, the remaining council, have determined you will face death by hanging."

My mouth opens in a disbelieving O. I don't care how many people Joe has killed. The answer is not more death. I turn to my pack and check its straps one more time. I can't watch this. I can't watch more people die.

"I'm going to check on Mother," I say. Thomas rubs my back for a moment before I'm striding away toward his family's cabin.

Another pair of footsteps comes up behind me, and then Grimley is walking beside me. We walk in silence. I try to focus on the mission ahead. In the map of the PSC that I've seen, Haman's offices are on a lower level. I hope there might be something left there, some clue, to help me find a cure.

"You know, I'm staying to watch over her," Grimley says.

"I didn't know that," I say. I steal a glance at him. His face is tight, serious. He looks older than when I first met him. I suppose we have all aged.

Inside, Mother is still huddled in the bed, Dr. Bowman at her side. I haven't seen her since that morning. Shame fills me as I realize how bad off she is. Her whole body shakes unrelentingly. The tremors are unmistakable. This is more than a chill.

Memories fill me of another time I was at her bedside, another time I watched her die. I can't do this again.

Dr. Bowman looks up at me. "Have you had any luck?"

"Yes," I say. "I'm leaving in a few minutes. I think the cure is at the PSC."

"That is an excellent place to start. Most of my work was at the Institute and prison. It makes sense the other studies would be there."

I nod.

"Imani, she's going to be all right," Grimley says. "I'll be here. I'll watch over her."

"I'll be here as well," Dr. Bowman says.

"And me."

I look to the soft female voice and realize for the first time that Adelaide is in the room with us as well. The hatred is gone from her eyes. In its place is a look of sorrow, possibly sympathy.

"Adelaide—" I start to say.

"Just don't. Get out of here and take care of things. Got it? If this were my mum, I don't know what I'd do. So, get out there and fix it if you can. I'll make sure she's all right."

"These are the end stages before she will reawaken. We'll need a secure place to put her," Dr. Bowman says.

"Somewhere that she can't hurt herself, please," I say.

"Of course," Grimley promises.

"I'll hurry as quickly as I can," I say. Tears threaten but I wipe them away. Then I lean in and kiss her on the forehead. She is clammy and cold despite the blankets piled on her. It's all too familiar. I have to get far away from this house.

"Thank you," I manage and trudge toward the door.

Once outside, my tears fall more quickly than I can keep up with. I don't stop to see the spectacle of the hanging, although I can hear the sounds of execution from deeper in the forest. Thomas is waiting for me on the hand cart. Our whole party is already gathered and waiting for me. Apparently, none of them wanted to watch the hanging either, which is some small comfort.

Thomas reaches down for me and I climb onto the platform.

"You all right, love?" he asks.

"Yes, I'm fine. Let's go," I say.

"Take care and radio when you can," Maire calls. She's standing a few paces away. I didn't see her when I passed. I'm too much of a mess. I need to focus on this job.

"Will do, Mum," Thomas calls then gives the signal for the first two men to start pumping us down the tracks.

Maire looks tired. Her eyes are puffy—she's been crying as well. Whether for her executed one-time-friends or Thomas or just the state of our world in general, I might never know. I raise a hand, kiss my fingers, then wave to her. She repeats the gesture and, somehow, we are one in our sorrow, our pain, and our hope.

TWENTY FOUR
Marian

Marian awoke to a new sound. The night had been riddled with moans and bangs. The creatures below them were relentless, but the day's march and the events of the previous week had caught up to her and she had fallen into a fitful sleep. Her dreams were full of attacks—Leaders in black uniforms, citizens in stained and torn white smocks, even her friends accusing her of ruining their lives. Yet she slept on.

Sometime well after sunrise, a sound she'd never heard before penetrated the walls of their shelter and woke them all.

Ethan squatted at the edge of the trap door, peering down. Emily and Charlie were where Marian had left them the night before, only now they were sitting up.

The noise came again, a deep bellowing that wasn't human but wasn't any animal that Marian could identify.

"What is that?" Marian asked as she made her way to Ethan's side, hoping to see something.

"I think it's a cow, but I can't see to be sure," he said.

Marian couldn't see either. The sound was coming from outside the barn and all that was visible was the floor below, thousands of footprints scraped and pressed into the dirt, but not one mindless person left.

"Where do you think they all went?" she asked.

"I'm not sure, but I have an idea."

"What's that?" Marian pointed to a machine with large tires off to one side. She hadn't paid much attention as they hurled themselves up the ladder the night before, but now that she had slept and wasn't being chased, it was much easier to take inventory of their options.

"That's a tractor. It's solar powered, built for working the fields and hauling heavy farm equipment," Ethan said. "My family unit had one for our community."

"Do you know how to drive it?" Marian asked.

"Yeah. I'm trying to figure out if it's worth risking a drop down there to check it out."

"We don't have many other options," Marian said.

The sound came again, only this time louder and it repeated, frantic and strained.

"Whatever is happening out there is not pretty," Ethan said.

Marian shuddered. If it was a cow, she didn't want to see it, and she couldn't think about a human making that kind of noise.

"Do we have any water or food left?" Charlie asked.

"Yes," Marian said and got him one of the last water pouches.

They needed to get to the PSC today. Hopefully there would be supplies there. She watched as Charlie used his good arm to hold the pouch up for Emily, who was sitting up but staring at the space between her feet. She drank some without any coercing, which was a relief and a change from the day before. Marian hoped they could get her to eat, and if not, at least she knew the PSC had medical supplies, possibly a liquid nutrient solution they could feed her.

Marian closed her eyes and took a deep breath in her nose, letting it out her mouth slowly. She had to remind herself that this was a good plan. There was nothing at the school, not even any shelter. At least here there was a barn, a tractor, and the possibility of more supplies across the tracks.

"Let's do it," Marian said to Ethan.

She handed him the other water pouch after taking a sip for herself.

"Does this mean you're all right with me?" Ethan asked.

"It means we need to get out of here and we have to work together if we want to make it, 776."

"You called me Ethan last night," he said.

"Whatever." She held out her hand for more water.

He handed her a protein packet from his hidden pants pocket, then passed two to Charlie and Emily.

"Marian, let it go, all right? No one is punishing anyone for anything anymore. Let's drop the numbers. The Leaders are gone, so we don't have to do that anymore," Charlie said.

Marian ignored him and started folding her blanket from the night before.

"How's your arm?" Ethan asked Charlie.

"Hurts like hell," he said.

"I bet," Ethan said.

"Let me look at it," Marian said. She set her blanket down and knelt by her friend. He lifted his arm out from his chest and she slipped off the ripped fabric turned sling to better look at the swollen limb.

"Good news is it looks like it's mostly your wrist or close to it," Marian said. "Bad news is it will probably have to be set, but I don't know how to do that."

"Yeah, I was thinking that," Charlie said.

"Did you sleep at all last night?" she asked.

"Not really. I listened to the mob down there and drifted in and out."

"What about Emily?" Ethan asked.

"She slept most of the night."

"Right. Let's check it out then," Ethan said. "I'll lower the ladder down one rung at a time until I can see. That way none of them can grab it if they are still down there out of sight."

"Do you think they're hiding? Trying to lure us out?" Marian didn't know what they were capable of.

"I have no idea," Ethan said.

"They don't seem to be very intelligent—more of a mob mentality," Charlie noted.

"That guy yesterday acted like he wanted to eat me," Ethan said.

"Eat you?" Charlie shuddered.

"It was rough. I definitely don't want to get near any of them. But we need to get to the PSC. That's our only hope at this point," Marian said.

Ethan frowned. "I think that tractor is our only ride."

"What do you need me to do?" Marian asked.

Together they figured out a way to maneuver part of the ladder down and Ethan carefully made his way one rung at a time until he could see more clearly.

"The tractor seems operational. It's been used recently—the controls are clean and the battery indicator says full."

"What about the mob?" Marian asked.

"Uh, I don't really want to talk about it, but I know why they left now."

"What happened?" Charlie asked.

Ethan climbed back up the ladder and sat on the edge of the opening. "All I'm going to say is that a herd of cows got loose in the field. If those guys were hungry before, hopefully they won't be now."

"Is there room for all of us in the cab of that tractor?" Marian asked.

"Should be," Ethan said.

"Then let's get going. Ethan, you go down first and get the tractor ready. Charlie, do you think you can climb down on your own?"

"Maybe if you help me get started."

"No problem," Marian said. "We'll have to lower Emily down the same way we pulled her up."

"We won't have much time. I'm guessing as soon as I start that engine, the creepers will be crawling at us again."

"Some of them weren't crawling. Some of them can flat-out run," Charlie said.

Ethan nodded. "Right, so we have to be quiet, fast, and hope that this all works out."

"Do the doors on the tractor lock? Once we get inside will we be able to lock them out?" Marian asked.

"Yes, they should. They did on the one we had back at my home pod," Ethan said.

"Let's go then," Marian said. "Emily, are you ready?"

Emily didn't say anything, simply stared at her feet and breathed little, shallow breaths.

"Maybe she hit her head in the explosion," Ethan said, forehead creased in concern.

"It doesn't matter. Let's just get going. Charlie, help me get this rope back on her."

Marian tucked the blankets in to keep Emily from bruising while Ethan made his way down the ladder to the tractor as quickly and quietly as he could. They heard the click of the door opening and closing on the big machine. Marian looked out the opening and saw Ethan's indication for them to come down. The people in the field either hadn't seen him or didn't care.

Marian helped Charlie slide to the edge and turn over on his stomach while Ethan stabilized the bottom of the swinging ladder. She positioned the rungs under his feet and held his good arm, spotting him as he slipped his bad arm over the first rung. She could see the pain echo across his face, but he didn't cry out. Marian couldn't believe his pain threshold. It had to be higher than anyone she knew. The purple and red arm, swollen to twice its natural size, looked more painful than anything Marian had ever experienced.

Soon he had a rhythm and was almost to the bottom. Marian just had to push Emily to the side and position her rope so that she could be lowered down.

"Emily, you have to help me. We need to move quickly. But the good news is we are almost to a place with beds and medicine and real food," Marian said and hoped she wasn't lying.

Emily didn't respond.

"I know you are so very sad and broken, Emily, but we need to fight. We need to keep going." Marian tried looking her in the eyes, but the girl's stare was far away, back at the Secondary School with her twin sister's dead body.

The rope was secure; she only had to loop it over the rafter and drop it down. Before she did, she leaned forward and kissed Emily on the lips.

"We're going to make it," she said.

Emily shifted her gaze to meet Marian's. There was a moment of connection. Her friend was still in there. She was just traumatized and in shock.

"Hang on," Marian said, and threw the rope over the rafter then down the opening. She made her own way down the ladder, and with Ethan's help they pulled until Emily was dragged from sitting to hanging in the air high over the barn floor. They slowly let the rope out, lowering her through the opening and to the ground with all their blankets and what little food was left inside Marian's black confiscation bag.

Marian couldn't help it—at a snap and a cry, she looked out the big doors to the field still swarming with people. They weren't very near, at least a few minutes' walk, but she could still see crawling and pawing humans, their faces red, their once white uniforms stained brown and red, and bloody chunks of something being tossed around and fought for in the crowd.

She looked away. It was a horrible sight. There had to be more than one dead cow out there. She'd seen hungry people riot before, but nothing like this. Not to this extent.

"Hey," Ethan said. "Don't look at that. It's not worth it. You don't want that in your head."

"I'm fine," Marian said. "Let's just get her down."

Charlie was already in the cab waiting. Once Emily touched down, Marian helped lift her onto Ethan's back and he climbed up the four ladder steps to the cab of the tractor. Charlie held the door open for them and the two squeezed in: Ethan in the driver's seat, Charlie on one side, Emily on the other.

The terrible truth sunk in at last: there was no room for Marian.

"Come on!" Ethan called to her in a frantic whisper.

"There's not enough room!" she replied.

"We'll make room, just get up here. We need to get going," Ethan said.

"Marian, we'll make it work. Just climb up," Charlie said and motioned with his good arm.

"Hold on," Marian said.

There were more tools on the wall where she got the rake the day before. She grabbed the most lethal-looking one with seven sharp prongs at the end of a long handle. Then she ran to the tractor and climbed up the small ladder to the door.

"We definitely don't have room for that," Ethan said.

"It's not going in there. Just get this thing running," Marian said, and she closed the door.

"Marian! What are you doing?" Charlie called, but his cry was muffled by the closed door, and Marian was already climbing the rest of the way to the top of the cab. Bars were set into the roof, perfect for holding onto up there. Marian banged on the cab and hollered, "Let's go!"

She crossed her fingers and closed her eyes, hoping the engine would start.

It fired up without hesitation, roaring to life and attracting the attention of the bloody mob before them. Heads turned and bodies rose from the carnage they were climbing over.

"Go!" cried Marian. She clung tightly with one hand and braced her weapon on the edge of the cab as they lurched forward.

Bodies moved toward them before they were clear of the barn. Marian had to lean forward and duck down to miss being scraped off by the door opening, but she made it. Ethan was moving much too slowly, and the first attacker came at her from the side without a ladder. It clung to the metal, growling, as Ethan picked up speed. Marian swung the sharp end, scraping its fingers. It howled but didn't let go. Changing tactics, she started thrusting down as hard as she could, aiming for its face, closing her eyes when the sharp points punctured skin. A thud told her when the body fell to the ground. By then, several more had a hand somewhere on the tractor, trying to climb up, and more were coming.

They were around the building now, heading for the fence, but they were on the far side of the barn, where there was no gate. Ethan was speeding up. Marian could hear Charlie shouting from the cab but couldn't understand what he was saying. Between the roar of the engine and the moans and shouts of the wild throng beneath her, details of other sounds were blocked out.

"He's going to drive through it," Marian said to herself.

She swung at one attacker and stabbed another. For a moment she thought she recognized someone behind the blood and shrieks, a woman she knew from somewhere. Her black braids were coming loose, her smock ripped at the neck and her arms scratched, bruised, and reaching up.

How did these bare-handed humans take down and kill full grown cattle? Marian wondered. It had to be adrenaline and a psychosis of some sort.

The tractor was moving fast enough that Marian stopped swinging her weapon at the people around them and held onto the rail with both hands. They were almost to the fence. Its thin wires would be no match for the large rubber tires and steel frame… she hoped.

And she was right. They crashed over the fence and climbed up the hill to the tracks, only slowing slightly. Marian held on until they got to the top, level ground, before she began beating off the arms and faces straining for her. A large man was pulling on the handle of the cab door. Marian stabbed him in the top of the head, her prongs sinking past his skull deep into his brain. He cried once then fell backward off the tractor, almost taking her tool with him. A quick tug on the handle, and it came free in time for an arm to grab her ankle.

Marian swung around, connecting the handle with the side of another man's face. He looked stunned and tumbled off onto the rails below. The woman Marian thought she might know rolled next to him. Both immediately got back up and started walking more slowly behind the tractor, still in pursuit.

"Why won't they stop?" she cried.

The tractor picked up speed, and Marian worked to clear the remaining hangers-on from the sides and back of the tractor. As they moved faster, fewer were able to grab on and climb.

"Yes!" Marian cried and jabbed her weapon in the air as the last mindless person fell from the tractor with a scream. They were cruising toward the bombed-out psychology center and away from all the chaos at top tractor speed.

And between the PSC and her tractor was an entire horde of moaning, shuffling people. As she watched, two stumbled out of the ruins.

"Where are they coming from?" she said to no one and shifted her position to have better leverage. She estimated at least two hundred of them and one of her. At least she had the high ground, and at least the others were locked in the cab.

Beyond the staggering bodies, the blackened earth and rubble of the PSC still smoked. She tried to make out where the entrance used to be. Stairs had led up and down in the glass breezeway. She hated to think of what happened to the entrance workers when the bombs hit. There was also an elevator in the center of the facility. It wouldn't be operational, but the shaft could give her some bearing.

The people ahead were starting to get closer as the ones behind fell back. The side window rolled down and Charlie stuck his head out.

"Where should we go?" he yelled.

"Anywhere that looks safe. Look for openings and stairwells. We need to go underground, to the bunkers," she said. "Roll your window up. If I see something I'll bang on the roof."

Charlie gave her a thumbs up, the ancient symbol for all was well, and pulled his head back inside the cab, closing the window behind him.

She didn't have much time. She wouldn't be able to search for a passage to the bunkers while fighting. The people were almost on them again. Building debris littered the ground and Ethan swerved around some larger chunks on the tracks. Marian held on tightly.

"This is ridiculous," she said.

Then she spotted it, off to the left—the twisted metal beams that at one time held a sliding elevator aloft. She banged on the top of the cab just as the first attacker slammed into the front of the speeding tractor and slid off, getting run over.

Charlie's head poked out again. Marian pointed to the elevator shards sticking up in the piles of mess.

"Head for that," she called. "There should be stairs close by."

Charlie nodded and moved back inside to relay to Ethan. The tractor lurched sideways, making a sharp right toward the building and plummeting down the gravel hill to the trimmed grass below.

Marian wasn't ready for the quick move. She tried to catch herself, grabbing at the rail, but missed. She tumbled off the tractor, hitting her head on the side on the way down and landing sprawled on her back in the gravel. The large rear tire barely missed crushing her arm and leg as her friends sped off without her.

TWENTY FIVE
Imani

Thomas and I and four others are on the platform with our gear in trunks strapped to the ancient frame covered in recently replaced wooden planks. The plan is for two at a time to take turns pumping the handles while a third person runs the brakes. The other three will sleep, or try to, and we'll trade off in four-hour shifts. It takes five men to get the car moving, but once it does, the steady downhill grade makes it easy to maintain a decent speed. The extra men bail, and Josh and Mark continue at the handles while Sam works the brakes.

I'm not looking forward to my turn. My head still aches from the man kicking it, my shoulder stings from the bite of a wiper before rescuing Mother—which seems like it happened a lifetime ago—and there are a myriad of other aches and pains that morph into one total body ache.

The cool air whips our hair back from our faces, and I pull my hat down farther on my head. I lean into Thomas and close my eyes. He is holding a shock rifle, as is the brake woman. Everyone else has one accessible, but we don't anticipate needing them until we cross the northern bridge to the flat lands. Mine sits next to me, my hand through the strap, my gloved fingers ready to react if needed.

The plans I'm able to recall of the Psychological Studies Center show upper floors with classrooms and study labs. Much of the layout is identical to the Secondary School. The main difference between the two structures is the PSC is built on top of a prewar college with a nuclear grade basement that survived the last wars. If Haman has secret labs and supplies, paperwork, subjects, or anything else useful, we have a good chance of finding it there.

A single light, powered by the turning wheels, illuminates the track ahead of us for several feet. Other than that, the night is dark and heavy around us. Through the trees overhead, stars shine and some race across the sky. There must be a meteor shower.

Twinkle, twinkle little star
How I wonder what you are.

The children's song comes to mind unbidden. I've exhausted the documents I can understand regarding Haman's research, so I let myself drift down a mental corridor of beauty from the past. Music and art float under my eyelids and in my ears. Now that I can relax and enjoy them, it helps me pass time.

I wake to the sound of brakes—metal scraping against metal. I sit up and stretch as we come to our first stop. It is still dark, and the cold is thick upon us. I'm grateful for my warm coat and boots. The others have undone their coats. Apparently pumping is more work than we anticipated, even downhill.

"I still don't think we should stop completely," one man, Mark, says.

"We need to change places and I need to pee," Sam says.

"You might have to learn how to pee on the move," Mark replies.

"Enough." It's Jason, the guard who apologized to me earlier. We haven't spoken since the first awkward exchange, and I don't feel the need to remedy that now. "We are almost to the flat lands. I doubt there are wipers this far north in the hills, but once we cross the bridge, we're going to have to keep an eye out." He turns to Thomas and me. "Are you two ready to work?"

"As well as can be expected, I suppose," Thomas stands carefully and stretches before looping his shock rifle over the shoulder on his uninjured side.

I don't feel like doing anything except sleeping in a dark room with a soft bed. My shoulder, ribs, and face ache, but Thomas and I aren't the only ones injured and we have a lot to do.

"Where are we?" I say and follow his lead, standing unsteadily.

"Just east of the north bridge. We will be crossing it in about an hour or so," he says. He looks to the redhead. "Have you radioed in yet?" Mark is a specialist in mechanics and electronics. He's here to maintain our radios and try to find any other technology we can bring back to make our lives on the mountain better.

"No, was just about to do that," Mark says, retrieving the radio.

"Hey, if you need to relieve yourself, this is a good time to go. I'll watch your back if you watch mine," Sam calls to me.

"Sure," I say and hop down after her.

The gravel under the tracks makes a loud crunching noise as we make our way into the bushes. I keep my rifle ready as she ducks behind a bush in front of me. She comes out sooner than I expect and taps my shoulder.

"Your turn."

When I'm done, we start back to the car.

"You're the human library, right? You've got all that stuff in your head from the past. Right?"

"Yes. I have a head full of artificial memories," I say. I haven't had many people ask me this directly. She's older than me by quite a few years and several knotty scars line her right arm where she's pushed up her coat. She seems like she's been through some hard times. But she also seems like the kind of person I could trust. I like her.

"Does it hurt?" she asks.

"It used to," I say. "I've learned to deal with it."

"Can I ask you something?"

"Sure."

"Were unicorns ever real? Those horses with a single horn in the middle of their forehead?"

I look at her in surprise. I didn't expect anything like this. Such a strange question.

"Give me a second," I say, my pace slowing. I let my mind go soft while looking at the dark branches of the trees in front of us, and visions of beautiful white horses with flowing manes and tails dance before me. They are in stories for children, movies, books for adults, legends, tapestries, clothing. Apparently, a subsection of our ancestors were obsessed with them. I dig further and find academic information about their existence.

"Come on, Sam. Let's go," a man calls out, probably Josh, and I am pulled back to the present moment.

"Sorry," I say.

"It's a stupid question." She is marching back up the hill to the platform.

"No it isn't."

She looks at me sideways, this tough woman holding her shock rifle like she'd rather kill you than talk to you, and she wants to know about single horned horses from little girls' stories.

"Why do you ask about them?" I ask.

"My mother used to tell me stories when I was a girl. I wasn't allowed to repeat them, but I always wondered if she made them up or if it was true that they used to live in the woods around our community."

My heart melts a little bit at the thought of a tiny soldier girl daydreaming about unicorns. I know what that felt like, to hide with your mother in the bathroom and trade secrets, to have forbidden dreams and snippets of the ancient past held in your heart that didn't dare see the light of day.

"Yes," I say. "They were real."

"Really?" She looks at me with amazement. "Well, I'll be."

I don't feel bad about the lie. It's not a lie, actually. There's no proof either way. Some scholars actually believed they had found scientific evidence of their existence before the modern age, and doesn't our world have enough room for what's real and what's imagined? Her face is soft with nostalgia, and she smiles at me before she jumps on the cart, then reaches her hand down to help me up.

"You ready?" Thomas asks.

"Yes," I say.

I take my place at the handle across from Thomas. Jason works the brake while the other three try to get some sleep. I don't envy them having to relax while we cruise through possibly wiper-infested woods. I wish them well in my mind and push down as hard as I can on the handle. We start to roll down the hill.

It's not safe to talk—we have to keep an eye out for wipers—so we just pump. We get into a rhythm as we become comfortable with the pumping, and soon the car picks up enough momentum that we can step back and let go, the handles moving up and down on their own. Jason works the break to make sure we don't go too fast and risk derailing. I smile at Thomas. He winks and points up at the stars. I look up and see more streaks across the sky. It's breathtaking. For a moment I forget that all these beautiful night lights are shining over a war zone. We are heading into the midst of countless dead bodies and many living ones who will hunt us down.

It occurs to me that a blast could have taken out part of the tracks, especially near the capital. If that is the case, we will have to go the rest of our way on foot, which is far slower. I'm hoping that won't be necessary. There could also be a train on the tracks anywhere along the route. We have to be ready for this as well. The light ahead shows more trees and occasionally the hind legs of a deer or fox jumping away.

Soon the trees give way, and we are on a bridge over a canyon, the river rushing below us. As I pump to keep the car moving, I scan the opposite shore for movement, the cliffs for bodies. But it's not like back at the Institute. The land is untouched by bombs and there are no wipers wandering here. I'm relieved but also nervous. I wonder when the devastation will begin.

Another hour and the trees thin. The slope we've been coasting down is tapering off and I can smell the smoke of war. I had almost convinced myself that the bombs may not have done as much damage as we imagined, but as we begin to cruise by the communities on the edge of the capital, even in the dark it's clear that there was once a world teeming with people here and now it is gone.

Along the tracks, patches of ground are charred black, some spots still smoking or flickering with flame. Shapes—people, I think—move outside our light, but no one suggests we stop. They might be wipers. I keep my eyes peeled for anything in the tracks, but nothing appears. Eventually, we come to the train yard. What is left of two sleek white trains covers the side tracks where they had been waiting for deployment. Half of a car, its jagged edges reflecting the light of our car, bars our path forward.

"Hold up," Thomas calls out. He's still on main lookout duty since he is closest to the light. "Debris ahead."

Jason has been staring at the passing wreckage but turns to follow Thomas's indication. "Looks like part of a passenger car." He pulls back on the brake to slow us.

"If it's just the melamine cover, we can punch through it," Thomas says.

"But if there's metal behind that, we're screwed. We have to stop and check it out," Jason says, and I agree with him. This mission is too important to gamble on anything.

I think of my mother and wonder how she is. What stage is she in the disease? Is Grimley taking care of her like he said he would?

Jason pulls hard on the brake, and loud screeching fills the night air.

Josh sits up, bleary. "I know it hasn't been four hours."

"We've got something in the tracks," I say.

"Ahh, of course," he says. "I figured this would happen."

"I need two of you with shock rifles ready and on guard, the rest of you down here to help push," Jason commands. He looks us over and nods. "Imani and Mark, that'll be you two."

We are the smallest of the group, so it makes sense, but we're also the only two without guard experience, so I'm not sure we are the best shots. I do my best to stand at attention and look sharp, watching the land around us for movement as the other four make their way to the debris. I can hear them chatting quietly as their boots crunch down the gravel. The night is still except for us. It must have been melamine, the white plastic we use to build all our shells, because they shove a few times and it slides easily off the tracks.

Relieved, I sweep around the area again, straining to see anything in the dark. A clicking comes from my right—Mark's messing with a radio dial.

"Hey," I say. "We need to be watching for wipers."

"I did," he says. "There's none here. This place is dead… literally."

I hate the pun and hate that he's not watching out for something that could hurt Thomas. He's now officially my least favorite person on this trip.

"Yeah, but they could come up at any point. You don't understand. You haven't seen them."

He grunts. "Sick humans stumbling around in the dark don't really scare me."

"They don't all stumble," I say. "Some of them are fast and strong. I was tackled by one once. It bit my shoulder."

He nods like he doesn't believe me but needs to humor me.

"I'm not kidding. It was—" A sudden movement behind him catches my eye. I point my rifle and Mark jumps to the side.

"Hey! Don't shoot me just because I'm not as worked up as you," he says and drops the radio, fumbling for his gun.

"No! Behind you," I say and take aim.

It's a woman. She's jogging slowly but her gait is lopsided. I can't tell if it's from fatigue or illness.

Mark takes aim.

"Okay, let's verify—"

He fires.

"Mark! No!" I cry.

The woman drops like a sack of rocks. The others run toward her, their rifles at the ready.

"Why did you do that?" I ask, shocked.

"You just told me how awful they are. Did you want her to chomp on your boyfriend?" He's picking up the radio again.

I really hate this guy. I push the radio down, and he looks up at me, annoyed.

"We don't know if she's a wiper or not! What if she was a survivor? We have to find out before you shoot."

"Relax. My gun is set to stun. She'll be fine and..." He trails off, staring at his gun.

"What is it?" I ask.

Thomas hops up onto the cart before he answers. The others are still gathered around the woman.

"Is she okay? Is she sick?" I ask.

"She's dead," Thomas says.

"What? How?" I ask, staring at Mark.

Thomas holds his hand out for Mark's gun, and Mark gives it to him. Thomas checks the setting, sighs, and hands it back. "You had the settings turned up, you techy goof. In that mode and the right angle, the shock can kill. Especially if you have a weak heart."

The others are jogging over. Jason gets to us first and leaps nimbly aboard. "What happened, you two? I thought the guns were set to stun."

I scowl at Mark. "He fired before I could get a good read on her."

"We didn't even see her coming. At least he spotted her," Sam said.

"No, I spotted her, he shot like a maniac. You need to talk to him, Jason," I say. I don't want to even look at the redhead. "We're here to save people, not kill them."

"I think he learned his lesson, Imani." He eyes Mark, who nods obediently, and Jason continues, "Let's deal with the body and get moving. Wiper or not, I don't like this place."

We don't see anyone else as Sam and Josh move her body and cover it with a piece of tin. We don't have shovels to dig a grave and the sun will be rising soon. We push the cart back into motion. Thomas and I pump for all we are worth while the others hop on and try to get comfortable. A fresh blanket of apprehension covers us, and my stomach is churning and tight from the loss of another life. *I could have saved her*, I think.

"You realize this is all going to be up hill on the way back, right?" Sam says before settling down to finish her turn of rest.

"Yeah," I say. "I'm trying not to think about it."

"Don't worry. Maybe we'll find a truck or something. That will be better," Sam says. "As long as the sun still rises on us. This smoke might mess with the solar cells."

She sits with her back against a trunk and I look forward again. We are cruising at a good pace through what used to be our capital. Nothing but fire and ruin remains. We pull our shirts over our noses and mouths in an attempt to filter out the smoky air. Not a single person is visible, dead or alive, in the destruction. Images of long lost cities flash through my mind, overlaying the destruction before me. Great buildings full of people, leveled in blasts from the great war my ancestors survived. This destruction has been repeated throughout history. War after war, bomb after bomb, death and more death. In long distant wars, people wandered the streets wiping up ash, their skin burning. Maybe this is better.

I try to stop thinking at all.

Other bits of debris on the track are small. Thomas is running the brake now and he's getting good at jumping off and moving things, so we don't have to stop completely. He jumps back on and we continue pumping away. Soon the sun is rising behind us and to our right. We've made a full half circle and our destination is approaching. I am exhausted but vigilant. As the world around us lightens, we reach the other side of the capital, finally leaving the bombed buildings and businesses. Ahead, fields and fences, little sheds and barns, and more black spots and fires show where communities full of the little round white pods I grew up in used to stand in rows, homes for the people who lived there. Now nothing is white. Only gray and black and the green of the fields remain.

We see our first wipers just after the sun breaks over the mountains. The group of five are stumbling along the tracks. They screech and stretch for us, and one tries to run alongside, moaning and grabbing at the sides of the car. But we are going too fast for them, and Thomas fires a stun shot at each one. He made sure his gun was set to the lowest effective setting. They roll into the grass and I silently wish them well.

I'll get the cure and I'll come back to you, I promise in my mind to people I don't even know. Ahead to the right, a massive pile of rubble is in the same place where the Psychological Studies Center should be.

"What on the bloody morning is that?" Thomas says and points ahead.

A large gray farm vehicle is racing toward us on the train tracks. A large group of wipers—maybe twenty-five to thirty, I think after a quick count—surrounds it, and atop the vehicle is a small shape beating at the wipers with a long pole. The vehicle turns sharply, heading toward PSC. The person on top flies off the roof, strikes the side of the vehicle, and lands in the middle of the tracks.

TWENTY SIX
Marian

Marian couldn't breathe. She landed hard and for a moment didn't know what happened. Then they were on her.

A man with golden hair turned dark brown from dried blood jumped on her, reaching for her throat. A woman shoved him away, Marian's tunic getting ripped as the man scrabbled at it. One of them bit her arm; she wasn't sure which. More scratched at her as she fought to get the handle of her weapon out from underneath her body, but the weight of those pressing down on her made it impossible. She felt hot breath on her neck and started screaming.

The load suddenly lightened, and as she drew in breath to scream again, a strange sound—*zap... zap... zap*—filled the air. Some of the people had moved away from her, and a screeching sound cut through the moans and snarls followed by more *zaps*.

A new face leaned over her and made eye contact. The massive man wasn't covered in blood, and he wore strange clothes. He nodded at her, then turned to throw off a charging woman. She curled into a ball, her arms shielding her face as she waited for more grasping hands to tear at her, but the man grabbed her wrist and pulled her to her feet.

"Ow!" she cried.

"It's okay. I've got you," he said.

Marian's head throbbed as he pulled her down the tracks, past many motionless attackers in dirty white. She still had the pole firmly in her hand. It dragged on the rocks and ties as they made their way to a primitive train car, gear stacked on the edges and people with shock rifles firing on the mob of people that had been attacking her. By the time they reached the rail car, they were all unconscious.

She glanced back at the tractor, which had nearly made it to the wreckage of the PSC. They hadn't even realized she fell off.

"We need to get these guys tied up," an older woman called from the platform of the train car. "We don't want them waking up and surprising us in half an hour."

"I'm not sure if we have enough rope," said a younger man with a thick accent and red hair. Marian recognized the lilt from her research visits to the prison. He was from the mountains.

"I've got some in my pack," a girl said, throwing her long black braid over her shoulder. She was wearing a blue cap and had her own shock rifle slung over her shoulder. She stopped when she saw Marian and stared at her like she'd seen a ghost. "23?"

The voice was familiar to Marian. Take away the hat and the gun. Put her in a gray school tunic and a lost look in her eye and Marian knew this girl.

"4254?" she said.

"Yes! What are you doing out here?" 4254 rushed to Marian and put an arm around her shoulders, helping her walk.

"We're heading for the PSC. The school was bombed—there's hardly anyone left. Do you know what happened?" Marian said. "Wait, how did you get out of prison, 4254?"

"Call me Imani," she said. "It's a very long story and we have a lot of other issues to deal with first."

"Imani, okay," Marian said. "I'm Marian."

"That's right." Imani smiled and helped Marian to the side of the train car where she sat down.

An older woman gave her water and Imani began cleaning a wound on Marian's head. She didn't know when that had happened, but it explained the throbbing pain and intermittent blurry vision.

"Who's in the tractor?" Imani asked.

"Other kids from the school, Charlie, Ethan, and Emily."

"They have names too, eh?"

"Not everyone, just us."

"Wait, 12?" Imani's eyes widened further as she recognized Emily. "Where's 13?"

"She's gone," Charlie said.

Imani closed her eyes for a moment, then opened them, jaw set. "Did anyone else survive there?" she asked.

"A few teachers and house mothers were alive when we left. More people were in the rubble, but we had no way to get them out."

"Do they have food or a plan? Did they send you for help?"

"We left in the night. I was tired of having adults tell me what to do. I figured if the whole place had gone to hell we might as well take our chance at survival. I knew there would probably be supplies at the PSC, maybe shelter if we were lucky. This place was—"

"Built before the first war. Right." Imani nodded.

"I can't believe you're here. I never thought I'd see you again. This is probably the weirdest day of my life." Marian shook her head as she spoke and immediately regretted it as the throbbing intensified. After the explosions, chases, and fighting for her life, seeing Imani here was hard to accept. She felt like she was in a dream and she couldn't wake up.

Imani spoke as if she had read her mind. "I thought about you when I heard about the bombings. I wondered if you survived. I never expected to actually see you again."

"Why are you here?" Marian asked.

"I knew about these bunkers as well. We came for supplies and answers. Where is Haman?"

"Who?"

"Professor 789," Imani said.

"He has a name too? What the hell is going on?"

Imani took a few minutes to briefly fill Marian in on the Blue Spider rebels and Haman's plans gone wrong. Marian knew some of it, but the rest about the information in Imani's head, a One Shot to cure all illness, and subjects from the Shops was hard to believe. Still, she had to. It was the only information they'd had in days and as far-fetched as it sounded, it made sense. It tied together Haman's strange movements and facilities, his connections to more than just the school and psychological industries, the rush for med production, and the bombing.

"So, the mountain people had an arsenal all this time?" Marian said with wonder.

"Yeah, except only a couple of people knew it. They found it after the first raids happened and they moved underground."

"This is just so…ironic," Marian said.

"I know," Imani said. "Listen, we need Haman and those meds. I think we can save these people if we can find the rest of his research." She gestured at the inert forms around them. "I only have parts of it."

"In your head?"

Imani nodded.

"I have no idea where he is, but I know his offices were somewhere on the lower levels. There were also vaults down there. We were hoping to get supplies. We didn't count on all these walking loonies attacking us."

"The mountain people call them wipers. They thought the Mind Wipe did this to them, but it's actually an inoculation Haman gave people who were sent to the Shop for final use. He had a network of spies smuggling them into his facilities."

"And he did all this right under the Leaders' noses?" Marian asked.

"Yep," Imani said.

"Love, we need to get moving. Most of these folks are taken care of but we have to hoof it to the ruins if we want to find shelter or answers before nightfall," the boy with the thick accent said to Imani.

"Love?" Marian raised her eyebrows and Imani blushed.

"Thomas, this is Marian. She was my roommate at the secondary school," she said.

"Well, fancy that. What a small, ruined world this is," he said and smiled, his whole face alight and shining. Marian wished a boy like that would call her *Love.*

"You guys got her?" the first big man asked.

"Yeah," Imani said. Then she spouted out a bunch of names as the rest of her group gathered around. "This is Josh, Mark, Sam, and Jason."

Marian knew she wouldn't be able to keep them straight.

"Mark, radio in that we made contact with survivors and we're heading to the PSC," the big guy said.

"Will you ask about my mother?" Imani said.

"I thought your mom was dead?" Marian asked.

"Like I said, it's an awfully long story. Can you walk?" She stood and offered a hand to help her up.

"I have to, don't I?" Marian said.

Mark called in their location and reported their status. He asked about Imani's mom as requested. A woman's voice cracked in reply.

"Tell Imani she's stable. Not good, but stable. She's awake and we moved her to her own space, but she's still talking numbers and she's crazy hungry."

Thomas squeezed Imani's shoulder and she nodded.

"Tell her thank you," Imani said, and Mark relayed the message. "She's definitely got it," Imani whispered.

"Yah, but we're here and she's going to be okay," Thomas said.

They were soon making their way on foot to the mess that was once the Psychological Studies Center. They stepped over debris and rocks. Craters pocked the ground.

"Those must be where individual bombs fell," Imani noted as they passed three large holes.

"How many did they have?" Marian said. "It seemed like just one big one hit us, but this looks like a lot of little ones."

"There were lots of other explosives in the head. They are made to clear large urban areas. At least twenty were launched," Imani said, her voice haunted.

Ahead, the tractor had stopped in front of a large pile of debris. A couple of wipers were banging on the doors to get in. Charlie was bent over Emily and Ethan was doing something with the controls.

"Those your friends?" asked the big guy.

"Yeah, we all came from the secondary school," Marian said.

"With that tractor?" he asked again.

"No, on foot. We found the tractor this morning in the shed over there." She pointed to their shelter from the night before.

"You walked all this way through wiper-infested fields? Damn, girl. You should sign up for guard duty," said the older woman.

"We only saw wipers when we got close to here," Marian said.

"So, maybe they haven't spread as far as we thought," Imani said, looking at Thomas.

The two younger guys, Josh and Mark, jogged ahead and shocked the two wipers then tied them up with the last of the rope from Imani's pack. Charlie opened the door and climbed out.

"Marian," he called when he saw her. "Are you okay?"

"Nope," she said. "But I'm alive."

"We need help getting her out." He pointed to Emily. Ethan lifted the girl up and Josh and Mark reached up to help her down.

"What's wrong with her?" asked the older lady—*Sam*, Marian thought—as she examined Charlie's crooked bandage and swollen arm.

"We don't know, probably shock," Marian said.

"I bet you'd like a pain killer for this, right?" Sam asked Charlie.

"Yes, please," Charlie said with relief while the woman pulled out a bottle of pills from her pack. She handed a couple to Marian as well.

"For your head," she said. "I don't have much water left. Can you dry swallow these?"

"Gladly," Charlie said.

Marian followed suit.

Sam got a new sling for his arm and patted him on the back. "Once we get somewhere secure, I'll set it for you. Can you handle that?" She raised her eyebrows.

"I don't have a choice, do I?"

"Good answer," she said.

"Let's get inside." Thomas had moved ahead of the crew and was motioning at a beam lying at an angle on a pile of concrete.

Marian introduced Ethan and Charlie to the rest of the group, and soon they were climbing over boulders and beams, shuffling carefully through broken glass and ignoring the dead bodies visible here and there in the rubble. The big guy, Jason, had Emily thrown over his shoulder like a sack of potatoes. His shock rifle rested in the other hand, ready for anything.

Thomas found the elevator shaft, but the stairwell next to it was full of debris.

"Those wipers had to have come from somewhere other than here. There's no way some of those big guys fit through these holes," Mark said.

"Imani, can you pull up a map or something? Is there another stairwell?" Thomas asked.

Imani closed her eyes and rocked a little.

"What is she doing?" Charlie asked.

"I have no idea," Marian said.

"She's our walking bank of knowledge. You want it, she's got it in that pretty little head," Sam said.

"When I worked here, these were the main elevators and stairs, but there were also sets on either end of the main halls." Marian indicated left and right.

"Ack!" Mark cried as an arm reached out for him through the debris in the stairwell. The person attached to it moaned and snarled. Mark fired immediately.

"So there are more. How long was this guy collecting supposedly dead people?" Jason asked.

"He'd been doing it since before my mom got sick," Imani said. "Dr. Bowman said more than a year."

"Let's do this," Jason said. "Half of us go to the left and half to the right. If you find a way down there, alert the others."

"What about Emily and Charlie?" Marian said. "I don't think they can get over all this rubble."

"Unless they want to sit here and wait for us, they're going to have to—" Jason started.

"I've got it. There's a secure entrance to the left, like Marian said. It was made for escaping after a bombing." Imani opened her eyes.

"All right then, everyone this way. Watch out for survivors and wipers. And grab any food or water rations you see."

They all followed Jason as he picked his way over and around the bombed-out area. It was slow going. They had to double back out to the perimeter and then to the far end of the complex, where they found a reinforced steel door surrounded by a mountain of concrete and glass. The debris in front of it had been pushed aside, indicating that the door had been opened and closed a few times, just wide enough for an average sized adult body to squeeze out.

Marian tried the handle. "It's locked. Traditional key lock, no magnets to blow."

"No sweat," Thomas said and stepped forward, his hand jingling through the items in his pockets. He pulled out a small metal device with two prongs. After a moment of concentrated wiggling, he turned the knob and pulled the door open.

No arms reached out for them. No moans filled the dark air.

"All right, I want Mark to stay here with this girl and the radio. It won't work underground anyway," Jason said.

"Emily," Charlie corrected him.

"Right, Emily and this kid. You're both staying up here." He nodded at Charlie.

"Charlie," Charlie said sounding slightly annoyed.

"Sure, Charlie with the broken arm," Jason said. "Once we are down there, I want Sam and Josh on supply recon. We are looking for anything to help us survive—water, food, and weapons. Got it?"

"Yep," Sam said.

"The rest of you, go find whatever it is you're looking for," he said.

"What are you looking for, Imani?" Marian asked.

"The cure. I know there is a cure here. Haman was working on one right before he messed with my head. I just don't have the rest of the story."

"Do you know what it looks like?" Marian asked.

"I have no idea," Imani said, sighing.

"That's great," Mark said, rolling his eyes.

Marian gave him a dirty look. She did not like this guy in his red hat and greasy hair, one hand on the radio, the other on a rifle. Then she gasped.

"Imani, the last time I was here, Haman's wing was on high alert. They were mass producing a batch of a new med. That could have been it."

"How long ago was that?"

"Just a few days. He said something had gone wrong and there were subjects that needed the meds as soon as possible. We need to look for vials of green liquid."

"That has to be it!" Imani cried. "I was right, Thomas. I just hope Joe didn't blow it all up."

"Me too, love," he said.

Marian had that pull in her gut. She couldn't help but wish someone felt that way about her and wasn't afraid to share it. Her gaze drifted to Ethan. She didn't know why she did it, it just happened.

He was staring at her too.

It's dark and we only have small handheld lights to guide us down the stairs into the bunker. Our footsteps echo and the dust in the air makes it hard to breathe. I pull my shirt up over my nose and mouth, the others doing the same.

"Where should we go, Map Lady," Sam asks.

For the most part the passage looks like it wasn't affected by the blasts, the pre-war architect's design doing an amazing job. I make a note to look up the plans for future use.

"Up ahead there is a fork in the hallway. It starts branching into three main sections; holding cells are to the right, labs and storage to the left."

"So, this is where he kept all the crazies?" Josh says.

"Here and two other facilities," I say.

"I can't imagine being locked up down here. It would make anyone lose their mind," Josh says.

I look at Thomas, and we share our own memory of being locked up without having to say anything at all.

"You guys okay to split up?" Thomas asks.

Everyone nods in agreement as we come to the first intersection in the passage.

"Take note of what you find and mark the door if it's too big to carry. Let's meet back here when you are done, see if this place is inhabitable for the time being. We need a base."

Jason, Sam, and Josh head down the far-left passage. I ask Marian, "Do you remember where they might have kept the meds?"

"I don't know the exact room," she says. "But it's in the middle passage and a door in the middle of the corridor somewhere."

"Well, let's start opening doors," Ethan said. I haven't talked to the tall boy yet, but he seems nice enough.

There are only three lights between us, so Marian takes one, Ethan takes one, and Thomas and I have the third. We open each door and explore the rooms as carefully as we can. Most are labs and offices, nothing but desks and paperwork. Some are empty. Marian finds water storage in one, and she props the door open with a crate of bottles. We each take one to celebrate. It is stale, possibly older than our civilization, but it's clean water in sealed packaging and we're grateful. The bottles can be reused to distribute water to other survivors once we're organized.

Thomas and I keep opening doors, but nothing resembles medicine in any form. It occurs to me that I've never seen medicine before. It was such a precious commodity in our community before I went to secondary school that I never had any. Of course, I was always grateful not to be sick enough to need it, but at the same time I had to wonder if maybe I wasn't looking for the right thing. My artificial memory indicated bottles of white or colored capsules, but a lot had changed since then.

"Marian, come look at this," Ethan called.

Thomas and I look in their direction to see their lights moving into one of the doors on the left behind us.

"Should we go look too?" I ask.

"If you were an evil genius, where would you hide your stockpile of meds to cure the monsters you accidentally created?" Thomas asks then knocks on the door in front of him.

I look at his light shining on the knob. There is an old-fashioned tumble lock above it with space for seven numbers.

"In a locked room," I say.

"Everything else down here has been open except this one," he says.

"But how do we get in? Can you pick it like you did the other one?" I ask.

"I can try, but I'm not sure," he says and pulls the tool out of his pocket.

"Imani?" Marian calls. "Come see this."

"Can you hold the light and do that at the same time?" I ask.

"Yah, I got it, go ahead." He smiles and I feel warm all over. We are so close. There is a lot still at stake, but we made it this far. Things are looking up.

I make my way carefully back down the hall to where her light is shining on an open door.

"Do you think maybe this is it?" she says, and I stick my head inside.

There are two carts full of small boxes. We open the closest box and Ethan's light reflects off a deep blue liquid in little bottles.

"This could definitely be some sort of medicine. Is it labeled?" I pick up a bottle and turn it over, looking for writing, but there's nothing. Marian is searching the box.

"Nothing," she says, shrugging.

"What if it's not a medicine?" Ethan says.

"Well, we can't do anything without knowing what it is," I say, feeling hope squeeze out of me. Hopefully, Thomas can open that lock.

A cry from deep in the complex draws all our eyes off the blue bottle and to each other.

"What was that?" Marian whispers. In an instant, she transforms from larger-than-life 23 to a fearful teenage girl. Just like me.

"I don't know," I say.

I walk to the door and look for Thomas. His light is still there, moving while he works on the lock.

"Thomas is okay," I say. "It must be Jason and the others.

There's another cry, coming from the opposite end of the hall as Thomas. Then we hear the *zap zap* of a shock rifle and more feet.

"Something is up. Let's mark this door and get out there," Ethan says.

"You think those guards need our help?" Marian says. "They are pretty tough looking."

"I'm not sure, but we should be ready." I lift my shock rifle to the ready, but all is still now. Thomas's light is still as well. Then it shines toward us and back down the other side of the hall.

"What was that?" he calls.

"I don't know," I say.

"Let's go check it out," Ethan says.

"Have you guys checked all the doors on this side yet?" I ask.

"Just about," Marian says.

"Let's prop this one open—" I start but am cut off by another cry then more feet and gun fire.

"We better see what's happening," I say.

All three of us make our way to Thomas, who meets us halfway. The sound of footsteps echoes around us.

"Turn off your lights," Thomas says, and the other two follow his lead.

It's so dark I can't see anything at first, then lights at the far end where we came from flash in erratic patterns.

"They must have run into more wipers," Thomas says and takes my hand in the dark, leading me forward. "You two want to wait in the water room?" he asks. "I wish we had more shock rifles."

"Maybe, can we lock it?" Marian asks.

"I don't know," I say but another cry cuts us off. Now there's yelling and multiple sets of feet are running.

"Let's all go in the water room," I say and feel Thomas pull us in that direction when a flashlight comes around the corner ahead of us and bobs down the hallway, moving fast.

It's Sam. I can just make out her face.

"Get to cover," she cries. More shots zap behind her.

"What's going on?" I ask, but Thomas opens the door to the room with the water and we all pour in. Ethan pulls the door closed behind us before she can answer.

"Where's your shock rifle?" Thomas asks and I realize she's not holding one before she shuts off her light, plunging us into darkness.

"I think I got it locked. If we're quiet, they can't find us," Ethan says.

"But who is they?" Marian whispers.

"Humans," Sam says. "I mean, regular ones. Not wipers. They ambushed us and took our weapons. Jason and Josh are still back there—I don't know what happened to them."

"Why did they jump you? And how did you get away?" Thomas asks.

"I don't know why they jumped us. We were checking rooms and I was on my own—wait, I hear something," she says. We all hold our breath as footsteps of a group of people walking sounds down the corridor.

TWENTY EIGHT
Marian

Marian made her way to Ethan's side in the dark. She pressed her head against the door, trying to hear the voices on the other side, but only muffled shuffling came through. Ethan started to say something, but she held up her hand to cover his mouth, taking a few moments to find it. They listened again, and this time hushed whispers could be heard from the other side, though nothing distinct.

They heard doors opening and closing. Marian stiffened. Ethan said he locked the door, but what if it wasn't? What if they had the key? And what did they want anyway? Wouldn't anyone still alive now be on the same team? Why would they have attacked Jason, Josh, and Sam? Unless Sam wasn't telling the truth…

Marian decided not to think that way until she had proof. There had to be a better way to spend what little brain power she had left.

The door to the room next to them opened and closed, and someone said, "Nothing. I don't think she's down here."

"She couldn't have gone far. Are you sure you saw her turn down this corridor?"

"I think?" said the first voice, more muffled and far away.

"Let's finish checking each room, then head over to the cells. We need to find out what these mountain people are doing down here and how they knew to come to the PSC."

"Got it." The voice sounded close, and the knob to their room rattled. "This one's locked."

Marian could feel everyone in the room holding their breath. Something brushed her arm, startling her. It was Ethan. They found each other's hands in the dark and squeezed.

"Move on," the other voice said. "The boss always locks his private storage. She's not going to be there."

The footsteps moved on and a few more doors opened and closed before it grew still again.

Marian gave Ethan's hand one more squeeze, then let it go before walking toward Imani, feeling out in the dark for her friend's head. She bumped up against her after a few careful steps then whispered, "I think they're gone."

"Better wait a bit longer," Sam said through the inky black.

Marian nodded in agreement then realized no one would be able to see the gesture.

After several more minutes of silence, Marian felt Ethan move closer to her and sit on the floor with the group. She could hear the breath of four other people, but nothing else. She started to doze off, her head throbbing. Either the meds Sam gave her didn't last very long, or she just didn't have anything to distract her from her earlier injuries now.

"I think we should give it a peek." Thomas's thick accent cut the silence.

"I think you're right," Sam said.

The group rose together, and someone moved past her toward the door. She heard the lock click. It was much too loud for the silent space.

If they are still out there, they've heard us now. But they didn't hear anything except the sound of the knob turning and the door swinging open. What sounded like a shock rifle bumped a wall and someone cursing under their breath.

"Looks like we're good," Thomas whispered back into the room just before he clicked his light on. The small beam was blinding in the thick dark they'd been hiding in.

"I need to go back and check on Jason and Josh," Sam said.

"Let's make a plan first," Imani said, and Thomas returned to the room, closing the door but leaving his light on.

"What happened, Sam?" Imani asked.

"We were ambushed. There were at least six of them. They had their own shock rifles and didn't ask any questions. Just came up behind them in a room full of food rations and started shooting. I was near the door, off to the side, so they didn't see me right away. Jason and Josh tried to hold them off, and I tried to help from behind, but there were too many. I got away to warn you, but clearly, at least two followed."

"What were they wearing?" Imani asked.

"Light gray tunics. Definitely not mountain people," Sam said.

"You are sure they weren't in black?" Imani asked.

"Yes. Light gray."

"Professor 789's men," Marian said, forgetting he has a proper name too.

"Sounds like Haman is still alive and giving orders," Imani said.

TWENTY NINE
Imani

"If Haman's still alive, then we have an even better chance of finding the cure. If he created it, then he certainly will want us to use it. We just need to find him," Marian says.

"Were you able to get the locked door open?" I ask Thomas.

He shakes his head. "It's not like a regular lock, nor an electro one. We're gonna need the code to get in. But it's seven digits long so there's going to be…"

"Ten million possibilities," Marian finished.

"Sure," Thomas says. "We don't have all day for that."

"Then we need to find Haman," I say.

"We at least need to know why his men attacked us," Sam says and gets to her feet. "I'm going to go check on Jason and Josh. See if they took them."

"I'm going to find Haman." I feel like I'm repeating myself.

"Don't go getting yourself shot. Let's take it easy," Thomas says.

"I agree. We should take a logical approach," Ethan says. "Let's stay together this time and try to follow their movements."

"What about Charlie and Emily?" Marian says. "What if those guys went out that door and got them too?"

Sam looks at me and Marian. "You two girls go check on your friends and meet us back here. Thomas and Ethan, come with me. Let's see if Jason and Josh made it. I might need your help carrying them if they are stunned."

She hangs on the word *stunned* like it's an unrealistic hope. I wish I'd talked to Jason a bit more, accepted his apology. I'd avoided him since realizing who he was and didn't want to believe he was a good guy. I was so wrong.

Marian and I trace our steps back to the surface, carefully watching and listening for guards and wipers. We reach the door leading outside without problems and turn the knob slowly before peering out.

Mark is on his feet, gun ready and pointed at my head.

"Easy, it's me," I say, glad he didn't shoot first and find out who I was later. "Has anyone else come this way?"

"Not anyone worth talking to." He indicates several bodies on the ground around them.

"They keep coming out of nowhere," Charlie says. "Mark has been picking them off as best he can, but we couldn't get inside. The door locked behind you."

Marian is holding the door open and I shove a rock in the frame to keep it from latching.

"Have you heard back from Maire yet?" I ask.

"They are holding steady," Mark says. "They wanted a report on what we've found."

"Yeah," Charlie says. "Are there any supplies or other people?"

"Yes, to both," Marian says. "But let's move you guys downstairs, so you don't have to deal with more wipers."

"Can I radio in the report?" I ask as Mark gets his gear together.

"I suppose so," he says and holds out his handheld radio.

I follow the instructions, holding it upright and pressing two buttons at once then giving my call sign. Maire answers immediately. Of course she's waiting for any word we can send. Her son is out here, and the fate of our people is hanging in the balance.

"Imani, love. Is that you?" she asks.

"Yes. We found water and some intact parts of a structure," I say. "The rail lines are clear all the way through the capital, and there are some survivors. Just wanted to let you know. We're going back underground for a while."

"All right. Thank you for checking in. Radio again when you can but don't waste the battery."

I can hear other voices in the background, weird repetitive chanting.

"What is that? Where are you?" I ask.

"I'm with your mother, dear. Thought I'd check on her myself," she says, and my gut clenches.

She is moaning and I can make out her voice now. She's still repeating herself, that string of numbers that she started saying on our last night together.

"Imani, we've got her. You go get done what needs to be done," she says.

"You're right. Thank you, Maire." I sign off, trying to focus on the job at hand, not losing my mother again.

We all make our way into the dark shaft, letting the door close and lock behind us. The small silent Emily clings to the stout, younger Charlie with the broken arm, and everyone makes it to the bottom of the stairs just fine.

"Let's take them to the water room," Marian suggests, and I agree. That's as good a place as any to wait in the dark.

Thomas is there when we return but the other four are not.

"Where's Sam? What happened to the other guys?" I ask.

"They were gone when we got there. Sam and Ethan are looking for supplies and I was waiting for you."

"We decided to just rally everyone here," Marian says.

"I'm going to find Haman," I say. I can't wait any longer. He is here somewhere, and my mother is suffering. The sooner I find him and his magic pill, the sooner I can get home and help her.

Thomas pushes open the door. "Anyone else coming?"

This is why I love Thomas. He's always ready to go no matter how crazy my ideas are.

Marian stands up. "I'm coming as well," she says. "I'd like to let him know how I feel about his *programs.*"

We cover our small handheld light with fabric to dim it a bit. The passages we've been exploring lead deep into the underground complex. As we come to areas familiar to Marian, she takes the lead.

The structure is easy enough to navigate, even in the dark. It consists of one main hall stretching the entire length of the former building above with occasional hallways branching right or left. We follow multiple sets of large footprints in the dust. At one point there are signs of a fight and then drag marks after that.

"Looks like someone lost pretty bad," Thomas says.

We walk for a lot longer than I expected we would before we finally see a light ahead. It's moving—someone else walking. We push up against the nearest wall, turning off our light, and watch. The light continues toward us until it turns right and disappears.

"Let's check out where it came from," I say, and we start our creep again.

Eventually there are voices and the sound of footsteps. Thomas and I hold our shock rifles at the ready, but I'm not sure what to do. What if we can't find him? How do we get these guys to talk to us without shooting us?

The choice is made for me when Marian pushes past both of us and walks down the hall toward the noise and another dim light.

"Marian, wait!" I say. But I'm too late. She's around the corner and we can hear her shout.

"Who's in charge here?"

There's a scuffle and Thomas and I hold back while we wait to see what happens. Mostly male voices echo through the chambers and Marian cries out in pain. I can't stand here listening and not do anything. I meet Thomas's eye, then step out and point my rifle at the group in front of me.

Ten to fifteen men in dusty white uniforms are in the space, which is bigger than a corridor. Two of them are trying to subdue Marian while the rest are going through boxes of supplies stacked against the walls. Jason and Josh lie on the ground, tied up and gagged, still unconscious from being shocked.

In the center of all the chaos, holding a cup like a king's chalice, sits Haman. A pile of books lay at his feet, a reader in his hand. He is pointing for a guard to do something when he looks up at us and a half smile spreads across his face.

"Imani," he says. "I hope you brought your mother too."

THIRTY

Marian

arian rarely regretted anything, but that day she regretted charging into a literal den of bad guys.

"Professor 789," she said as two men held her arms by her side. But she couldn't think of anything else to follow with.

"23," he said. "Or do you prefer Marian?"

She narrowed her eyes. "What? How did you know?"

"How do you think I got to be where I am? I know everything about everyone, including your little group meetings and secret names and initiations."

Marian was dumbstruck. "But how? We were so careful."

"Just because an auto-eye doesn't report to the school office doesn't mean it's not reporting anywhere. Did you really think no one noticed all your infractions? How could you get away with so many and not get caught? I was intervening on your behalf."

"But why?" Marian asked, both baffled and embarrassed. She shuddered to think of all the things he'd watched them do and wondered who else had been privy to the videos.

"Because it's all part of the plan. You have discovered the future on your own. I didn't even have to prompt you, just keep you from wrecking yourselves while I got everything else in place. Would you please lower your weapons?" He directed this toward Thomas and Imani.

"Release Marian and we will," Thomas said.

The professor waved his hand and the guards let Marian go. Imani and Thomas let the front ends of their guns drop. Ten of

Haman's henchpeople in white suits watched their movements, and a few more dug through boxes. They were very outnumbered.

"Haman, where is the cure? We need to help the wipers," Imani said.

"There will be no cure for those savages," Haman said, dismissive.

"You can't just leave them all to die if you have a way to save them. That's horrible," Marian said.

"If you have a cure, we have to use it," Imani said. She started walking toward Haman, her rifle still in her hands, but another white uniformed guard stopped her before she could get close. She turned the gun on him.

"You would attack us to save those who attack you mindlessly?" Haman asked.

"You are nutters," Thomas said, gun aimed at the man near Imani. "How can you do that to your own people then leave them to pull each other apart?"

"I watched them kill a live cow and eat it raw, Professor. This is wrong. If you can stop it you should," Marian said.

"Enough," he said. "Do you know what is really horrific? Starving to death. And that is what we are facing if we cure all of them and have to share our limited resources. We have other things to worry about right now. I assume you came from the mountain colony. Are there many survivors there? Were you attacked as well?"

Thomas started to say something, and Imani cut him off. "We aren't telling you anything until you give us the cure."

"Passion really is wasted on the youth," Haman said.

Marian was having a hard time accepting this smooth-talking man with dirt on his face and a group of guards at his command as Professor 789. He was the most duplicitous person she had ever met. She couldn't help but admire him a little. He had pulled off a fantastic coup right under the nose of the Leaders.

"Haman, let us cure them. We will do all the work. There will be plenty of resources left for everyone. It's spring, we can plant crops and rebuild," Imani was almost begging now.

"Absolutely not. I'm guessing that since you are all here, that means the mountain colony is at least partially intact."

Marian could see this was going nowhere. "What do you want, Haman?"

"Well, that's simple. I want your cooperation."

"Okay. You've got it," she said, pulling her arms from the guards with looks of contempt. "Now what should we do?"

"Marian," Imani said.

Marian held up her hand and gave Imani the look she was famous for—*trust me, I've got this.*

"I want to know the status of the mountain colonies and anything else you've seen since the attacks," he said.

"Full report, great," Marian said. "All I know is that the Secondary School is completely gone. Maybe ten people left there. On our way here we saw one heard of cattle and one herd of people you damaged eat the herd of cattle with their bare hands and teeth."

"Preposterous," Haman said, and his guards looked at each other with raised eyebrows.

"It seems like all the major communities were bombed, leaving only the fields. The capital is leveled." She looked at Imani for confirmation on this point. Imani nodded.

"What about the mountains?" Haman looked to Thomas and Imani.

"The lower levels of the mines collapsed and flooded. We lost quite a few folks, but we are used to being attacked and regrouping." Thomas's thickly accented words were laced with acrid sarcasm.

"We need to find the source of this attack and make sure it doesn't happen again. I have a team gathering supplies here. What other resources do you have to report?"

Marian looked back at her companions. They were steely eyed. No one said anything, so she spoke up again. "We have some supplies at the other end of the building. We can go get them and come back here to figure out our options."

"Perfect," he said. "Rodrigo, go with them. Imani, stay here. I want to ask you a few questions."

"I don't know why you think you're in charge now. Last I checked the whole world blew up and no one picked you to lead the leftovers," Thomas said. "She goes with us."

"Imani, I imagine you have some questions for me as well?" Haman said ignoring Thomas.

"She's going with us," Marian echoed.

"Where's your mother, Imani? Is she here? I can't imagine you'd leave her behind again," Haman said. "I'd like to have both of you with me again. That was always the plan."

"I'll stay," Imani said. "Just let them go get their gear and we can talk."

"Is your mother with the gear?" Haman said, clearly a rhetorical question.

"I think you already know that," Imani said and walked past the guards to Jason's side and started untying him.

"Pity," Haman said. "You'll have to take me to her at some point. You both have something I need."

"Don't touch him," one of the guards said, grabbing her arm.

Imani him off. "We're all on the same side now. He doesn't need to be tied up. Jason is a good guy."

"Rodrigo, follow them so they don't get lost on the way back," Haman said.

"We don't need Rodrigo," Marian said as she pivoted and took Thomas by the arm.

He looked at Imani, who tipped her head toward the door and mouthed, *I'll be fine*. The three of them understood the plan without having to speak it.

Marian and Thomas walked out the door and down the hall, leaving Imani with Haman. Rodrigo was close behind them, his shock rifle at the ready. Marian looked back at him a few times and side-eyed Thomas, but Thomas was staring straight ahead, clearly upset.

"So, how long have you been taking orders from the professor?" Marian asked.

"I don't take orders," Rodrigo said. He was medium height, just a bit shorter than Thomas. His hair was light brown and curly but cut very close to the scalp.

"Looks to me like you do." Marian waved her hand at him in a dismissive way. "Did he do you a huge favor or something?"

"Haman knows more than anyone I've ever met," he said.

"Well, now you know Imani," Thomas said in a low grumble then looked at Marian. She nodded.

"I don't know what you two think you're planning. But I have my shock rifle primed and ready to go. Just show me where your supplies are and let's get everything back to the base."

Marian put her hands up in the air. "Listen, all I'm planning is to stay alive and enjoy some freedom for once. You must be looking forward to that, right? I can't believe Haman would set up the same kind of rules that the Leaders had. Look where it got them."

"Right," Thomas said. "Fat lot of good all those rules did for them. Look at this mess. We went ahead and blew each other up anyway."

They walked on in silence until they came to the turn for their hallway. If they followed the plan, the rest of their group was waiting around the corner in the water room. Marian walked faster and spoke again, only much louder this time.

"It should be right around here. Was it this corridor, Thomas?" she asked and indicated the correct one.

"I'm not sure," he said, matching her volume. "What about this other one?"

"I guess it's a good thing Haman sent you with us, Rodrigo. Look at how lost we are and we're not even heading back yet," Marian said.

"Why are you yelling?" he said and poked Marian with the tip of his shock rifle. "Shut up and just get to the room."

"Hey, I thought we were going to be friends," she said.

"It's definitely back here. Yes, this one," Thomas said and doubled back to the original passage before turning sharply and rattling the knob on the door. "Rats and bollocks, it's locked."

"Are you sure?" Marian said. "Maybe this isn't the right door." She rattled it herself.

"Let me see," Rodrigo said and pushed Marian out of the way to pull it open himself.

Several things happened at once. Thomas quick stepped behind Rodrigo and had his rifle at the ready in the same moment that Rodrigo pulled open the door that wasn't locked, just in time to see Sam with her shock rifle aimed at his head, ready to fire.

Sam hesitated, but Thomas didn't. He fired just as Rodrigo pulled his gun up to shoot Sam. He fell to the floor in a crumpled heap.

"Nice!" Marian said.

"Who is that?" Sam asked.

"One of Haman's flunkies," Thomas said. "Such a dolt. Fell for the oldest trick in the book."

"The fake locked door?" Marian asked.

"No, the helpless prisoner. Never believe someone you've got a gun pointed at. They will lie as much as possible and will shoot you the first chance they get."

"Harsh," Charlie said from the dark of the room. "Where's Imani?"

"She stayed with Haman. I don't think he poses any kind of risk yet, and she had stuff she wanted to talk to him about."

"Did he tell her about the cure? Are they implementing it?" Sam asked.

"Nope," Thomas said. "We need to get back there, get the code out of him for that locked room, and get rid of him. He's caused more issues than all the Leaders put together."

"You're quite the bloodthirsty little mountain rat, aren't you?" Marian said.

"Nobody messes with my girl," Thomas said and shifted his gun to his back. "All right then. What's our plan?"

Haman is making me sick. I can't stand to look at him, but I have to. Why did I think this would ever be easy? Why did I think I could just walk in here and offer to do the dirty work and he'd agree? He's clearly out of his mind. I have to figure out how to get around his visions of grandeur and get the code into that room, because I'm certain those vials of meds Marian described are there. Only someone really disturbed wouldn't save the people he destroyed. I'm dealing with a mad man.

"Where is your mother?" Haman asks again.

"Why do you care? Why are you so obsessed with her?" I ask.

"Because she's a part of me. We are a part of each other. She was there at the beginning of this journey. I need her here at the end."

"That makes no sense," I say.

"That's because you think you know everything, but you don't."

"Why did you have her locked up in that facility like a wiper then? She said she didn't even see you very much in all the months you had her there."

"I thought you'd be grateful to me. I gave you everything you wanted. What more can I do?"

"What are you talking about?"

"You wanted to know you weren't alone, I got you into the secondary school. You wanted knowledge, I blocked tapes of you sneaking into the archives. You wanted to see your mother again, I sent you her picture and gave you a chance to be with her. You wanted a different world, I placed all of human history in your mind—at the mere thought of anything you want, you can have it. And yet you've fought me every step of the way."

"I didn't ask you for any of those things and they weren't yours to give," I say.

"You thought you got a perfect score on those exams on your own?" He watches me, amused.

At first, I can't remember what he is talking about. Then it hits me. My entrance tests were perfect. It's the only reason they let me into Secondary School.

My face must register my understanding because he laughs and nods. "She remembers now."

"Why would you do all of that?" I say. "I didn't want any of this, I just wanted some medicine for my mother." *And that's all I want now too.*

The humor drains from his face, leaving an embittered old man. "You're such a fool, Imani. I thought you'd be much more intelligent than this." His tone is harsh, unforgiving.

"Haman…" I say.

"Your mother is the love of my life. I couldn't be with her. She didn't want to take my assignment. She wanted to have children, so I watched you from the moment you were born until the day I lost contact with you in prison. Even then I got reports and updates and I made sure you weren't harmed."

I think of all the things I went through in prison that could have easily been classified as harmful and laugh.

Haman seems to understand. "It could have been much worse."

Three close calls that could indeed have been worse come to mind, but I push them aside. Focus. "Haman, the love of your life needs that cure."

"What are you talking about?"

"Why do you think I'm here and not with her?"

He snorts. "Because you've always been selfish, more worried about your *feelings* than your mother's needs. You make an excellent subject, a miserable daughter."

"She's got the sickness, Haman. Whatever you gave her when she got out of the Shop finally caught up with her. She's locked up in a closet shredding her own hair and nails trying to get out and kill someone."

Haman is silent, but only for a moment. "You're bluffing."

"Why would I lie? What do I have to gain?"

"The cure," he says.

"You're worried that all these people are going to be healed and they will remember that you're the jerk who ruined them, aren't you? You don't want me to save anyone because you're afraid they will all hate you and you'll lose control."

"Enough. What are you really here for?" he says.

I want to scream in frustration and have to work to keep my voice calm. "The *cure*. I just want one bottle for Mother, and I'll do whatever you want."

Haman considers this for a minute, then shakes his head. "This is unacceptable. How do I know you're telling the truth?"

"Spoken like a true liar," I say.

"If I give you one vial and send you back to her, how do I know you will return?"

"You don't," I say. "You just have to have faith."

Haman chuckles. "Faith," he says. "That is such an old word. So overused and meaningless."

"Funny you say that now," Imani says.

"Why?"

"Because Imani means faith, and I know that's the name you gave Mother."

THIRTY TWO

Marian

The group was huddled in the water room, heads bent together, occasionally looking up to listen for outsiders.

"Jason and Josh are tied up down there. We need to get them and Imani and if we can sway any of the guards, we'll need their help too," Thomas said.

"We'll need everyone to help us move Jason and Josh to safety in case they aren't awake yet," Marian said.

"Ethan, Mark, Thomas, and I can move them if you and Imani cover us with your shock rifles," Sam said. She was muscular enough to look like she could carry at least Josh on her own, so no one questioned this plan.

"What do you want me to do?" Charlie asked. Marian could tell he felt a bit useless with his arm in a sling and clearly still hurting him. She didn't want to tell him to stay behind and watch Emily again, but she couldn't think of any other choices.

"You can man the radio. If we aren't back in an hour, call for backup," Mark handed him the handheld device. "Do you know how to use it?"

"He's the smartest person I know," Marian said. "He probably knows how to build one of those things."

"How are we going to administer the meds if we can get them?" Charlie asked. "I'm assuming they are intravenous? Do you know if there are medical supplies here as well?"

The group looked at each other in confusion. Clearly, no one had thought this far ahead.

"I helped extract some of the ingredients, but I don't know anything beyond that," Marian said, shrugging.

"I'm sure Imani has a plan for that," Thomas said. "She's got it all up there." He tapped his temple.

"Well, if she doesn't, I'll see if I can find anything useful. You guys get in the room, I'll work on disbursement. You said it's a liquid, right, Marian?"

"Yes, the process we worked on was creating liquid vials that looked like the mouthwash containers we found, but green."

"Got it," Charlie said.

"Are you guys ready?" Sam said.

"I'm not sure we have much of a choice." It was Ethan's first contribution to the planning session. Marian wished she could read his mind. She didn't dare ask him what he was thinking in front of all these people. Something was bothering him, but she couldn't guess what.

"I mean, you could always lie yourself down and have a nap in here with the water bottles if you fancy," Thomas said. The joke was lost on Ethan.

Why was I so attracted to someone so serious? Marian thought.

"Let's head out," Sam said.

"We better leave a rifle with Charlie and Emily," Ethan said.

"Good point," Sam said and looked between Mark and Thomas. She wasn't offering hers. "Mark, you have the least experience with one. Give it up and stay in the middle of the group."

Mark hesitated, then thought better of arguing and gave his gun to Charlie, who was trying to shove the radio in the pocket of his trousers.

"Let's just get going," Mark said.

Marian started to leave the room, then thought twice and doubled back. Everyone else was in the hall waiting for her, but she needed to do this.

"Charlie," she said.

"Yeah?" he said.

"I think you're amazing. I just want you to know that." She threw her arms around him, gun and all, and kissed him on the lips.

He was stiff as a board and his face was puckered, his lips tight as a line. When Marian pulled back and looked at him, he was blushing and looked very confused.

"What was that?" Charlie asked.

"Just in case," she said. "Will you take care of this? You can put the radio in it." She slipped her black bag over his head and patted its contents. "Keep it safe for me. I want to know how the story ends."

"Get out of here," he said.

Marian did as she was told and headed out the door. She glanced back quickly and saw Charlie touch his lips, smiling as he looked down.

They made their way cautiously back down the hall. No one spoke and they froze whenever they saw a light or heard a noise. Eventually the light from Haman's corridor was visible. Voices were starting to become clear. They halted.

"There are about ten guards in there, plus Haman," Thomas whispered. "When we move in, Ethan, Marian, and Mark, you need to go right for a weapon. See if you can get one away from one of the guards. They won't be expecting us, so it shouldn't be hard. If you can't get one away from them, at least keep them busy until we can get Haman caught. Then they should all fall in line." He looked around the group. "Got it?"

"Yes," they all mumbled.

"Okay, we'll go from there," Thomas said.

"Thomas, you and I will lead the charge," Sam said. "Everyone else fall in as quickly as you can after us."

"Let's do it," Marian said. She had a goal and a purpose, and she knew fate was on their side. It had to be. Something had to go right, for her, for their world, for the future.

"All right, ready?" Sam said. "Go!"

They charged into the lit space without any kind of cry. Thomas and Sam stunned as many guards as they could, Sam barely missing Imani with one shot. Thomas was on Haman before anyone could stop him, shock rifle to his head. Ethan and Mark were each locked in their own fight with guards trying to wrestle away their weapons. Imani joined in the fray, grabbing the man next to her from behind, wrapping her arms around his neck and squeezing to cut off his air.

Marian targeted a woman her own size. She was carrying a crate, her gun slung over her back. As soon as she saw Marian come at her, the woman dropped her crate and fumbled for her weapon. The boards broke open, spilling its contents. Marian didn't have time to see what was inside as she jumped over the mess and grabbed at the woman's gun strap. They wrestled there, jerking and pulling at each other, limbs locked in struggle, too close to get in a punch. The woman finally twisted sideways, shrugging Marian off and leaning low before rising back up with all her body weight to elbow her in the face.

The floor was slick. The contents of the crate were liquid and had escaped to cover the concrete beneath their feet. Marian's head jerked back, pain everywhere, and her feet slipped out from under her. She felt like she was falling in slow motion. The battle around her was coming to a close. Sure, she'd failed to take down her target, but she was going to be all right. Even if the woman shocked her, she'd be all right eventually. They were going to win this. They would all be all right.

The back of her head hit the floor with an unmistakable crack.

"No!" Imani cried as she let go of the man she had nearly dropped to the ground and ran to her friend. There was so much blood. And her face… her face was empty.

Ethan had successfully wrestled the shock rifle away from his opponent and didn't waste any time shooting the woman who had shoved Marian down, then man Imani had tackled, then Haman, and then Sam, by mistake.

"Ethan!" Thomas called, "Stop!" and drew his weapon up to site Ethan in his targets. "Stop, man."

His shoulders slumped and in two steps he was at Marian's side, on his knees, looking her over for signs of life. Blood pooled on the floor behind her head, mixing with the liquid from the broken crate. It was all over Imani's arm and legs as she cradled her once roommate and tried to find a way to help her.

"Cripes," Sam said as she stunned the guard she had kept at bay and walked to their side to help. She stooped and felt Marian's wrist and then her chest. "She's dead."

Ethan stared at Marian's body, unmoving, rifle slack in his hands, his eyes wide and searching. Imani continued to rock back and forth on her knees, Marian's head cradled in her arm, her other hand on Marian's chest.

"How?" Imani gulped in a breath.

"Blunt force trauma to the head, an accident, but still…" Sam didn't finish her sentence.

Suddenly, Ethan was on his feet and shooting Haman's body, unconscious from his first hit. His rage was palpable in the room, more powerful than the current coming off his repeatedly fired rifle.

"You did this!" he cried.

Thomas was on him in a moment.

"Ethan, stop!" He grabbed the boy's gun, pushing the barrel upward. "There's been enough death today."

Imani was up now too, running to Haman. "Ethan! What did you do?" Her bloody hands searched Haman for signs of life. No pulse, no breath. "He's the only one who had the code to that door!" Her grief for Marian turned to rage, and she turned on the dumbstruck boy with tears running down his face as he held his rifle close to his chest.

"How are we supposed to get the meds now? How am I going to get in that room?" She shoved him and Thomas grabbed her next, holding her to his chest as she sobbed.

"We'll figure it out, love. We'll figure it out," he said.

Imani looked into Thomas's eyes, surprised to see him crying as well.

"I don't care anymore," Ethan said quietly. "My life was quiet and simple until you people came into it. Until she," he thumbed at Marian, "came into it."

"You all need to get it together," Sam said.

The room was strewn with bodies, most of them unconscious but not for long. Jason and Josh were already starting to wake up. Two guards had immediately surrendered when they saw what was happening. The rest were on the floor.

"We need to get these guys contained before they wake up and make sure we have what we need for phase two. Right?" Sam said.

"Sounds like a good idea," Mark said. "You guys with us?" he asked the two remaining guards.

"Yeah," one said, staring at the growing pool of blood around Marian. He tore his eyes away, pale, and looked at Mark. "It seems pretty useless to be fighting each other. We just want food and somewhere safe from the people Haman screwed up."

"Same," said the other one.

"You think your buddies will agree?" asked Thomas.

"I'm sure," the first one said.

"Good," Sam said. "Just in case, help us move their bodies into one area. We'll tie them up and take their guns with us."

"What about Marian?" Imani sniffed. "What about my mother?" Tears ran in rivers down her face as she wiped her nose and mouth on her blue sleeve.

"One thing at a time, love," Thomas said. "Let's get back to Charlie and get that door open. All right? Then we'll take care of them."

They made quick work of the unconscious guards and moved Haman and Marian to a separate corner, a trail of blood marking her body's path on the floor. Mark and Josh stayed to watch the guards and question them when they awoke. Imani wiped at her face a few more times, leaving streaks of Marian's blood, and then everyone else made their way back down the hall to meet the others.

I can't feel my palms as we walk back down the corridor. My fingers are numb and tingling. Marian is still in that room, only she's not. She's dead. It's just her body left, laid out next to Haman. She's gone forever, and we'd only just found each other.

Funny, I hadn't thought of her much since I was taken from the school, but seeing her again brought back deep feelings of warmth and friendship. It was almost as good as seeing my mother again. And now she's gone. One minute here, fighting beside me. The next, gone.

I walk close to Thomas. My arm and hands are sticky with blood, and I find myself pinching my fingers together and pulling them apart over and over in time with our footsteps. I don't know how to proceed. No code, the only two people who knew anything about this facility dead. Haman is dead. That realization is just sinking in as well. He was the only one who had answers to so many questions. I'm left with what's in my head, and Thomas.

I look up at him. His face is tear streaked as well. He glances down at me and gives a halfhearted smile.

"It's going to be all right, love," he says. I know he wants that to be true, but I'm not sure.

Charlie's face is drawn and pale when he sees us. He scans our faces. He is looking for Marian. But she's not there. When he sees Ethan, he seems to understand.

"How?" Charlie asks. His voice is flat and unemotional.

"She fell and hit her head. It was fast," Thomas says.

The stout younger boy clenches his jaw and takes a deep breath in through his nose. He blows out slowly and then looks at me.

"Did you get the code?" he asks.

He's trying to be brave. He's trying not to feel the pain I know is pulsing through his veins. Next to him, Emily begins to sob, her head in her hands.

Charlie and Ethan are next to her in an instant. Charlie loses all his self-control and wraps his good arm around her, his own tears bursting forth.

Sam looks at the rest of us. Jason rubs his head. He's been quiet, but now he speaks up. "What's the plan?" he asks no one in particular.

"We need to get that door open, get those meds out, and get them back up to the mountains. Report what we've found here and possibly leave someone here to hold down this fort, gather more intel," Thomas says.

"I still can't believe I let those guys get the jump on us," Jason says.

"Doesn't matter now. We've got you back and we need to regroup, figure out what happens next," Sam says.

I cautiously approach Charlie, who looks up. "Were you able to make any headway with the lock?"

He shakes his head and my heart plummets. He sniffs. "I found some possibilities for distribution though. If you can get me the meds, I can create a system to deliver it at a distance."

"That would be amazing, man," Thomas says, impressed.

"But we need the meds," I say. Every passing minute brings more pain and anxiety, less clarity. I need to think, I need to get out of here. I need to see the sun and feel the breeze, even if it's smoky.

"Charlie," I say. "Give me the radio. I'm going to call in. I need to get outside."

"I'll go with you," Thomas says. "Let's take some water and get you cleaned up." He grabs a bottle from a case and readies his rifle.

Thomas, always there, always thinking clearly, always ready. I can't remember how I ever lived without him.

"We'll keep working on the door and gather supplies for the trip back," Jason says, taking his spot as natural leader again.

Thomas props the door open even though I know Thomas can easily pick it again.

"Just in case we need to hurry back in," he says.

I nod and press the buttons on the radio then speak in my call sign.

Maire answers. "Imani, love. What's the report?"

"Hello, Mum." Thomas leans over my shoulder.

"My Thomas! Good to know you're still alive. What's the update?" she asks again.

"We are fine," I say, because we are. No one Maire knows has been killed. "We have some supplies and shelter here. Will be heading back tomorrow hopefully."

"That's very good news," she says. "Have you found anyone else?"

"We have. There are a few survivors other than wipers. I think we're all on the same page now."

"What does that mean?" Her voice is tense.

"We'll explain it later. How is my mother?" I ask, trying to keep my voice from cracking.

"She's good, love. Nothing has changed. She's eaten the food we gave her but is showing signs that she would attack us if she were able."

My heart sinks like a rock in a stream, everything else moving too quickly around me.

A wiper stumbles upon us from behind the entrance to the stairwell. Thomas loses no time turning and firing at her—a young woman, barely older than me, with dirt-streaked hair and a torn white tunic, also smudged in brown. She falls with a quick convulsion and lies before me, still now.

I can't help it. I start to sob again.

"Imani, love, don't cry. She's going to be all right. At least she's still talking. That's more than the rest of them do," Maire says.

"What is she saying, Ma?" Thomas takes the radio from me.

"It's just that string of numbers. Same seven ones over and over again, but at least we can understand her."

I cease crying, the world around me snapping into place. I snatch the radio back from Thomas's unsuspecting hands.

"What numbers, Maire? What are they?" I say, desperate to be right.

"Lands, I've heard them enough times over and over I expect we all have them memorized. Five, three, one, eight, zero, zero, eight."

I repeat the sequence out loud twice then press the button again, "Thank you, Maire! We'll check in again before night."

"Don't bother. Just let us know when you're on your way back or if something happens. Save the batteries," she says.

I hand the radio to Thomas and sprint for the door, not even waiting to see if he's following me.

THIRTY FOUR
Imani

The code was successful. Inside, the large room was full of not only several boxes of green vials of medicine, but also food rations, seeds, tools, precious metals, and books.

"I think my plan will work," Charlie says after we plunder the supplies and combine everything we've found in the vault room. "This is an aerosol medication. It's meant to be breathed in for quick absorption and rapid response."

"So, we spray it up their noses?" Jason asks.

"Theoretically," Charlie says.

"How the bloody biscuits do we do that?" Thomas asks. "I can't even get close enough to see their eye color, much less shoot something up their nose."

"That's where this comes in." Charlie held up a small machine with four propellers.

"That's a crop drone," Ethan says. "We used those back home all the time."

"I know. I'm very familiar with them," Charlie says. "I've modified them in the past. Marian said it was some of my best work."

"So, you're going to spray them with the meds, like bugs in a field?" Ethan says, comprehension dawning.

"That's the idea," Charlie says.

"Brilliant," I say.

"Huh, that's what Marian said too." Charlie's face falls and he looks close to tears again.

"She knew your plan?" I ask.

"No, I did something similar at school before we left. Actually, it had to do with you," he says.

"How?" I ask.

"I spray painted a big red message on the train side of the Secondary School. It said: 4254 LIVES."

"Are you serious?"

"Yep, it was Marian's idea," he says.

"That's wild," Thomas says and laughs heartily.

There are only four drones in the underground supplies, and one has a dead battery, but we retrofit them all and head to the surface. Everyone wants to see this work.

Charlie is in the lead carrying two drones. Everyone else has at least two boxes of meds. I take Emily by the hand and gently lead her to the stairs. Her fingers are chilled, and her skin is pale. *She needs food and sunshine,* I think. *She needs Maire.* I wonder if they will let me take her back to the mountains with me.

It is dark outside. We've been in the bunker for so long with only our flashlights, we forgot that the sun would go down out here. The drones are outfitted with lights, so Charlie is able to test them out anyway. It's not long until he has one loaded with two vials of the medication, enough for six shots if they hit directly in the face. The sprayer has been tightened, changing the output from a fine mist to a more direct spray.

"We should be able to get at them from outside of arm's reach but still have a pretty accurate shot," Charlie explains.

The drone is only in the air for a few minutes before the first wipers start crawling out of the rubble and making their way toward us. Charlie navigates the flying machine through the dark sky to the face of a man, bloody and bruised, his hair short but still greasy, his clothes torn, and his mouth open, drool rolling down his chin. He looks angry as the light from the drone hits his face. He holds his hand up to block the light from his eyes, tipping it back, as Charlie predicted they would do, giving the perfect shot at the mouth and nose.

"Ready, fire!" Charlie cries with a bit more enthusiasm than I expected.

It's a direct hit. The man groans then sways and falls to the ground again.

"Whoa," Thomas says. "What is in that stuff?"

"There were labels on the vials. That's how I knew what it was for. It's mostly valerian root and velvet bean. The concentrated valerian puts them to sleep and the velvet bean is a high-density form of dopamine that is supposed to heal the frontal lobe of the brain, which is what Haman figured was damaged. Pretty sure he was right. Once they're unconscious, we should administer a second dose by hand."

It is strange to see adults nodding and taking orders from a short, stout kid. He can't be more than fourteen years old, yet he has the maturity and intelligence of someone much older. He gives me hope for our future.

We spend the next hour learning to operate the drones, each of us taking a turn at the controls. After that, I take Emily back down to the bunker. The guards from Haman's group are waiting for us. They are just as lost as we are, and when I tell them that we are eradicating the wipers for them, they drop their shoulders and tense looks. I think we are finally achieving unity.

They show us where there are cots and pillows and blankets. Most are from cells, so we drag them away to the water room and vault room. We share stories and hopes and ideas. The others join us from above one by one, until we are all camped out together, two people sitting watch at a time through the night.

It's morning, and laughter rouses me. I am one of the last to wake. Thomas didn't wake me for my watch shift. Someone has brought a trunk down from the train car. They are making real food instead of canned rations—warm bread and eggs and cheese.

"Where did you get all this?" I ask.

"Campfire outside," Thomas says.

"How long did I sleep?" I ask.

"Days," he says and laughs.

I punch him playfully on the arm and he kisses me.

"I'm assuming your good mood and the fact that you're cooking outside means the meds worked?" I can't help but feel that old nervous clench in my gut, preparing for bad news.

"There are quite a few groggy people out there. Sam, Jason, and a few of Haman's people are taking stock of wounds and med needs. They're going to move them down here and send out word for more survivors to come this way."

I'm afraid to relax, to believe this is really happening, but as the day wears on, I start to feel lighter and lighter. Teams of three are sent to scout for wipers and survivors. There aren't many. Mostly what we find are bodies or body parts.

There aren't enough of us to bury them all right now, but we do what we can for Marian and Haman. It's a bittersweet moment. This girl I felt I owed so much to and this man who may have saved my life—or ruined it. I still don't know. No one has spoken of the fact that Ethan killed Haman in cold blood, out of anger.

I think of the time so many years ago when we laid my mother to final rest. A little wooden box planted under an apple tree in the Field of Yesterday. I remember the beautiful colors of green and blue and wet brown earth, the Leader who came to speak and didn't know anything about her. Charlie speaks for Marian. No one speaks for Haman. Ethan wipes at his face, but we know it's not for the dead or for regret.

The next morning, Thomas, Emily, and I load up the tractor and head to the mountains along the tracks. It's much faster than the hand car on the hills. The hand car becomes the perfect vehicle for scouting for survivors and supplies in the flat lands.

I carry a satchel with me filled with the precious medicine, some food, and a book I found in Haman's vault called *Lord of the Flies*. The description seems appropriate—a group of children learning to govern themselves and survive. My artificial memories try to dribble the story into my mind, spoiling the enjoyment of reading it for myself. I push those thoughts away and browse the thin paper pages, reading aloud as Thomas operates the machine.

We stop along the way for survivors. Most come running at the sound of the engine. We direct them to the PSC and tell them more help is coming. We assure them that there is a cure for the madness plaguing the dead who walk among them. Most are grateful. Some are angry. All look as weary and battle worn as we are.

We make it into the village after dark on the last dregs of battery. The sun had kept the batter charged during the day, but now the headlights are low, and we are barely getting enough power to make it up the last hill. The road ahead of us fills with people, not crazed survivors or desperate refugees, but Thomas people, in bright colored clothing, confused then excited when they realize who we are.

Maire is the first one to greet us.

"You're really here! My loves!" she cries and embraces each of us individually, even Emily. "Who's this now?" she asks as she looks over the slight pale girl.

"That's Emily. She needs a mother," I say, and Maire nods. It's not a question of if, but just how much care she will give this lost girl.

Grimley is also there. He takes me by the arm and leads me to my mother. She's in a shed behind one of the newer houses. I can hear her mumbling and moaning as I approach. My gut turns and I steel myself for what I know I will see when he opens the door.

"I'm going in first. I'll hold her and you administer the meds, all right?" he says.

I nod.

"You have everything ready?"

I nod again. We couldn't afford to take a drone back with us when most of the wipers were centered around the PSC, so I took a couple of vials and a syringe without a needle. Charlie had shown me how to tip her head back and squirt the meds down her nose.

I close my eyes as Grimley slides open the barred door and steps inside. I can hear Mother scream as she sees him, and I know she's lunging for him, trying to bite and maim and kill. But in just a moment, he calls my name and I step inside.

He has her from behind, his arms wrapped tightly around her gaunt frame. She seems so much thinner than when I left, yet it's only been a few days. There are scratches on her arms and face. She still has on trousers, but they are sagging off one hip and her shirt is torn. Her eyes are wild and she's thrashing to be let go.

"Come on, Imani," he says. "You can do it."

"You've got this, love." Thomas is behind me, making his way to Grimley's side to help hold her legs out of the way.

I walk carefully to her side and have to pull on her long, tangled hair to get her head back at the right angle. She screams again, a wild beast trapped in madness and sorrow. I shove the syringe in her nose and push the plunger all the way in.

She coughs and gags, spitting and hissing. *Like a wildcat*, I think. I'll have to remember to look up wildcats later. I force myself to stay present. To watch her mellow before our eyes, eventually sinking into Grimley's arms and closing her eyes.

"Now what?" he asks, holding the once squalling thing tenderly.

"Now we wait. She should sleep for an hour or so, then wake up calm. I'll give her another dose before then," I say. Tears come as he nods and carries her out the door.

Thomas wraps his arms around me and kisses my hair.

"We did it, love," he says.

"I know," I say.

"Can you believe it?" he asks.

"No," I say.

"Why not? I thought you were the one who was supposed to be all full of faith?" He smiles at me in that boyish way I love so much.

"Because even though I have faith in you and me, I didn't have a lot of faith in other people."

"Some of them proved you wrong, eh?"

"Yes, some of them did."

"And some of them proved you right?"

"Yes. Unfortunately," I say.

"Would you like to chat a bit about it?"

"No," I say.

"Me either," he says.

And we walk out of the shed hand in hand.

ACKNOWLEDGEMENTS

This series is so much more than just a series for me. It tells Imani's story, but mine is woven between the lines as well. I've been through many changes over the ten years I've been working on these books, and this final installment was never meant to be. Which is oddly fitting because so many things that have happened to me in the last few years were "never supposed to happen." And yet, here we are.

I'd like to thank Emma, for her tenacity and faith, Olivia Swenson, editor extraordinaire, for her flexibility, creativity, and insight, and especially my kids for their inspiration, cheers, and tissues when needed. I also need to thank my writing buddies. I'm very blessed to have many talented people in my life, but those who worked closely with me on this project are the Kidlit Drink Night hooligans, Karen, Amy, and Stephen; My Converse Amazons, Linda, Angela, Kay, and Katie; and the Straightjacket Writers, Eric and Chris. And the best for last, Blake, a man of power, honor, and prestige. Jämoré.

Lastly, I'd like to thank the brave taxi driver in France who picked me up in the middle of the night—with my four kids and a lot of luggage in tow—to take us to a safe place to sleep. It just seems fitting to thank him here. If I would have died that night because of my own stupidity, this book wouldn't be here for you to read. Thank you, French taxi man, for being a decent human being. There are many of you out there. You have my thanks as well.

Leigh Statham

was raised in the wilds of rural Idaho but found her heart in New York City. She now resides in North Carolina and has an MFA in Young Adult literature from Converse College. She is the winner of the 2018 James Applewhite Poetry prize honorable mention and *Southeast Review* 2016 Narrative Non-fiction prize.

Girls of War is her fifth YA novel, and her essays, poetry, and short stories can be found in the *Remington Review*, *Southeast Review*, *North Carolina Literary Review*, and several anthologies.

Follow Leigh Statham on

leighstatham.org

#d4254 | #GirlsofWar